"When all is said and done, the money is yours by right."

"That's handsome of you, Lyndon." Chloe sounded surprised. "I don't know of another man who'd make such an offer."

"As long as I have enough for my needs—they are expensive needs, I'll grant you—I'm content." They strolled a few moments in silence, both of them, Michael imagined, thinking of the situation. "Tell me something, Chloe. How is it that your brother doesn't know you've taken control of your money?"

"He wasn't one of the trustees."

"I'd think one of them would've informed him."

"No."

"How the devil—my apologies—did you convince them not to?"

"I batted my eyelashes at them?" she suggested, and did so in such an outrageous manner that he burst out laughing. "No?"

"No," he said firmly, though he smiled. He thought he'd laughed more in this last week than in many a month. She was unpredictable, his Chloe—*his Chloe?*

<u>BOOK YOUR PLACE ON OUR WEBSITE</u>
<u>AND MAKE THE</u>
<u>READING CONNECTION!</u>

We've created a customized website just for our very special readers, where you can get the inside scoop on everything that's going on with Zebra, Pinnacle and Kensington books.

When you come online, you'll have the exciting opportunity to:

- View covers of upcoming books
- Read sample chapters
- Learn about our future publishing schedule (listed by publication month *and author*)
- Find out when your favorite authors will be visiting a city near you
- Search for and order backlist books from our online catalog
- Check out author bios and background information
- Send e-mail to your favorite authors
- Meet the Kensington staff online
- Join us in weekly chats with authors, readers and other guests
- Get writing guidelines
- AND MUCH MORE!

Visit our website at
http://www.kensingtonbooks.com

MARRYING MISS BUMBLEBROTH

Mary Kingsley

ZEBRA BOOKS
Kensington Publishing Corp.
http://www.kensingtonbooks.com

ZEBRA BOOKS are published by

Kensington Publishing Corp.
850 Third Avenue
New York, NY 10022

All Kensington titles, imprints, and distributed lines are available at special quantity discounts for bulk purchases for sales promotion, premiums, fund-raising, educational or institutional use.

Special book excerpts or customized printings can also be created to fit specific needs. For details, write or phone the office of the Kensington Special Sales Manager: Kensington Publishing Corp., 850 Third Avenue, New York, NY 10022. Attn. Special Sales Department. Phone: 1-800-221-2647.

Zebra and the Z logo Reg. U.S. Pat. & TM Off.

First Printing: June 2002
10 9 8 7 6 5 4 3 2 1

Printed in the United States of America

*To the members of the Rhode Island Romance Writers,
for the support, the laughter, the chocolate,
and, most of all, the friendship.*

One

Lord Michael Lyndon blinked his eyes in surprise. "You wish me to marry whom?"

"I believe you heard me," the Earl of Grantham replied. "Miss Chloe Russell."

"Good God, sir, you couldn't have picked anyone more ineligible!"

The earl looked at his son from under bushy eyebrows. "To the contrary. Not only does she have a handsome dowry, but she has a competence from her grandmother, as well."

Michael rose and paced to the fireplace, drumming his fingers on the mantel. "She is the worst possible match for me."

The earl waved that off. "You don't have to live in her pocket, boy. Just get heirs on her."

"While leg-shackled to the clumsiest girl in the *ton*."

"She won't interfere with your athletic pursuits. Though why you must wear that hideous spotted neckcloth when you go driving is beyond all understanding."

Since Michael had no intention of explaining, again, the rules of the Four in Hand Club to his father, he merely frowned. "But why her, Father? Surely there must be someone else more suitable. If I must marry, that is."

"High time you set up your nursery," the earl said gruffly. "High time you gave me heirs."

Michael's lips tightened. He had a brief, nightmarish vision of his future offspring, sons who were enthusiastic about athletics, but hopelessly inept at all games. "That is not what I meant, Father, and well you know it."

The earl shrugged his elegantly clad shoulders. "Her father and I had an agreement—"

"The devil you did!"

"—that my oldest son would marry her, should she reach the age of one and twenty without a husband. That is you."

Michael stared fixedly at his fingers, still tapping on the mantel. "That grandfather would so drain the estate—"

"Precisely." The earl nodded once. "You know, boy, that I have labored mightily to bring it back to its former state." His lips pursed in distaste. "I am, however, no farmer."

"Then let me at least have Chimneys," Michael urged. "You know it should be mine."

"You're no farmer, either. No, boy, the only thing that will help us is an infusion of money," the earl went on. "Which is why I have chosen Miss Russell for you."

"Father, surely if I looked for myself—"

"In the Marriage Mart? When, boy? And how much success do you believe you'll have?"

"As to that, I believe I am not totally repellent," Michael said dryly. "Nor is my title."

"Pray attend to me. There isn't any money to match the title. I'll grant you it is old and respected, but the money is more important. No father will allow his daughter to marry a penniless man, no matter his rank."

"Then I may as well choose a Cit."

"Do not be impertinent. Miss Russell's family is well established, but she has not a title. Her brother wishes one for her. You will provide it. She will provide the money. She is worth, I believe, some five thousand a year."

"Really." Michael regarded his father straightly. "I'm surprised such a paragon has not been snapped up before this."

"You know why. Because of her ridiculous nickname."

"Miss Bumblebroth."

"Precisely."

"A well-earned name, Father."

The earl waved that off. "A few trifling incidents."

"Tripping over her train and then falling nearly into the Queen's lap while being presented at Court? Spilling lemonade all over herself—and, I might add, Lady Cowper—at Almack's? Casting up her accounts at a *ton* ball? A well-earned name."

"A cruel one," the earl said quietly, making Michael look at him in some surprise. Rarely could he credit his rational, urbane father with any sensitivity. "It is no wonder the girl has gone into seclusion."

Michael frowned again and paced to the drawing room window, which overlooked Grosvenor Square. He wasn't in the petticoat line; he was not one to do the pretty. Instead, he was known as a noted Corinthian, a label he rarely applied to himself.

Still, he had always been interested in sports, and he'd immersed himself in the pursuits at which he excelled since he was a mere stripling. He was a bruising rider, a member of the Quorn, an expert boxer who often sparred with Gentleman Jackson; he was deadly with pistols and sword alike. Yet he was expected to marry the least graceful girl to be presented in living memory.

That was a facer, he thought. He'd known he'd have to marry someday; that had been borne in upon him after his brother's death. Lately, if truth were told, he'd felt that day coming closer. To be presented with it like this, though, was stunning. To be asked to marry such an unlikely girl was outside of enough.

"Father." He turned back from the window. "I believe I am capable of choosing my own bride."

"Oh, I quite agree." The earl looked at him from over steepled fingers. "Arranged marriages are archaic. But who will wed her, else?"

"Apparently only a penniless viscount, heir to a penniless earl."

"Precisely." The earl nodded, completely missing the rare

edge to Michael's voice. "As I said, it is an advantageous
match for all concerned."

Michael stared balefully at his father. "What you are saying, then, is that it's all arranged."

"Oh, no. You still must propose to the girl."

"Ah. Is that all?"

"Of course you'll speak with her first," the earl went on.
"If you feel you won't suit, you needn't go through with
it."

"Oh, indeed," Michael said. *Needn't go through with it?
Hardly,* he thought, unconsciously mimicking his father.
"And if I say I will not do it?"

The earl sighed. "Why must you always be this way,
boy? You know I want only what's best for you."

"Unfortunately, we don't always agree on what that is."

"I am older and more experienced than you—"

"And I know myself," Michael snapped.

"Damme, boy, must we always come to blows on everything?"

Michael was quiet for a long moment. "I know you wish
the best for me," he said finally. "But I cannot be what
you want. I am not like you."

"I have done rather well with my life," he said dryly.

"Against your own father's tendencies."

"There is that." The earl looked down at his fingers. "If
you were more like James . . ."

"Yes? I would do what?" Michael asked in a bored voice
that masked his surprise. James was rarely mentioned in
this house. "I'd not question you?"

"You'd listen to me."

The room was silent for a moment. Then Michael looked
over at him. "I am not like him, either," he said softly.

"I'm sorry, boy. I shouldn't have said that."

Michael waved that away. "You are set on this?"

"I think it best. As I have spoken to Miss Russell's
brother about you—"

"The devil you have!"

"—I believe you have no choice but to see the chit."

"Very well," Michael said after a moment. "But I will decide whether to ask her or not." He held the earl's gaze with his own. "Are we agreed?"

The earl sighed, then nodded. "Yes, boy. We are agreed."

"Who is it you wish me to marry?" Chloe Russell demanded, looking up from her easel and sweeping back a strand of hair that had escaped from her untidy bun. Inadvertently, she left a streak of carmine red paint across her cheek, to harmonize with the daub of cobalt on her nose and the ochre on her forehead.

"You heard me, Chloe." Stephen, far more neatly attired than his sister ever was, rose up on the balls of his feet and then rocked back down, his hands tightly clasped behind his back. "Lord Michael Lyndon. And you have paint on your face again."

"Yes, yes." She brushed impatiently at her chin. "Have your wits gone begging, Stephen?"

"I believe 'twill be a good match," he said stiffly.

Chloe stared at him for a moment, and then began to laugh. "Oh, Stephen! You cannot be so foolish as to believe that. Why, the man's a veritable Corinthian!"

"So he is. I hope you don't intend to meet him looking like that."

That made her head snap up, all laughter gone. "He's not here, is he?"

"No. But if you would but look at yourself, even you must agree you look less than your best."

"I never look my best," she said, picking her way through the cluttered studio to the small mirror she kept on the wall, to check for such minor details as a brush used to hold her bun in place, or a smock she'd forgotten to remove. "Oh, my." She touched the tip of her nose and grinned. "Really, it's not so bad, Stephen. There are only three pigments today, and at least I kept close to the primary colors."

"Pray be serious for once in your life, Chloe. Levity is ever your besetting sin."

"Levity is what has often saved me," she shot back.

"I doubt it will appeal to Lord Lyndon. We wouldn't want him to take a disgust of you."

"Oh, no, that would be terribly disastrous."

"So it would," he agreed in all seriousness. "His father and I have agreed—"

"His father?" She twisted to look at him, all laughter gone. "You could not be so stodgy as to arrange such a thing!"

"Actually, Father did. I am merely carrying out his wishes." He rose up on his feet again. "Someone has to look out for your future. Helena believes the match is suitable."

"She would," Chloe muttered.

"She cares only about your well-being, Chloe, as do I. She would see you comfortably settled."

"She would see me making the social rounds again," she shot back.

"And would that be so very bad?"

She stared at him. "Stephen, even you can't be so insensitive."

"I wish only the best for your future."

"So do I." She crossed the room to him. "If you would but let me set up my own establishment—"

"Out of the question, Chloe, and well you know it," he said sharply.

"Of course. We both know I'm far more valuable to you here than I'd be on my own."

"Dash it, you're my sister! You talk as if I use you."

"You would if you could." She paused. "Or my money."

"That is a nasty thing to say, Chloe," he shot back.

"But true. How wonderful for you that the marriage settlements are likely to be generous."

He looked uncomfortable. "Well, true, there are debts. Helena's clothes alone cost a fortune—"

"Stephen, how could you do this to me?"

"You talk as if I am a monster, when all I've done is arrange a good marriage for you."

"Bosh. No one wished to marry me before. Why now? Oh, don't bother answering," she said bitterly. "We both know the Lyndons are pockets to let."

"A young lady should not concern herself with such matters."

"But this lady does, and well I should, when it concerns my future. Why, if Lord Lyndon had not his own income from his estate he wouldn't be able to live as he does." She frowned as a thought struck her. "How does he feel about this?"

For the first time, he looked away. "I believe him to be agreeable."

"You believe," she said. "Then you don't actually know?"

"No"

"Oh, good Lord! Stephen, we live in modern times now. People choose whom they wish to marry."

"Not always. Father chose Helena for me, and look how that has turned out."

Chloe shuddered. Helena, their second cousin, was a pretty but brainless goose whose penniless state had made it unlikely she would marry elsewhere. She and Stephen had known each other forever, yet that mattered not. The marriage was not a happy one. "Yes, just look at it."

"There is no need for you to use that tone of voice," Stephen snapped, finally goaded by her intransigence. "You will meet with him, if nothing else."

"Very well," she said with deceptive docility. "And just when is this meeting to occur?"

"Helena has invited him to take tea with us tomorrow."

"He must be overjoyed."

"He certainly must be anticipating it," he said, making Chloe wish, once again, to bash him over the head for his lack of understanding. "I will, of course, depend upon you to be there. And not," he frowned, taking in her appearance yet again, "looking like that."

"I shall be in good looks," she said, knowing that would be inadequate at best.

"Very good." He bowed and turned to the door. "Remember, Chloe. We depend upon you for this."

"Yes, Stephen," she said tonelessly. As the door closed behind him, she whirled and flung her paintbrush against the wall. It fell to the floor, leaving a streak of carmine that joined a rainbow of other streaks left from her occasional fits of temper at a painting that wasn't going well. She stared at it balefully and then turned away, taking a deep, calming breath. Temper would not help. The only thing she could do was to think this thing through rationally.

After pacing across the floor, she slumped into a chair and pulled out the brush that held her hair in place. It tumbled upon her shoulders, unruly, tangled, and an undistinguished shade of brown. Oh, she was no beauty. She knew that. She was also clumsy, as all the world knew. *Miss Bumblebroth,* she thought with the dispassion she had trained herself to use. Why in the world would someone like Lord Michael Lyndon wish to marry her?

Chloe reached up to twist a strand of hair, stopping herself just in time. Paint there would be extraordinarily difficult to remove. For the money, of course. What other reason could there be? The Lyndons were nearly bankrupt. It would behoove her to find out exactly how serious their financial situation was. They'd welcome the money left her by her grandmother. If they had any idea . . .

No. She shook her head and her hair swirled, catching golden highlights she wouldn't have guessed she had. No one knew, and that was the way matters would remain. Never would she give over control of her entire fortune to her husband. Never would she allow him such power over it, lest he gamble away all her hard-earned gains. She would have to speak with her man of affairs about establishing another trust.

Of course, she didn't have to accept Lord Lyndon's offer, she thought, then rejected the idea with another shake of her head. Stephen and Helena both would pressure her to accept—Stephen because he truly cared about her future, Helena because she had long wished to be sole mistress in this house, with none of the servants owing their allegiance and affection to Chloe. Though why they did was a mystery to her. She was only Miss Bumblebroth.

The thought made her rise. After all this time, the name still hurt, and it was likely she'd hear it were she to go out into the world again. Her past mishaps would always be remembered and held against her, her own particular burden to bear. The only thing she could do was to refuse Lord Lyndon's offer, which would likely be a reluctant one. She doubted he would want to sully his reputation by association with her, no matter her fortune. No matter that she had increased her grandmother's legacy far beyond its original amount, though few knew of that.

The paint-splattered wall loomed up before her, proof of the side of her personality few ever saw. Fits of temper did her no good, she thought, bending to pick up the paintbrush and carefully examining the bristles for damage. Women had little power in this world. No matter that she wished to set up her own home and had the means to do so. The only way she would ever be allowed to leave this house would be through marriage, or by taking some dreary position as governess or teacher. Lord knew that didn't appeal to her. She was far too fond of her comforts and her relative freedom. Marriage, then? Her brow furrowed as she began to unbutton her smock. Mayhap. Mayhap it wasn't so disastrous an idea as she thought.

That gave her pause, as she stopped in front of the mirror to check her appearance. Patience, her maid, so aptly named a person, would likely scold her for the damage she'd done to herself, from the paint on her face to her hair, hanging loose and lank. How Patience ever suffered her she didn't know, she thought with her first genuine smile. She wondered if Lord Lyndon would do the same.

That thought made her frown as she turned away from the mirror. It always came back to that, did it not? What Lord Lyndon thought of her had suddenly, and unexpectedly, become important. *Well, sir,* she thought, putting up her chin as she stalked out of her studio, *we'll see. We'll just see.*

"I don't understand why you're doing this, miss," Patience said the following day.

"I've a plan, Patience," Chloe said, glancing at her reflection one last time. There, her hair was exactly right, and the dress was perfect. "I simply want to control my life."

Patience had been with Chloe for enough years that she felt free to speak her mind. "You never will if you continue so," she muttered.

Chloe turned. "Oh?"

"Do you think you'll ever be allowed to leave this house?"

"Who will stop me?" Chloe demanded.

"Mr. Russell."

"Not when I decide to go."

"Oh, miss." Patience looked at her sadly. "But will you ever decide to?"

"Of course I will," Chloe said sharply. "I simply will not be forced into marrying someone I don't even know. Would you care for that?"

"If it was a lord wanted to marry me, I might, and him looking as he does."

"That's of little moment. I believe I still have some say in my future." She moved away from the dressing table. "He should be here soon. Wish me luck."

"I wish you well, miss," Patience said.

Chloe frowned at her, but decided to save her energy for Lord Lyndon's visit and his probable offer of marriage. She was rather anticipating it.

"Oh, no," Helena moaned when Chloe walked into the drawing room a few moments later. "Why did you pick that dress, and on today, of all days? And when I specifically told you to wear your pink? You never did have a sense of style, but was this made by the village dressmaker at home? Not

that village dressmakers can't be good, I've had some per-
fectly lovely frocks made in the country, but—"

"Actually, this is a London frock," Chloe said, smiling.
She knew her dress of plain beige book muslin was neither
new nor flattering, and that it had never been in the first
stare of fashion. That was, of course, the point. So was her
hair, which she had deliberately left tousled. Not that that
made much difference.

"But not from any modiste I would acknowledge. Chloe,
you look a veritable quiz."

"Why, thank you, Helena," Chloe said, settling herself
on the couch. "Coming from you, that's high praise."

"Stephen, please talk with your sister."

"Chloe, do you wish to ruin everything?" Stephen asked
through clenched teeth.

"Actually, yes."

"Dash it, the man has a title! You'd be a viscountess."

"As if I care for that." She looked at her sister-in-law.
"Shall I go change?"

Helena took another look at her and shuddered again.
"There's not enough time to repair—that."

"Oh, good," Chloe said brightly, and picked up her embroidery. Lord Lyndon should see her at a ladylike pursuit,
particularly when she did so poorly at it.

"I will be very annoyed with you if things do not go
well," Stephen said.

"Oh, dear."

"Don't try me, Chloe. Helena."

His wife looked up. "Yes, Stephen?"

"Try to make her understand how important this is, if
you will." He glowered at Chloe. "I shall be in the library,
awaiting Lord Lyndon," he added, and stalked out.

"I simply do not know why you are so opposed to this
match," Helena fretted. "He is quite an eligible *parti*."

"Yes, Helena." Chloe fixed her attention on her tangled
embroidery silks.

"I needn't tell you that this match is quite important,"
Helena went on.

Chloe looked up. "Why?"

"Need you ask? Chloe, my dear, we wish to see you established in the world."

You wish to be rid of me. "There are, of course, the marriage settlements to think of."

"As if we care about such a thing! I'm sure I don't know why that should matter to you. We are your family."

Chloe's lips tightened. "I apologize, Helena, but I do so dislike the idea of being penniless."

"Really, Chloe, you are the most ungrateful chit! When we have fed you and housed you for all this time."

" 'Tis my house, too."

"Oh, my dear, do not believe that we would pressure you into something you do not wish."

"Of course not," Chloe murmured, frowning at a particularly complicated knot.

"We simply wish only for your own good. Your silks are all tangled again," she added.

"Oh, really?"

"Perhaps 'twould be wise for you to put that away. We don't wish Lord Lyndon to believe you to be inept."

"I daresay he already does."

Helena eyed her with suspicion. "Chloe, surely you aren't thinking of refusing him."

Chloe looked up, and their eyes met. "I might."

"You might?" It was very nearly a shriek. "Oh, I fear I am about to swoon. Chloe, my vinaigrette! Please!"

Chloe let out a sigh, but she crossed the room to fetch the vinaigrette. Helena needed recourse to one quite often. Though she could appear entirely weak and helpless, Helena ruled the household with an iron hand. Doubtless it was her idea that Chloe marry, although Stephen probably thought that the inspiration was his.

For now, though, there was nothing for it but to hold the silver-chased object below her sister-in-law's nose. "Here," she said. "Take a deep breath. 'Twill revive you."

Helena did as ordered, eyeing Chloe balefully. "Really,

you are the most ungrateful chit," she said again. "When we have worked so hard on your behalf."

"I don't know what I could be thinking of." Chloe returned to her chair as Helena again sat upright.

"Nor do I. He is a fine catch, especially for you."

Chloe's lips twitched. "Yes, Helena," she said, somehow gaining control of herself.

"Mr. Russell and I believe—yes, Horricks, what is it?" she broke off, as the butler came into the room.

"Excuse me, madam," he said, bowing as he proffered a silver tray bearing a calling card. "Lord Lyndon is here."

"Oh, dear," Chloe said before she could stop herself, and Horricks glanced at her, his features softening marginally.

"He appears quite the gentleman, miss," he said daringly. Helena might think she was mistress of the house, but even she knew, deep down, who the servants favored.

"Of course he does. He is a viscount," Helena snapped. "You are getting above yourself, Horricks."

"I am sorry, madam."

"So you should be. Well? Why are you keeping his lordship waiting? Show him up."

"Yes, madam," he said, and, his back stiff, left the room.

"Chloe, do sit up straight," Helena ordered. "And put that horrible embroidery in the workbag. Why you needs must persist in trying embroidery—yes, Horricks?"

"Lord Lyndon, madam," he said tonelessly, again shooting a look at Chloe, this one brimming with conspiratorial amusement.

"Oh! Lord Lyndon, do come in." Helena held out her hand. "We're honored by your condescension in paying us this call."

Lord Lyndon bowed over Helena's hand, and then looked from one to the other, somehow making Chloe sit as straight as even Helena could wish. Although his face was blankly polite, she suspected this man was awake on all suits. "Mrs. Russell. Miss Russell."

Helena simpered up at him as he bent over her hand. From beneath lowered eyelids, Chloe studied him as he sat on the sofa across from her. Heavens, he was more handsome than she remembered, and so faultlessly dressed that he made her feel even more untidy than she already did. His bottle green coat was made of the best superfine, his boots of the best leather, and his pantaloons—Chloe suddenly looked away, hoping she wasn't blushing. Lord, but the image of how his pantaloons fit along his muscular thighs stayed with her. Neither could she forget the way they hugged his narrow hips, the hips of a true horseman. *Good heavens, Chloe,* she thought. *You've never had such thoughts before.*

"It is my pleasure," Michael said gravely, careful to keep his eyes blank. 'Twas a long time since he'd felt so diverted as he had when Chloe had sized him up so thoroughly. There'd been more feminine interest than he'd expected in her quick glance, but also something else. Speculation, but not what he was used to, for his title or his prospects. No, it was as if she were, for some reason, surprised.

"Would you care for a dish of tea?" Helena went on. "I daresay you would prefer something stronger, but I do so enjoy tea at this time of day. One is amazed to think of it coming from such a heathen country. I prefer orange pekoe myself—"

"Helena," Chloe said, her voice lower and more musical than he'd expected. "The tea?"

"The tea? Oh, yes, of course, you'll think me quite birdwitted, my lord."

Very much to his surprise, Michael met Chloe's eyes and saw them dancing with humor. For the first time, it occurred to him to question the dreadful frock she wore. "Thank you," he said, and settled back to enjoy himself.

"The Season has been fine so far, has it not?"

"Yes." He looked squarely at Chloe. "Are you enjoying it, Miss Russell?"

"I rarely go out in company, sir," Chloe said. "I'd rather paint."

"Paint?" *Interesting.* She acted as if she were not on the

catch for him at all. It was, again, not the behavior of the young misses he was accustomed to.

"Yes, our Chloe is quite the artist," Helena put in.

"Watercolors, I presume," he said, sounding deliberately bored.

Chloe set down her saucer so hard it rattled on the fine inlaid table. "Oils," she said flatly. "Watercolors are missish."

He blinked. "Are they any good?"

"Of course."

"Chloe!" Helena looked at her in dismay. "Do remember yourself."

"I am, Helena." Chloe's face was calm. "I remember Lord Lyndon has come here to discuss a proposition with me."

"Chloe!" Helena exclaimed again, and Michael laughed into his fist. Lord, but there was far more to the girl than he had known. A proposition, indeed. He might not actually be facing disaster, after all.

"Oh, my lord." Helena looked genuinely distressed. "I must apologize for Chloe."

"There's no use apologizing for me, Helena," Chloe said cheerfully. "I suspect Lord Lyndon prefers plain speaking."

"Quite." He looked directly at Helena. "May I have a few moments alone with your sister-in-law?"

Agonized, Helena looked from one to the other, and then reluctantly nodded. "Oh, certainly, Lord Lyndon. I shall be in the library with Mr. Russell."

"So," Chloe said, before the door had fully closed behind Helena, before he'd had a chance to turn back to her, "who's forcing you to this?"

Two

This time Michael's laugh rang out. "Are you always so outspoken?"

Chloe grinned unrepentantly at him. "Often. 'Tis so prodigious easy to shock Helena that I couldn't resist."

"It was really too bad of you," he said gently, and her hectic glee faded.

"I suppose it was." She let out a gusty sigh. "I shall have to apologize to her again. I do make Helena's life rather a trial sometimes." She looked up at him. "I apologize to you, sir, as well. I shall quite understand if my behavior has given you a disgust of me."

He sat opposite to her again, his crossed leg swinging freely. "No. Rather the contrary, actually."

"Oh, pity."

He blinked. "I beg your pardon?"

"I was hoping it would."

At that, he grinned. "You are more interesting than I thought. I'd not known that."

"No. You've heard other things."

"As it happens, yes."

"That I'm called Miss Bumblebroth."

"A cruel name," he said, again gentle.

"I earned it!" she exclaimed, and then glared at him as he let out a laugh again. "What?"

"My dear Miss Russell, are you defending it?"

"No! Oh." She collapsed against the back of the sofa,

her spine curving into the slump Helena so decried. "This will never do. We'll never suit, sir."

"I'm not so certain."

That made her sit up. "You can't be serious! Why?"

"You make me laugh," he said simply.

"Yes. At me."

"Oh, no, my dear Miss Russell. At the things you say, perhaps the things you do, but never at you."

"No? When I've embarrassed you enough, when your friends have had enough jokes at your expense, when our pictures have been in the broadsheets enough times because I've made us both look foolish, how will you react? Will you hide your eyes and pretend to be aloof, the way you do now, or will you laugh? Not at the things I say, but at me?"

He was staring at her in mingled surprise and speculation, though she wasn't sure why. "I'm not precisely sure," he said, after a moment. "Perhaps 'tis arrogant of me to say such a thing, except that I hope I'd be civilized enough not to make mock of my wife."

"Your wife!" She squeaked. "But you haven't even asked—you haven't even made me—"

"A proposition?"

She clapped her hands to her mouth. "Did I truly say that?"

"I fear you did. My grandmother would have liked you, I think. She'd have said you weren't one of those milk-and-water misses throwing themselves at my head."

"Do they?" she asked, with the first faint stirrings of interest and something else, an emotion that was new.

"Throw themselves at me? Oh, Lord, yes," he said, sounding bored, as he had earlier. "All simpering sweetness and shy glances, and all the time they're sizing me up like prime breeding stock."

"Like a cotillion being danced at Tattersall's."

He laughed now, displaying strong white teeth whose slight unevenness was somehow endearing. "Yes, rather like that," he agreed. "Do you know, I begin to think marriage is a fine idea, if only to protect myself."

"To me?" Her voice was a squeak again. How could she, inadequate as she was, protect him from anything?

"Yes, why not?"

"Because 'tis only something our fathers arranged."

"Such marriages have been known to thrive."

"Some haven't," she retorted.

"True. I think ours might be better than most. If we're always honest with each other."

"No fear of that with me, sir," she said ruefully. "As you've seen."

"Quite." He reached out to catch her hand, and a curious sensation, almost like a shiver, went through her. She tried to pull back, but his grip was too strong. "Will you do me the honor of becoming my wife?"

She looked down, a little surprised to realize that her hand was trembling. "I know this is the part where I'm supposed to tell you that la, sir, this is so sudden, but—"

"No buts." He tipped her chin up with a finger. He was not overtly forceful, and yet his eyes—dark brown, with thick, long lashes, she realized—were compelling. "Well, Miss Russell?"

Chloe looked at their linked hands again. Did she truly wish to marry this man? Half an hour ago she would have thought it unlikely, but things had changed. What further chance would she have of meeting or marrying anyone, let alone so superb a man?

More importantly, he seemed kind and good-humored, and he would not, apparently, turn that humor against her. But marriage? Lord!

Yet the future held few other prospects for her, other than dwindling down to become poor Aunt Chloe, so graceless and so tactless. It still wasn't her choice, but since society frowned upon a woman living alone, that option was closed to her. Marriage to Lord Lyndon was her only chance for a decent life.

She raised her head, hoping he wouldn't see how very

vulnerable she felt at that moment. "Yes, Lord Lyndon. I believe I will."

He bowed. "You have made me the happiest of men."

"I rather doubt that."

He laughed and raised her hand to his lips. The touch sent that shiver through her again, stronger this time. "Shall we go tell your brother?"

She nodded. "Helena must believe I tripped over you, or some such thing."

To her surprise he didn't laugh, but instead placed his hand on her shoulder, turning her. "Perhaps I won't be able to promise never to laugh at you," he said at her look of inquiry, "but I can tell you this: From this day on, I will challenge each and every man who calls you 'Miss Bumblebroth.' "

"Oh," Chloe said inadequately, and tumbled headlong, heedlessly, helplessly in love with him.

The news spread quickly through London—or at least the part of London that mattered. In clubs or at Almack's, at Vauxhall or in overheated, overcrowded ballrooms, the *ton* could talk of nothing else. Miss Bumblebroth had snared herself a husband at last, and such a husband! No one knew how. Certainly the prospective bridegroom gave nothing away, and one never saw her. She seemed never to step foot outside the Russell house on Curzon Street, not to go to Hatchard's for books or to Gunter's for ices, and certainly not to drive in the park at the fashionable hour. No one even knew if she were visiting modistes for her bride clothes, though she must be. Even Miss Bumblebroth must have some interest in clothes.

On the morning after the announcements of his engagement appeared in all the London newspapers, Michael rose earlier than usual and rode at a sedate pace toward Hyde Park. He did not go late to *ton* affairs, because his mornings and their activities were too important to him. Yesterday he'd had to face the reaction of his friends and acquaintances, their surprise and their jokes and their jeers. And even though he'd thought himself prepared for them, he hadn't been. He was a noted athlete, a true Corinthian. Why else would he be awake when most of the fashionable world slept? Yet here he was, engaged to Miss Chloe Russell, and all because his father and hers had made an informal arrangement. Of course, he thought dispassionately, his father had been thinking of James at the time. James, who had been dead now—Michael closed his eyes and calculated. Fifteen years, ten months, and four days.

London, like Michael, was already awake and bustling, and Mayfair was no exception, with traffic and vendors crying their wares. Still, he was surprised, as he turned into the park from Park Lane and prepared to break into a canter, to see another rider coming toward him. He pulled Thor aside to allow the other man to pass, and then stopped altogether as he spoke. "Good morning, Lyndon."

"Good morning, Hempstead." His answer was merely polite. Michael had never particularly liked him, though he wasn't sure why. It had little to do with Hempstead's being a member of the dandy set, making their acquaintance slight. All they had in common was Chloe, Hempstead's cousin. "You're up early."

"The other way around. Up late, went home, and couldn't sleep. So." He made a slight movement of his shoulders that might have been a shrug, had he wanted to disturb the set of his riding coat. "I decided to ride instead."

"I see." Michael nodded, and dug his heels into Thor's sides. "If you'll excuse me."

"I gather we're to be connected, in a manner of speaking," Edwin interrupted.

The man sat his horse well, Michael would say that for him. "Relatively speaking."

"Relatively—oh. Oh, yes, that's good, Lyndon." Edwin's laugh held not the slightest bit of humor. "Yes, I suppose it is that. Good gad, man, why Chloe?"

"Why not?" Michael answered coolly.

"Why not?" He gave that humorless laugh again. "She hardly fits into your way of life."

Something about this man set Michael's teeth on edge, made him forget the doubts about Chloe that yesterday's remarks and jokes had awakened in him. "I believe she and I will rub along together tolerably enough."

"Do you?" To Michael's annoyance, Edwin turned his horse alongside Thor. "She doesn't ride. Did you know that?"

Michael trained his gaze ahead. "Yes, I do."

"Poor Chloe." He laughed. "She always kept falling off. We used to tease her about it."

"Did you?" Michael glanced sidelong at him.

"All the time. She should have been tied on. Then mayhap she wouldn't have fallen so much."

"Did you know her well when you were young?"

"Know her? Good gad, we're practically brother and sister. Not really, of course. My mother was Chloe's mother's stepsister. But we all grew up with her, my sister Helena and Stephen and I. We all played together."

"Quite," Michael said, his jaw tight as he gazed ahead.

"None of us were very surprised at the things she did during her come-out," Edwin continued, leaning forward as if imparting a great secret. "Appalled, of course, but never truly surprised. She's always been clumsy. No wonder she's called—"

Michael glared at him. "Careful."

"You've heard it before, Lyndon." Edwin grinned. "You knew it when you proposed to her."

And had used the name himself. His grip on the reins tightened briefly, and Thor sidled. "I intend to challenge anyone who calls her by that name."

Edwin reared back. "Good gad, why?"

"It matters not. You might wish to tell your cronies of my intentions."

"I do believe you have a *tendre* for her, Lyndon."

"Believe as you wish," Michael said carelessly. "The

challenge stands. Now, if you'll excuse me, I wish to seek more congenial company."

"That was unnecessary, Lyndon," Hempstead called as Michael cantered away, making Michael smile grimly. So he was discomposed. Good. He deserved it, after what he'd said about Chloe.

What kind of life had she had, growing up? Lord knew his own had been difficult, but it sounded as if hers had been a constant torture. He didn't love her, and probably never would, but he could undertake to protect her from the Hempsteads of the world. If nothing else, his challenge stood.

The lamps from the Grantham town carriage gave faint illumination to the scene outside, of imposing town houses and mansions. In spite of that, Chloe looked firmly out. Her hands were tightly clasped in her lap, her shoulders hunched. Although the announcements had already appeared in the newspapers, she had yet to meet Michael's parents. She wished she were going anywhere else—well, almost anywhere else—than she was.

"It will be all right," Michael said, laying his hand on hers.

Startled, she turned toward him. "Oh, of course," she said. "I'm n-not worried at all."

"Chloe." His grasp tightened. It was improper for him to call her by her first name so early in their acquaintance, and yet it suited her. "My parents are decent people."

"Oh, I know. At least, I assume they are. You're their son, aren't you? They'd have to be decent."

He was glad she couldn't see him smile in the darkness. "You'll find that my father can be distant at times. He's very much a rational man, not an emotional one."

"He also arranged the match."

"So he did, but I proposed because I wished to."

"Mm."

"And what, pray tell, is that supposed to mean?"

"He must be happy about the match."

"I suppose he is, in his way." Again, he smiled. "My mother, however . . ."

"What about her?" she asked, with the first real interest, however faint, she'd displayed all evening.

"She has been wishing me to marry for years."

"Oh." Chloe looked away again. "Of course. She must feel as your father does. You are the heir, after all. She would like you to carry on the line."

"She wants grandchildren," he said bluntly. "She'll likely tell you that tonight."

"Is she that outspoken?"

"She rivals you, my dear."

That brought a laugh from her. "I am not so terrible."

"Only at certain moments. Truly, Chloe, all she wishes for is my happiness."

"Does she really think you'll find that with me?" she said dubiously.

He was quiet for a time. "I think we'll deal well together. I'd rather we didn't have a marriage where I have my interests and you have yours, and so we never see each other. I'd like us to be closer than that."

"So would I. I wish I could ride, or drive a carriage."

"My dear, I can teach you those things."

"I don't think so."

"Chloe, I am not marrying you for your accomplishments."

"Then why?"

He let out his breath. Lord, she could be blunt. He'd have to accustom himself to that. "Because I do think we'll deal well together. Many marriages in our set have started with less."

"True."

"It will be all right," he said again. "Trust me."

Chloe nodded. She had her doubts. Anyone who could produce so splendid a male as Lord Lyndon must be formidable. "If this isn't what you want, Lyndon, I'll cry off," she said hesitantly.

Even through the darkness, she could feel his gaze. "Is that what you want?"

"No, or I'd not have accepted you." She hesitated. "Does it bother you that I have money?"

"It bothers me that I must marry for it!"

"Oh," she said, her voice sounding small even to her. If he felt that way now, with only her dowry to consider, how would he react when he knew the truth?

"Ah, Chloe," he said, after a moment. "Forgive me. We both faced pressure from our families. Well meant, of course."

"Of course." She grinned suddenly. "Who would ever think we'd actually like each other?"

He chuckled. "Scandalous, in our set."

"Indeed. But I'm used to scandal."

"And I believe I could grow accustomed to it, had I reason." The carriage slowed. "We're here."

Chloe's stomach felt suddenly hollow. Through Michael's window she could just see the grand mansion fronting Grosvenor Square, its windows ablaze with light. Though she was familiar with the house by day, somehow at night it seemed more imposing. "Is there to be company?"

"No. They are welcoming you." He jumped out of the carriage before the footman could come forward to lower the step, making her envy his lean, athletic grace.

She would be likely to catch her heel in her gown and tumble forward, she thought glumly, though it didn't happen.

He held out his hand. "Come."

The great front door of the mansion, its lion's head door knocker showing not a speck of tarnish, was opened before they could reach it.

"Evening, Foster," Michael said.

"Good evening my lord." The butler bowed. "The earl and the countess are in the drawing room."

"Thank you." He handed his cloak to a footman, revealing clothes that were in the height of fashion and yet managed to be elegantly restrained as well. Over white satin knee breeches, he wore a faultlessly tailored coat of midnight blue velvet. His linen was snowy white, unadorned by lace or by any jewelry save for a diamond stickpin; his waistcoat was pale blue brocade, shot through with gold threads. He looked splendid.

For the first time, Chloe, usually so unconcerned about her appearance, wished she had not let Helena choose her gown, an unfortunate froth of white watered silk trimmed with huge pink roses about the hem. The color made her appear sallow, while the cut gave her a deceptive appearance of plumpness. At least Patience had labored mightily over her hair, carefully threading it through with white satin ribbon, but Chloe knew well it would be falling down before evening's end. What Lord and Lady Grantham would think of her, she couldn't guess.

"Miss Russell?" Michael said, and she looked up to see that he was holding his arm out to her. Somewhat to her surprise, not only was he smiling at her, but his eyes were warm. The sight gave her courage. Returning his smile with more confidence than she actually felt, she placed her hand on his arm and let him escort her from the hall, tiled in gleaming black and white marble, up the U-shaped marble stairs with their gilded handrails. Far above them soared a dome, its paintings indistinguishable now in the dimness. There was nothing the least bit shabby about this house, nothing to show that the Granthams were pockets to let.

The butler announced them in the drawing room, and the two people within looked up. Chloe's breath was suddenly shallow. "Michael." The earl crossed to them, his hand extended. "Good of you to come."

Michael inclined his head. "Good evening, sir. May I present Miss Russell to you?"

"My lord," Chloe murmured, and curtsied. Thank heavens, she didn't fall or even wobble, she thought as she rose and took the earl's hand. "It is an honor to meet you, sir."

"Come forward, child, and let me look at you." Although the earl was not above medium height, his bearing was such that he seemed taller. His hair was iron gray with silver at the temples, his coat was of mulberry velvet, and his breeches were of silvery satin. Everything about him proclaimed him to be a man of substance, of importance. "I knew your father, miss," he said at last. "He'd be pleased with this."

"Yes, my lord, I believe he would." Uneasy under his probing gaze, Chloe glanced away, studying the room. Here again there were few signs that the Granthams were in need of funds. It was true that the golden silk draperies were a bit faded; the Axminster carpet was frayed here and there, but it was undeniably fine. So was the furniture, Georgian in style, well polished in beeswax and upholstered in red brocade. There were no lighter squares on the wall to indicate where paintings had once hung. In fact, those that were there were undoubtedly valuable.

Only as Chloe gazed at what she recognized as a Tintoretto did she become aware of something subtly wrong with it. The brushwork was characteristic of the old master, but not, perhaps, quite up to his standards; the colors were just a little too bright. Why, it was a duplicate, she realized, her eyes widening. A clever one, but not the original, and that made all the rest of the artwork in the room suspicious.

Chloe cast a quick look toward Michael, who was regarding her from under hooded eyes, and felt herself flush. Doubtless he had seen her expression and knew the trend of her thoughts. Well, no matter, she thought with an inward sigh. She'd known all along her betrothed needed money. It was simply lowering to know that it was all he wished from her.

"Miss Russell, may I also present my mother to you," he said at that moment, and escorted her across the room. Seated on a sofa was a slender, pretty lady of indeterminate years, just now setting aside her needlework. In contrast to the earl, she smiled at Chloe. If in the earl Chloe could see how Michael would look in future years, it was obvious he had inherited more than his eyes from his mother. She appeared friendly and not the least bit overbearing. Chloe's breathing at last slowed to normal, and her own smile relaxed.

"How delightful to meet you, Chloe. I may call you that, may I not? I do detest formality," the countess said, holding out her hand. "I made my come-out with your mother."

"Oh, did you know her?" Chloe said eagerly as she sat next to the countess.

"Quite well. You've the look of her."

"I do? But in her portrait, she's lovely."

"Tut, tut, do stop fishing for compliments."

"Mother," Michael said again, and Chloe suddenly relaxed. The countess was not so very different from herself. "Please allow Miss Russell a chance to become acquainted with you before you start frightening her."

"Why?" The countess turned to face him where he stood, his elbow propped on the mantel. "She may as well know the worst of me from the beginning. And you know quite well I never mean any harm."

"Oh, I'm not the least bit frightened," Chloe assured her.

Michael and the earl exchanged what could only be called exasperated looks, and Chloe thought she saw more than a hint of fondness in the earl's eyes for his wife. She hoped someday Michael would look at her like that.

"Good. I've been so hoping you aren't missish. I can see you are not. Ah, there goes the dinner bell," she said, and rose. "Come, my dear, let us go in together."

Conversation at the dinner table was dominated by the earl. He spoke of theater and the opera, of men he had met at White's that afternoon and what they had discussed, of politics and the mismanagement of the war on the Peninsula. Lady Grantham and Michael appeared to be used to it. They ate mostly in silence, though once the countess rolled her eyes at Chloe, who had to bite her lips to hold back a smile. The repressive look Michael gave her only added to her amusement. Any fears she'd had about fitting into this family eased.

At length the countess rose, signaling to Chloe that they would leave the gentlemen to their port and cigars. Though

Chloe and his mother seemed to go along well enough, still Chloe sent him a look of silent entreaty. It hit Michael, then, that their marriage would expose her to the scorn of a society from which she had hidden for three years. He would have to protect her from that.

"She isn't nearly as bad as you would have me believe, Michael," the earl said in a carrying voice, as a footman reached to close the dining room door. For just a moment Chloe's eyes met his, and then the door closed behind her.

In the hall, the countess sighed and linked her arm through Chloe's. "Men can be remarkably stupid," she remarked.

"Oh, yes," Chloe replied, more fervently than was perhaps proper. That the earl held such a low opinion of her came as no surprise. That Michael shared it, though, was unexpected, and more painful than she could have guessed. She knew he didn't love her. She had not known, though, until this moment, that he scorned her as well. "And it may be a good thing."

The countess arranged the skirts of her gown gracefully around her as she sat on the same sofa in the drawing room she had occupied before, and indicated to Chloe to join her. "How so, my dear?"

"How could we manage them, else?"

That surprised a laugh from the countess. "Do you know, I begin to believe you'll do."

"I believe I must, must I not?"

The countess shook her head, sighing a bit as her smile faded. "I cannot like these cold-blooded arrangements. It's not fair to you or to Michael. I do not mean anything against you, of course," she added. "All you need do is look at the Duke and Duchess of Trowbridge."

"But didn't Lyndon set his interest on her once?"

"Until her father arranged a better offer, though he must be thirty years older than she. A more simpering, sly young miss I've yet to meet."

"Few would agree with you, ma'am."

"And don't I know it. Oh, pray don't mind me. I am

known to be remarkably cross-grained, especially with my family."

Chloe smiled. "Then I must consider myself honored."

Again the countess laughed. "Oh, you will do, my dear. Michael needs someone like you, if he but knew it."

"But I cannot ride or drive or even dance. Sometimes I wonder if I am able even to walk."

"Oh, piffle, a few trifling incidents." Lady Grantham waved off what had been to Chloe the most mortifying moments of her life. "Of course you've no sense of style."

Chloe blinked and then plucked at the white silk of her gown. "This was Helena's choice."

"Ah. That explains it. I can see I'll have to take you in hand. I shall bring you to Madame Celeste."

"Celeste," Chloe said in dismay at the name of London's most fashionable modiste. "Oh, no, ma'am. Could I not go to someone else? I've heard the new modiste Jeannette does wonderful work."

"So she might, but she does not have the cachet Celeste does. And then to Mademoiselle Therese for hats, and to a wonderful linen draper I know for stockings and such. Trust me, my dear," Lady Grantham said at her doubtful look. "I have the best in mind for you."

"Yes, ma'am," Chloe said, still doubtfully.

"Have you any preference in your clothing?"

"No, only that the necklines are modest." She paused. "Very modest."

The countess surveyed her. "I cannot see why. I suspect you've a lovely figure under that sack."

She's top-heavy, Helena had once said. *No wonder she falls so often.*

But what was her excuse before? another voice had answered, and they all had laughed. All these years later, the memory still had the power to hurt.

"Never mind, dear," Lady Grantham said, patting Chloe's hand, as if she had heard the words herself. "Trust me, men are drawn to such figures. I see I've embarrassed you."

"Oh, no, ma'am," Chloe murmured.

"Oh, yes, ma'am. Put yourself in my hands, and you'll see." Head tilted to the side, she regarded Chloe. "You may not have a sense of style, but you do have something better."

"What is that, ma'am?"

She looked straightly at Chloe. "A brain. Mind you use it, now."

"How will I manage, else?" Chloe asked, relieved that the subject had turned. Both women were laughing when the door to the drawing room was opened and the gentlemen came in.

"Manage?" Michael asked as he came to stand behind Chloe. His touch on her shoulder was feather light, and yet she felt a jolt go through her.

Chloe's gaze met that of her future mother-in-law's. "Nothing so very difficult," she said, and they smiled conspiratorially at each other.

Three

A ball to announce any engagement was de rigueur. Chloe knew that, and yet for days before her stomach turned hollow whenever she thought about it. It didn't help that she had both Lady Grantham and Helena, in alt about a connection to such an illustrious family, fussing about her, or that their ideas of style were so very different. Their tussles were sometimes so vehement that Chloe, who never had been prone to the headache, sometimes developed one and happily escaped. She was relieved when the issue was settled, with the countess the victor, though Helena sulked for days.

Thus as she stood next to Michael in the receiving line at the top of the stairs in the Grantham house, greeting the guests for the ball, her hands were clammy inside her gloves. All the cream of the *ton* was present, from Sally Jersey to Beau Brummel to the Duke of Devonshire. It was even rumored Prinny himself might make an appearance, a thought that made Chloe quake with terror. Her last encounter with royalty had been disastrous. At least while she was standing still, there was little chance of her tripping.

She glanced up at Michael, so tall and straight beside her, only the fact that he shifted from one foot to the other betraying his restlessness. He was dressed in his usual restrained style, tonight wearing a coat of burgundy velvet as a concession to the occasion, over a waistcoat of white and gray striped satin, and satin knee breeches. His neckcloth was tied with deceptive simplicity, and his hair was, for now, brushed back from his face. For decoration he wore only a diamond stickpin in his neckcloth, making nearly all the other gentlemen who passed through the receiving line, wearing coats in peacock shades and adorned with an abundance of fobs, watches, quizzing glasses and the like, look overdressed and faintly ridiculous.

Chloe's gaze was wistful as she took in his broad shoulders and his legs, well muscled from his various sporting activities. He was hers, but was she his? So far, there had been nothing the least bit loverlike in his attitude toward her. Oh, he smiled at her, laughed with her, took her for drives, but just so would he treat a younger sister. He didn't love her as she loved him, and, given the circumstances of their engagement, she shouldn't expect him to. But she could wish for it.

The receiving line was growing thin, with nearly all the invited guests already arrived. Michael turned to her with a smile. "Such is my mother's idea of a small, select gathering."

"Did you expect else?" She returned the smile. "It is an honor to you."

Michael, both concerned and exasperated by such an answer, looked at her, frowning. "And to you, as well."

"Of course," she replied lightly, and then went suddenly still and pale, gripping Michael's arm. His gaze sharpened on her before he turned to see just who was passing through the receiving line to provoke such a response in her.

"Lyndon," Edwin Hempstead made him a slight bow, and Michael's lips tightened. He'd known Hempstead, as Chloe's cousin, had been invited, but he wasn't pleased about it. "A pleasure to see you again."

"Mr. Hempstead. Of course you know Miss Russell."

"As you know. Well met, cuz," he said, bowing over Chloe's limp hand.

"Edwin," she said through bloodless lips. "I haven't seen you this age."

"No, not since you began hiding away." He took in her

appearance in one quick, dismissive glance. "You look quite well."

Utter rage went through Michael, and his hands clenched into fists. He thought Chloe, in her gown of some soft, silky rose stuff, with an overdress of lace, looked more than well. At her throat she wore only pearls, and her face was framed by softly curling strands of hair, artfully teased from the knot about her head. She looked attractive. She *was* attractive. The thought made him take a second look at her.

"I believe everyone has arrived, my dear," he said, smiling down at Chloe in a deliberately proprietary way. "We're to open the ball."

"Do keep a space open on your dance card for me, cuz," Edwin said.

"Yes, of course," Chloe said automatically, but in her gaze Michael read terror.

He smiled reassuringly at her. "Come, my dear. We must go into the ballroom to open the ball." His bow to the other man was infinitesimal. "If you will excuse us."

"Of course. I shall see you later, cuz."

Hempstead's faintly mocking smile made Michael long to hit him again. "Not if I can help it," he muttered, more determined than ever to protect her from such people, and saw Chloe glance quickly up at him.

"What dance is it?" she whispered as they entered the ballroom, which glittered with the light from the polished crystal chandeliers and the jewels worn by the various ladies present. The countess had kept the decor simple, rather than drape festoons of silk everywhere, as some hostesses had been known to do, or garlands of flowers. She had made artful use of plants, having set flowers and shrubs in pots placed around the room, along with small trees gaily draped in ribbons to match Chloe's gown, but in the press of people Michael could barely see them.

"A cotillion, if there is room to move," he whispered in return. At that moment the orchestra began to play the stately measures of the dance, and the throng took to the floor as the two of them, joined by his parents and two other couples who were particular friends of the Granthams, made up a set. The guests did the same, though Michael was aware that they watched him and Chloe. "Buck up, my dear. We'll brush through this together."

Together they went through the opening steps of the dance. He was a competent dancer, and he watched Chloe in delighted surprise as, head lowered, she followed his lead, if less gracefully. It was a complicated dance, allowing little conversation, and he knew she was watching her feet and concentrating on performing the steps. Until, as they turned, she lost her balance and nearly fell.

"Oh, dear," she whispered, biting her lip.

" 'Tis not important," he whispered back. "Relax."

"Easy for you to say," she muttered, but she lowered her head again. For perhaps three steps she did well enough, but then disaster stuck again. This time, she somehow stumbled over her gown and nearly fell into him. He righted her quickly with his free hand, just as he heard a distinct snicker in the crowd. His head snapped up, and his gaze was furious, accusatory. How dare anyone laugh at his Chloe?

"Fools. I wish we'd never invited the lot of them," Lady Grantham said.

"Then there'd be no ball," the earl said, unbending so much as to smile at Chloe.

"Edward, I don't know why you ever persist in taking me seriously. Though I own it would have been a far better idea."

"Oh, my lady," Chloe put in, her face scarlet. Buttressed now by his parents' support, she was dancing correctly, if not smoothly. "You've done me such an honor."

"I've exposed you to ridicule. I should have remembered how cruel and thoughtless society can be."

"It doesn't matter." Chloe's tone was gallant, but Michael could see from her eyes how hurt and frightened she was. And there was still the entire evening to be got through.

"Pray save another dance for me," he said abruptly.

"But you've this dance and the supper dance, and that is all that is allowed."

"Save one for me, regardless."

"And for me," the earl said.

"I'll sit one out with you, if it keeps another bas—fool away," the countess put in.

"Mother!" Michael exclaimed, choking back a laugh. "Your language."

She raised her head defiantly. " 'Tis true."

Chloe looked from one to the other of these people, championing her as no one in her life, except her mother, ever had, and felt her eyes sting with tears. If Michael didn't love her, he was at least a decent, honorable man, and so were those now gathered about her. She was lucky to have them as friends and, soon, as family. "You're all so wonderful," she exclaimed.

"Yes, aren't we?" Lady Grantham beamed at her as the music ended. "You're part of us now, dear. Best you get used to the idea of being wonderful as well."

Chloe laughed, giddy with happiness, something she'd not expected to feel tonight. "Of course I am. Lyndon." She turned to Michael. "I will graciously accord you another dance."

He inclined his head gravely. "I shall mark my dance card. Will that suffice?"

"I suppose it will do."

"Adam." He gestured toward a young man standing some distance away with a group of other people. The man, Lord Adam Burnet, turned and began walking toward them. He was much of an age with Michael, though his heavy-lidded eyes and languid posture made him appear sleepy against Michael's athleticism and restlessness. However, Chloe, who had met him earlier in the receiving line and had been the recipient of an unexpectedly keen gaze, wondered if there weren't something more beneath that lazy exterior. "Miss Russell desires a dance with you."

"Lyndon," Chloe protested.

Lord Adam bowed. "I'd be honored. Miss Russell?"

Chloe looked from Michael to the arm Lord Adam held out to her, and then laughed again. "You give me no choice, do you?"

"No quarter asked, none given," Michael said.

"Then, my lord, I'd be happy to," she said, and laid her hand on Lord Adam's arm.

"She is delightful," Lady Grantham said later, as she and Michael, standing beside her, watched Chloe trying to perform the intricate figures of a contredanse. Though she failed more often than not, there were moments when her face glowed with laughter. "How very lucky you are to have found her."

"Mm." Michael's gaze followed his fiancée. She *was* delightful, his Chloe. He hoped the *ton,* so often fickle in its tastes, would agree, not for himself, but for her. Though he hadn't known her for very long, already the thought of anyone calling her by that insulting name enraged him. If he heard of anyone using it again, he might not simply challenge him. He might kill him. And that, he thought, going still, was astonishing.

She was a success. She, Chloe Russell, who had been scorned by the *ton* and was engaged partly because of a prior arrangement, was a success. Of course, it helped that Michael had a number of friends who had been happy to stand up with her, but even without that, she had partners. Shy Mr. Wentworth, who, though nearly thirty and with a tidy fortune to his name, was still unmarried, had approached her with so much nervousness that she'd forgotten her own fears. She sat out a set with Sir Roland Parker, an older man who, like her, was the target of the *ton's* malice, because his deafness made him speak loudly and mispronounce his words. Finally, she danced with Lord Farrow, who had lost his wife several years earlier and still grieved. For the first time she could remember, her card was filled. Best of all, her remaining dance with Michael was yet to come.

She was fanning herself between sets, using a fan of ecru lace, intricately embroidered with rose and gold flowers, when a bored voice spoke beside her. "Well, cuz," Edwin said, looking down at her with that expression of disdain he affected, "you seem to be doing fairly well."

"Yes, I am, aren't I?" She smiled, determined not to let

him spoil her pleasure in the evening. "I am having a marvelous time."

"Are you?" He looked out over the dance floor, where people mingled together, talking, during this brief respite. "I imagine you have a dance free for me."

"No."

"No?" He pursed his lips. "Are you refusing me? Not well done of you, Chloe."

"I've no dances left," she said, and had the satisfaction of seeing his expression darken, if only for a moment.

"Ah. Being betrothed to Lyndon helps considerably, doesn't it? Even after all the missteps you've made tonight."

That hurt, even though she tried not to let it. Her self-confidence, so hard won, began to erode. "Not everyone still considers me to be Miss Bumblebroth, Edwin."

"Don't let him hear you say that," he said sharply. "He'd call me out."

"But you'd deserve it." She smiled serenely. " 'Twas you who hit on the name, was it not?"

His brow wrinkled. "You've developed a sharp tongue."

"I learned it from you, cuz."

"I believe this is my dance, Miss Russell," a voice she would recognize anywhere said, and she turned.

"Lyndon. Yes, it is," she said, beaming at him much as she had earlier at Edwin, though his father was actually written in for this one.

He held out his arm. "The music is starting."

"Then we mustn't miss it. Good evening, Edwin," she called back over her shoulder, as Michael led her onto the floor.

"Was he bothering you?" he asked.

"Not terribly. Oh, dear." This as the music for a particularly intricate country dance started. Chloe looked down at her feet, glanced at the sets that were forming, and then shook her head. "If I try to dance this, I'll likely knock over half the people here."

Michael chuckled. "Shall we just stroll, then?"

"Yes, I'd like that."

"Here, let's just go out onto the terrace for some air." His hand at her back, he escorted her outside. "Was he bothering you?" he asked again, when they were on the terrace overlooking the darkened garden, away from other people.

"He wished to dance." She gazed straight ahead. "Please, may we simply leave it at that?"

Michael looked sharply at her. Her voice trembled, and he wondered why. *Damn Hempstead,* he thought. Damn anyone who had ever laughed at her. If he did nothing else, he would make certain that never happened again. "I see Sherbourne and his wife," he said, and slipped his arm through hers. "Come. Let's go talk with them."

Two days later, sitting beside her betrothed in his curricle, Chloe was still thinking about the visit she had paid to her man of affairs the previous day. A lady was not supposed to venture into the City, let alone trouble her head with such a thing as business, and yet to Chloe such a thing was routine.

What was not was something he had said to her as she left. He had told her she was remarkable. She didn't think she was. She was quiet and mousy and would not now be where she was had not the Granthams been in need of money.

Though her new carriage dress of sky blue, with a scalloped hem, worn with a darker blue spencer, was attractive, if rather fuller than fashion decreed, she was no diamond of the first water, or even a flawed one. Her figure was passable, her features ordinary, and her hair was impossible. That she felt moderately less plain than usual was beside the point. She was needed for a purpose that sometimes dampened her spirits. She suspected Michael felt the same.

"Well?" she said, when he had turned the curricle into the park, away from the traffic that had taken all his concentration. "What do you stare at?"

"Your eyes are blue," he said. "The other day they were gray."

She laughed. "No, they're really not. I'm not roasting

you, I promise," she went on at his look of surprise. "It depends on what I wear. If I'm in green, they're green."

"Really? How remarkable."

Chloe felt herself coloring. That word again. "I don't know. Fortunately they don't turn pink if I wear that color."

He didn't laugh, as she'd expected him to. "Then if the colors are dull, your eyes are dull."

"Lyndon!" she exclaimed, wounded.

"Hush, my dear." He chanced taking his hand from the ribbons for a moment to lay it atop hers, a gesture she noted was seen by two older ladies passing by in a brougham. The news would spread through the *ton* by evening, she thought. *Miss Bumblebroth is making a dead set at Lyndon.* "I didn't mean to hurt you. I merely wish you would dress like this more often."

She made a face. "You sound so like your mother."

"Sometimes she's right."

She looked away. "I'll never be beautiful."

"You underrate yourself, my dear."

Was she his dear? "I don't think so." She paused. "Lyndon, are you sorry to be marrying me?"

"Have you forgotten? I proposed because I wanted to."

"And for other reasons."

He was quiet. "Yes, well, we needn't discuss that now."

She was right, then. He did resent being forced to marry her. "Was there someone else?" she asked in a small voice. "Someone you would rather have had?"

That made him look at her, clearly astonished. "Whatever gave you that idea?"

"I wasn't your choice."

He took a moment to answer. "I knew I'd have to marry sometime."

"But not now."

"Chloe, are you always so forthright?"

"Not so very long ago you called it outrageous."

"So it is, compared to most people."

"Most people of *ton,* you mean."

"Most people in general, I suspect."

"I'm not asking to gain compliments. I genuinely want to know." She lowered her head. "I cannot help wondering what our marriage will be like."

"The same as most people's, I imagine."

Chloe bit her lips. She so wanted it to be more than that, yet he seemed to be comfortable with the idea of a marriage of convenience. "Lyndon, might we get down and stroll for a bit?"

He glanced quickly at her. "Are you scared?"

"Of what?"

"Of being so high in this carriage."

"Heavens, no! I quite like it."

"Good. I'll have to teach you how to drive."

"Lyndon," she began uneasily.

"Just a gig, of course," he went on, "but then something more dashing."

"Lyndon, I'm not a dab hand at such things, or haven't you noticed?"

"Cant, Chloe?" His eyes laughed at her. "You're likely just nervous."

"Mayhap, but I still doubt I'll be able to."

"Of course you will," he said, with easy confidence in his skills. "It's quite easy."

"For you, perhaps."

"For any number of people." He pointed ahead, to where the *ton* thronged the park on their daily promenade. "Even the veriest whipster is managing well enough."

She sighed and decided to let the subject drop. If she didn't, she would lose all courage to go on with what she wanted to tell him. "Please, could we get down for a while?"

He cast her a look she found surprising in its shrewdness, and then nodded. "Hold their heads," he called back to his groom. "Do you wish to join the others, or stroll in the park?"

"In the park, please." She took his hand to climb down, and disaster struck. Her skirt somehow got tangled about her foot as she stepped down, and she pitched forward against Michael's chest. He staggered back a pace, and then recovered, catching her about the waist. "Oh, dear."

"Are you all right?"

"Of course, dam—dash it." Irritably she shook off his hands, though the feeling of them remained, making her breathless. "Don't you dare laugh at me."

"I'm not," he said, but his eyes were suspiciously bright. "Dare I ask, was that an oath I nearly heard?"

She ducked her head. "Yes. I know it's too bad of me. I am sorry."

"Chloe, I'm teasing you."

"I know," she said, her head still down.

"I told you I'd never laugh at you, my dear. I meant it."

That made her look at him. There was no amusement in his eyes. They seemed to hold hers for a very long time, until she at last looked away. "I know," she said. "I believe you."

"Then, come." He tucked her hand through the crook of his arm. The simple, almost impersonal gesture caused her to catch her breath again. Why did his touch do such things to her? "Is there something in particular you wish to speak to me about?"

"Yes. There's something about me I feel you should know."

"What?"

"I'm wealthy."

He looked away, his set jaw confirming her earlier assumption. Oh, dear, telling him about herself would not be easy, yet he had to know. "I'm aware of that."

"No, you're not. Oh, you know about my dowry, of course, and I'll grant it's quite generous. There's something else, though."

His gaze when he looked at her was sharp. "Something your brother didn't tell me about?"

"I wish it were that simple." She took a deep breath. "Lyndon, the truth is I'm quite disgustingly rich."

Four

"What do you mean by 'disgustingly'?" Michael asked distractedly. His mind was still filled with the near disaster of her stumbling out of the curricle. His body, as well. Even now, his pulse had yet to return to normal. Her waist under his hands had been trimmer than he'd expected; her bosom rather more considerable than her shapeless gowns hinted at.

As to that, what was his mother about, choosing such an ensemble for Chloe? The dress was much too full and probably covered her to her neck, he thought gloomily. Even the evening gown she'd worn to their betrothal ball had been entirely modest. That hadn't bothered him before. Now it did.

"Lyndon, are you listening to me?" she demanded, and he realized that she had been speaking.

He patted her hand. "Of course, my dear," he said.

"You think I'm air dreaming," she accused him.

"No, not at all. If you believe there's money your brother knows nothing of, then I believe you. But, my dear, you know as well as I that a woman doesn't manage her own fortune, even if she has the capacity to do so."

"What utter rot!"

He looked at her in astonishment. Her eyes were blazing with anger. Lovely eyes, too, he thought, with equal surprise. Not their color, which she herself admitted was changeable, but their shape, their size. Pansy eyes, he thought, and then scolded himself for his fancifulness. "Excuse me?"

"I'll have you know I've been managing my fortune for two years, and doing quite well at it, thank you."

"Chloe, what are we talking about?"

"The competence left me by my grandmother. 'Tis quite apart from my dowry."

"Your brother and I discussed that."

"Yes, the original amount."

In spite of her earlier anger, he still felt amusement bubbling inside him. "Is it larger now?"

"I cannot tell you exactly how much," she said simply. "It fluctuates by the day."

"If you have such a fortune, why do you still live in your brother's house?"

"Don't you believe I wished to set up my own establishment? I wasn't allowed. Women, as you just pointed out, aren't given much freedom in this world."

"Chloe, it's not that I don't believe you, but—"

"You don't believe me."

"You're serious," he said, frowning.

"Entirely. What do you think I've been saying?"

"I'm not sure. You'll have to explain it to me."

"In words of one syllable?"

"Excuse me?" he said frostily.

"Your pardon, sir, but 'tis how you treated me until a moment ago." She walked ahead of him for a few paces. "If you'd rather speak with my man of affairs, I'll give you his direction."

"Your man of affairs? Not your brother's?"

"Yes, mine. He was one of the original trustees of my inheritance. When I came into the money, I convinced him and the others to break the trust."

He blinked. "Unusual," he said, cautiously.

"Yes," she agreed. "However, they agreed I had a compelling argument, since I'd doubled the original amount."

That made him blink again. "Doubled it?" he asked, feeling like an echo.

"On paper, of course." She sighed. "This might be easier if you just let me tell it."

"Very well. I'm listening."

Her gaze was suspicious, but the truth was she had his full attention. Thus he learned of how she had first become interested in finance, how she began investigating various forms of investments, how she gradually became more serious about it. She lost money, of course, as she admitted was only to be expected, but she gained more. And, yes, her trustees were quite as surprised as he was by the entire idea.

"So," he said when she'd finished, his head reeling. If even one tenth of what she'd said was true, her original statement was correct. She was wealthy. "None of this is protected by a trust, I presume."

"Oh, there are several trusts. More now that we've become engaged."

His lips tightened. "To prevent me gaining control of it, I presume."

"Cut line," she said, making him blink. "I doubt you're spendthrift, but I also know why you proposed to me. Of course I know that by law whatever I have becomes yours. How good are you at figuring?"

"I do well enough. I have wanted to manage one of our estates for this age."

"Why haven't you?"

"I've not been allowed. I daresay that sounds odd to you, but my father believes I'm no farmer."

"Does he think you'll race your curricle over plowed fields?"

He laughed. "No, nothing that bad." He grinned down at her, but her head was down and she didn't see. He was beginning to actually like this girl, much as one might feel affection toward a sister. "Chimneys has always by family tradition belonged to the heir, so it should be mine. However, before now there simply hasn't been the money to run it well."

"Is it self-supporting?"

"Far from it, though there is an income. From what I gather, work is needed everywhere. I'd like at least to restore the land to good heart, though I'd need a bailiff with greater knowledge of the subject than I have."

"Then you don't understand ledgers?"

"I can read account books, Chloe," he said dryly. "I am not, as you pointed out, spendthrift."

She stopped and looked up at him, her face aghast. "That's not what I meant!"

"No? You might." They walked again, her arm tucked safely through his.

"I doubt it. I feel quite safe with you."

Safe! An odd word. Did she mean her money, or herself? Chloe was a puzzle. In her own way she was formidable; in quite another, vulnerable and in need of protection. He was coming to believe he'd taken on more with her than he'd considered. "In the future I may wish to run a stud farm there."

"Where is Chimneys? Leicestershire?"

"No, Kent."

"Hardly hunt country."

"But I intend to breed the best. It would be expensive."

"Profitable in the long run, though."

"Until then, though, it would be a drain on your funds. It may be a good thing you have those trusts."

"I do hope you aren't vexed about them. I merely wished to protect myself, and our children." She blushed. "Our younger children, that is, if we're so lucky as to have any. It's terribly unfair that the eldest inherits everything."

"It's how it's always been."

"It's unfair," she repeated. "When they reach their majority, our children will know their futures are secure."

"You say you think I'm not spendthrift," he said slowly.

"Lyndon, pray forget I used that horrible word."

"Has it occurred to you that I might be an expensive husband?"

"I imagine you will be," she said serenely.

Anger flashed through him. "I wonder that you agreed to marry me, then."

"Don't be silly," she said, and surprised him by hugging his arm through hers, for all the world as if she were comforting him. Comfort was the last thing he felt, though, not with the fullness of her breast pressed against him again. "At least I know the money won't be gambled or wenched away. You don't wench, do you?"

He laughed at this bit of plain speaking, any remaining anger draining away. "Young ladies aren't supposed to know of things like that."

"Bosh. If you wish to marry a traditional young miss, then you should repair to Almack's, sir."

"I assure you, this is far more entertaining."

Pain appeared briefly in her eyes. "I am glad you feel so, sir."

"I don't mean to hurt you, Chloe," he said gently, laying his hand on hers.

"I'm sorry, sir, but I'm not likely to change, either."

"I think you undervalue yourself."

"I believe I know what my value is, and it's in the Funds."

"For God's sake, Chloe!"

"You'd not have looked at me twice, else."

That silenced him. "I'm not overly pleased at being a bought husband."

Instead of firing up at him, she peeped up from under the brim of her bonnet, the most flirtatious movement he'd yet seen her make. "I've offended you. I'm sorry."

"Thank you." He inclined his head, aware he was behaving badly, but somehow unable to stop himself. No matter how true it was that his family needed money, the picture of himself as a fortune hunter was an ugly one. "Unfortunately, Chloe, when all is said and done, the money is yours by right."

"That's handsome of you, Lyndon." She sounded surprised. "I don't know of another man who'd make such an offer."

"As long as I have enough for my needs—they are expensive needs, I'll grant you—I'm content." They strolled for a few moments in silence, both of them, he imagined, thinking of the situation. "Tell me something, Chloe. How is it your brother doesn't know you've taken control of your money?"

"He wasn't one of the trustees."

"I'd think one of them would have informed him."

"No."

"How the devil—my apologies—did you convince them not to?"

"I batted my eyelashes at them?" she suggested, and did so in so outrageous a manner that he burst out laughing. "No?"

"No," he said firmly, though he smiled. He thought he'd laughed more in this last week than in many a month. She was unpredictable, his Chloe—*his Chloe?*

"No," she agreed, sounding regretful. "I fear I've no talent for flirtation."

"Thank God."

"I don't know if I'd say that."

"Any girl can flirt, but you, my dear Miss Russell, are an original."

She made a face. "Why, then, was I on the shelf at one and twenty, before you proposed?"

"Because you hid yourself away," he said quietly.

She looked away. "Yes, well, let's not discuss that just now. As to the trustees."

"Yes?"

"I treated them like kindly old uncles."

He grinned down at her. "God help them."

"Why?"

"No talent for flirtation, Chloe?"

"Well, I haven't."

"I suspect you manage well enough when you wish to."

"Not always." She laid her hand on his arm. "Do you expect to manage the money, even if you consider it mine?"

"Lord, no."

"Oh, good!" she exclaimed, giving him such a beaming smile that he was stunned. It was a lovely smile, bringing life and personality to her face. It was also more sensual than he'd expected. Her lower lip was fuller than her upper, making him wish, for the first time, to kiss her. *Good God!*

He became aware that she was watching him warily. He must have looked deucedly odd, staring at her so, he thought, and smiled quickly in reassurance. "Good?" he queried. "What is good about it?"

"Oh, dear." She peeped up from under her bonnet again, so that he saw that her eyes were alight with mischief. "That leaves it to me."

"Chloe—"

"Well?"

"Would you unman me so?"

This time she was definitely grinning. "Is your manhood so delicate, then?"

He burst out laughing. He doubted she was aware of the double meaning in what she'd said. "No, 'tis upstanding when need be."

She frowned. "Really, Lyndon, do get yourself in hand. Now what is there in that to give you the whoops again?"

"Nothing," he said, his voice strangled, and, just like that, felt again the need to kiss her. It was so strong, so insistent, he actually leaned toward her.

"What ho, Lyndon!" a voice called. Startled, Michael turned. On the carriage path two of his friends were passing, riding showy horses. Habit made him dismiss the mounts as little more than hacks. It also awoke his desire to ride. That, more than the interruption, brought him back to himself.

He raised his hand in salute, and then turned back to Chloe, who looked wary again. That was another thing. Until he'd seen her relaxed, laughing, he'd not realized how she kept a protective shell about her. "Just some acquaintances," he said, as if she'd asked. "On a pair of nags."

"Oh? I thought them handsome beasts."

"The mounts, or the riders?"

She actually blushed. "Lyndon! Oh, pray do not fun me!"

"But 'tis so enjoyable," he said and, because he couldn't resist, lightly touched the tip of her nose.

Chloe drew back, her eyes suddenly wide. "I—of course you would know about horses."

Inwardly he sighed as he took her arm to return to the carriage. "Yes."

"You must have studied them?"

"Indeed. Since I was quite small."

"I fear I never learned how to ride."

"Oh, I'll teach you," he said again, as he had with driving. It was only a matter of applying oneself, after all. "Chloe, how do you feel about my running a stud farm?"

She looked up at him from under her bonnet again. Unfair, that. It made him notice again her eyes, and remind him of their beauty. "I've no objection to it."

"Thank you."

"Of course, I won't interfere in your choice of blood stock. If—"

"If?"

"If you don't interfere with my investments."

He grinned down at her. Since she had the head for money, he'd be foolish to disagree. "That sounds fair."

"Done, then?"

"Done.

"Chloe," a voice hailed her as she came out of a shop on Oxford Street a few days later. "Do hold up."

Chloe turned, her insides clenching involuntarily at the sight of Edwin, coming toward her in his perch phaeton of canary yellow. Her time had been so filled since the betrothal ball that she'd given little thought to the nasty things he had said. It seemed every day there was something new to do, from Venetian breakfasts to *al fresco* picnics to paying at-home calls with Lady Grantham. So full had her days been that Chloe had had little time for her usual activities.

Though she wasn't yet fully accepted by the *ton,* for the moment her life was blessedly free from mockery. She had a feeling that was about to change.

"Hallo, cuz." Edwin tossed the ribbons to his tiger and jumped nimbly down. "Well met."

"Edwin," she said warily. "How do you today?"

"Well." He flicked her cheek, as he had at the ball. "That shade of blue is becoming to you."

"A compliment, Edwin? I am amazed."

"Yes, sometimes I surprise myself. Where is your fiancé today?"

"He is racing to Brighton."

"Ah, that is right. I had forgot." He flashed his teeth at her in a smile. White enough teeth, but set too close together, she noted again. "I do hope he takes no injury."

"Really, Edwin? Such concern."

"Of course. Who else would have you, cuz?"

"I'm well aware I'm being married for my money." More money than he knew, she thought, and was filled with inner glee for one of the few times in her acquaintance with Edwin.

"Certainly. No one ever said you were stupid, Chloe," he said, and she braced herself for the barb that was sure to come. "I suppose you think you love him."

"No." Of course she loved him. She thought about him all the time, wanted to be with him, worried about him when she learned he was doing something absurd, such as his race to Brighton. The thought of him gave her a strange feeling inside that was both pleasant and uncomfortable, a yearning for something she couldn't name. She wished he would give her her first, and perhaps most meaningful, kiss. Not that he showed any signs of doing so.

When they were together away from the house and Helena's restrictive influence, they got on well. They talked together, laughed together, made plans for the future. She had the sense, though, that he still kept himself back from her, just as she still kept herself back from him. She needed the protection. She couldn't begin to guess his reasons. She knew only that he treated her much as he might treat a friend or a favored sister. He certainly was not in love with her, and she had no idea what to do about it.

"That is a surprise," Edwin said, for once not catching her out in a lie. "A noted Corinthian like him, and you don't love him?"

She raised her chin. "Perhaps he loves me."

He laughed. "Oh, that's a good one, Chloe." His smile was mocking. "Lord, you are still so easy to tease."

"Did you mean to tease me by that, Edwin? I rather thought you teased me earlier, instead."

"Oh, beyond a doubt." He continued to smile, an expression she once thought fitted him so well, before she came to know him better. "I see you're all togged out, too. Who has the dressing of you? Lyndon?"

"No one who needs to use my money, Edwin."

"Ha, a palpable hit! Your tongue is growing sharp, Chloe. I had better watch myself."

"Don't you ever grow tired of it, Edwin?" she asked, suddenly weary of his endless torment and her endless guard against him. "When are you going to grow up?"

His smile grew fixed. "I rather thought I had, cuz. Better than you."

"It bothers you, doesn't it?" Her voice was soft. "That someone might get the better of you? That you might not win an argument?"

"But that's the point, cuz. I always win. Certainly against you."

"Only if I continue to try to best you. You do not always need to be so afraid of life."

"Afraid! Ha!" He laughed mirthlessly. "I was not the one who retired from the world for three years."

"I don't believe it hurt me, Edwin."

"Look at me and tell me you're not afraid of going into society."

"Of course I'm scared, given the past. But I'm trying to get over my fears." She searched his face. "Will you ever get over yours?"

"What do you know of what I fear?" he said brusquely. "You don't know me."

He was far out there. She knew him better than he thought. "If you will excuse me, I have plans—"

"Pity you've nothing in common with him." The smile was back in place, putting Chloe instantly on her guard.

"Opposites attract, Edwin," she said, smiling brightly.

"They must. You're not up to his weight, Chloe."

That hurt, though she knew better than to show it. "I think we're well matched."

He laughed at that. "As you said, you're opposites."

"I'll not deny it."

"You can't do a thing he does."

"No, I cannot."

"You can't even drive. You did drive once, didn't you?"

"Yes." She watched him warily, wondering what this change of subject betokened. "A gig."

"Yes, I remember. Why did you stop?"

"Because Father died and we moved to town."

"Is that all? Then perhaps you could take it up again."

"Mayhap."

"Which, I assume, means no. Poor Chloe." He laid a hand casually on the shining surface of the phaeton. "You couldn't keep up with us at home, and you can't keep up with him now."

That did it, as perhaps he knew it would. Chloe looked at him, looked at the phaeton, and frowned thoughtfully. It would be an incredibly foolish thing to do, and yet she felt, as always, driven. "Maybe—"

"Miss, you really have to be at the modiste's for a fitting," Patience said behind her.

Chloe turned to see her maid grimacing. She knew quite well what Patience was trying to communicate. Of course she didn't trust Edwin. She thought, though, that she could handle the situation. "Edwin, would you let me drive your carriage?"

"*My* phaeton? Why don't you ask Lyndon to let you use his?"

"I'd rather like to surprise him, that I can drive."

"Oh, you would, that is certain."

She ignored him. "I admit, my skills aren't up to snuff."

"Chloe, you really must watch your use of cant."

"But I do remember how to do it." Now that she'd broached the idea, she looked doubtfully at the phaeton. "I've never driven a team, though, or a vehicle like yours."

"Of course not, and you never will. You can't do it."

"I'm sure I could, with a little help. But if you don't wish to give it me, I'll have to ask Lyndon."

A smile spread slowly across his face. "As if I'd miss this chance to see you fail."

"Miss," Patience put in again.

"I won't fail," Chloe insisted, and wondered why.

"If you're sure."

"I am."

He sighed. "Very well. I'll hand you in. Mind your step, now. We don't wish to have a disaster on our hands before we begin."

Chloe ignored him to concentrate on climbing into the swaying vehicle. The ground looked very far away from where she sat. "Aren't you climbing up?"

"In a minute. Let me explain some things to you."

"Such as?"

"You're used to handling one horse, not a team. Remember, now, that these two beauties aren't like the nags you're used to. They're high-strung and sensitive."

Chloe looked at the two quiet horses, harnessed to the phaeton. They had not once so much as stamped or shaken their heads. "They don't look it."

"That's because I've already driven them for a time. Their mouths are sensitive, Chloe. Don't saw on them."

"I won't."

"Now, you have two reins for each horse."

"Oh." Chloe looked at the reins gathered in her hands, and felt a twinge of unease. "Edwin, I don't think—"

"Don't worry. Do you think I'd let you do this alone?"

"I don't know, Edwin. I don't trust you."

"I wouldn't trust my team to just anyone."

In spite of herself, she felt that compliment glow through her, so rarely had he given her any. There had been a time when she'd longed for them from him. "Well, then?"

"The reins work the same way as when you're driving a single horse."

"Do you mean both sets of reins control the entire team, or each set controls each horse?"

"Exactly," he said, beaming at her.

"But—"

"I think you're ready to go now. Let go their heads," he said to his tiger, who stepped back.

"But—"

"Chloe, you have the ribbons, don't you?"

"Yes, but—Edwin!" she cried, as the team, let loose, suddenly surged forward. Without Edwin there to take over if needed, she was plunged into the busy traffic of Oxford Street, without any warning. Oh, but he'd meant it that way, she realized in dismay and fear. He had never meant to come with her. She didn't even have his tiger standing on his perch behind to help if he possibly could.

And how could he, with the team going as fast as they were? She did still remember some driving skills, but this was a different type of carriage altogether. It was so high off the ground, and it swayed so that it was all she could do to stay upright. Pedestrians leaped to get out of her way. Two other carriages collided in a wonderful tangle of reins and traces, while still other drivers called curses at her. She hardly heard them. All of her being was concentrated on bringing the carriage to a stop without getting into a collision herself.

Ahead was a slower carriage. She pulled back on the reins to stop with all of her strength, forgetting for the moment that she was sawing at the horses' tender mouths, and thus goading them on from the pain. At such a speed, she had no choice but to swerve around the other carriage. Remembered training made her turn the phaeton at just the right time, and, there, she was beyond it! Without any damage, either, she was exulting, when she heard the distinct sound of a loud horn. Looking up, she saw something that would live in her nightmares forever.

Coming directly toward her, loaded to the top with passengers and driving at as quick a pace as she, was an enormous stagecoach. They were, she realized with amazing calmness, going to collide.

Five

Michael was feeling well satisfied with himself as he rode carefully along Oxford Street. Anyone passing on the street, wide though it was, had to be careful at the best of times. Though the morning wasn't very far advanced, it was, as always, teeming with both humanity and carriages of various types. People bustled out of the shops on either side, middle-class folks mingling with those of the highest *ton,* who had carriages at their command and footmen to follow them about carrying their purchases. Heavy carts and drays trundled along, while an urchin child swept the road for someone passing, hand hopefully outstretched for a coin. Vendors everywhere cried their wares—meat pies here, flowers there. Add to this carriages driven with great dash, if not skill, by tulips of the *ton,* and the stagecoaches driven at great speed, but little style, and one had a confusing, complicated path. Yet Michael threaded his way in supreme self-confidence through it all as he returned to the Grantham stables near Grosvenor Square.

Later today he would be participating in a race to Brighton. He'd done so before, but he hoped to better his time, as well as his opponent. It was dangerous, true. He risked always the chance of meeting up with other carriages which, driven by someone who was either too reckless or too timid, posed a threat of collision. He risked, as well, the danger of overturning because of some unforeseen chance or damage to the road. He risked danger from his

opponent, who would do everything to best him. All of this
he knew, but he would pit his skills against any threat.
When all was said and done, he was an excellent driver,
and he knew it.

Of necessity, he would overnight in Brighton, returning
on the morrow. It meant he wouldn't see Chloe today. It
bothered him, which he found almost annoying. No woman
had ever mattered so much that she came between him and
his abiding interest in sports—not even the Duchess of
Trowbridge when he had, for a time, courted her.

Not that he felt he knew Chloe very well. When they
were together unchaperoned, as when they drove, they always managed to find a great deal to talk about. They
laughed—he didn't know when he'd ever laughed so
much—and they'd had discussions on politics or the events
of the day or some such, which showed both the depths of
her knowledge and of her intelligence. He liked being with
her. He had even come to be fond of her, as he might be
with a sister. Yet he always had the sense she held something back, just as he did. He wasn't sure why that bothered
him as much as it did.

Someone, a woman, off to his right, was calling out to
some lord. *Devilish piercing voice,* he thought, as he heard
the cry again. Wondering who it was and who she wanted,
he glanced over and suddenly realized she was calling to
him.

"Lord Lyndon! Oh, please, help me!"

What the devil? She was obviously someone's maid, no
one he knew. Frowning, he picked his way over to her.

"Oh, thank heaven!" she gasped, before he could ask her
what she was about. "You may just be in time—"

"In time for what, madam?" he interrupted, annoyed now
at being accosted by her.

"Pray, sir, there's no time to argue! Miss Russell—"

"What about her?" he demanded, suddenly alert.

"His carriage—she's driving—oh, my lord, she can't
drive, and not in this traffic!"

He went cold at the thought of Chloe driving at all, let alone on Oxford Street. "Where?" he said, urgently.

"There." She pointed again, and this time he saw what he had missed before: Edwin Hempstead, looking down the street, grinning.

Devil take it! he thought again. If Hempstead were involved in this somehow, and Michael would bet his last farthing he was, then Chloe was in danger. The thought made him spur Thor into a gallop.

All of his pleasure in the day was gone as he rode grimly on. To either side of him now he saw pedestrians scattered and dazed-looking, while the drivers of the heavy transports looked surly and two private vehicles seemed to have collided. The vendors had ceased calling their wares, and instead were yelling in confusion and anger. The only person who seemed the same was the urchin, who grinned as Michael galloped past. "Good show, guv'nor!" he called.

There was the distinctive sound of a horn being blown. Daring to look up, Michael saw a sight that would live forever in his nightmares. Ahead was a stagecoach, heavily loaded and approaching him at great speed; driving straight toward it was a yellow phaeton, with Chloe at the reins.

He took no time to curse, even inwardly, no energy to yell out at her, which might in any event startle her and cause even more of a disaster than the one that loomed. Instead he let his instincts, and his trust in Thor, take over. Gathering the reins in his left hand, he used only his knees to urge the horse to the side, in the hope he might catch up to the phaeton before the stagecoach did, and grab hold of its reins. Chloe obviously couldn't control it, or she would be out of harm's way by this time.

Faster, and yet a little faster, and the stage was looming ever closer, but—yes, he was gaining on the phaeton. Perhaps it was pulled by a team, but Thor didn't have the weight of a vehicle to slow him down. "Chloe, hang on!" Michael yelled as he came level first with the hind wheels of the phaeton and then with the front ones, over which hung the seat where Chloe hunched over, clutching the reins. What he was going to try was dangerous, but no more so than letting her drive to disaster.

Pulling Thor as close to the phaeton as he dared, Michael reached out for the reins. His fingers touched them, grasped them—and slipped, as the phaeton jounced over something in the road and swayed to the side.

"Damnation!" he swore, and pressed closer again. This time when he grabbed the reins his grip held. He put all his strength into pulling them back, controlling Thor only with his knees. The phaeton slowed, at first slightly, and then more noticeably, until, with one last effort, he pulled it to a stop at the side of the road. The stagecoach, its driver cursing the air blue, sped by with only inches to spare. They were safe.

Michael, his blood pounding in his head, gasped with the effort he had expended. Thor's sides heaved. He could only imagine what had happened to Hempstead's team. *Damn Hempstead, anyway.* And as for Chloe—oh, dear God. "Chloe?"

She turned toward him, her face parchment white, her eyes wide and dazed. "M-Michael—"

She was unharmed. *Thank God,* he thought, and erupted with sudden anger. "What the *hell* did you think you were doing?"

Chloe shrank back in surprise. "Michael? I—"

"You know damned well you can't drive this rig. You're not only not strong enough, you haven't the talent. You never will."

"Michael, please—"

"You'd be dead now if I hadn't come along."

"Damn you, Lyndon, must you always be so good at everything?" she yelled, to his astonishment.

"Lucky for you I am!" he yelled back, only vaguely aware of the crowd which had gathered around them. "You could have killed yourself, and people on that coach."

"And the horses, too?"

"And the horses, too, devil take it!"

"You needn't swear," she said, and, astonishing him again, burst into tears.

"The great brute," someone in the crowd said.

"She was my wife, I'd take her over my knee and wallop her," someone else said.

"Oh, you would, would you? You just try, Joe Tanner, and see what you get!" a woman's voice answered.

"Quality's got strange ways," yet another voice put in, and it was enough. Michael raised his head and glared at the people, who stared back with unabashed interest. Thank God no one he knew was there, but then, no one of breeding would watch such a brangle. Not openly, at least. He had no doubt pictures of this would be on all the broadsheets by tomorrow at the latest.

Exhaustion had replaced anger, at least for the moment. He didn't know why Chloe had tried driving Hempstead's rig, and just now he didn't care. "Chloe, for God's sake—"

"I know I was wrong, I know what I did was stupid, but you don't have to yell at me," she got out through sobs.

"Chloe—"

"I didn't mean for anyone to get hurt!" Her chest heaved; dimly he was aware of the interesting effect that had. "I— oh, Michael, take me home. Please!"

"Of course I will, dear," he said gently, climbing from Thor and into the phaeton. Thor, well-trained as he was, showed only by the flick of an ear that anything untoward had happened as the phaeton's team surged forward. He controlled them easily, though Chloe, after giving a little cry, pressed up against him. High-strung, overly sensitive beasts, he thought, automatically sizing up the horses. "Here. Give me the reins."

"I c-can't. If I let go—"

"I have them, Chloe. Relax, now." Making a little sound of exasperation, he looped the reins around his wrist and palm, and reached for her fingers, prying them free. Her arms fell, seemingly nerveless, into her lap, her fingers still curled, as if still holding on.

"Lyndon?" a voice called. "Is she all right?"

Hempstead. Michael didn't even have to turn his head to know that. "Yes, no thanks to you."

"Thank God. I'll take over—"

"Damned right, you will." Michael bent on him the same glare he'd earlier used on the crowd, to greater effect this time. "I'll settle with you later."

"I'll hold their heads." Hempstead went forward to control his horses. Even as Michael jumped down and then turned to Chloe to put his hands at her waist and swing her to the ground, he noticed that Hempstead's concern was more for his team than for his cousin.

"Do you have a carriage?" he asked, bending to Chloe.

"I—no. Where are we?"

"Well you may ask." He reached for Thor's reins, to lead him along, and Chloe shied back. "It's all right, my dear. You're safe now. I'll take you home."

"How?"

"On Thor."

"No!" She pulled back more violently than she had before. "I'll walk."

"Chloe, you're shaking," he said as reasonably as he could. "It must be a mile from where you started."

"I'll manage, thank you, only don't expect me to go near that great beast!"

Unwilling amusement bubbled up inside Michael. That was his Chloe, with her spirit. "Welcome back."

She looked up, startled. "I beg your pardon?"

"My lord," a feminine voice called. Michael looked up as a hackney carriage pulled to a stop near him, and the same female who had started this particular adventure for him got out. "Oh, Miss Chloe, are you all right? I was that scared when I saw you go off."

"I'm well enough, Patience," Chloe said, sounding calmer now. "Unhurt, as you can see."

"Thank heavens! We'll get you home, miss." She looked past Chloe to Michael. "My lord?"

He nodded. "Take your mistress home. It's all right, Chloe," he said, as she swung back to him. "I'll visit later."

"I'm sorry if I caused a fuss, Lyndon," she said humbly. "I never meant to."

"I know, dear. Go along home now."

"Will you still go to Brighton?"

"What?" he said blankly. "Oh, the race. No, I don't think so."

"Oh, but, Lyndon—"

"I rather think I had my race for today." He smiled at her, and had the pleasure of seeing her eyes light up. "One horse against a team. Quite a feat, I think."

"Yes, I think so, too."

"Go along, now. I'll see you later."

"Yes, Lyndon," she said, and obediently climbed into the hackney.

Michael watched as the carriage drove off, and then turned back to Thor, who had yet to move out of place. With one easy motion, he stepped into the stirrup and swung himself into the saddle. "Extra treats for you today," he murmured, leaning forward to pat the horse on its flank, and then straighten. He had things to see to. "Home, boy," he said, and turned the horse, his racing done for the day.

Some time later, his good mood evaporated, Michael stalked down St. James, swinging his walking stick furiously, his face so set that anyone who knew him decided not to speak with him. All the world knew already of Miss Russell's latest bumblebroth and could guess the reason for Lyndon's reaction. It was not often one saw him angry, but when he was, he was dangerous.

He took the stairs two at a time at Edwin Hempstead's lodgings, though the porter followed him, protesting. And when Hempstead's valet opened the door to his furious pounding, he pushed past the man. "You and I have something to settle, Hempstead," he said, swinging the walking stick again. He had never struck anyone with it in his life, but he was sorely tempted to do so now. The man could have killed Chloe.

Edwin, engaged in reading a newspaper, rose leisurely.

"Lyndon. I thought I might see you today. Care for a brandy?"

"No. What did you mean, letting Miss Russell take your phaeton?"

He shrugged. "She wished to do so."

"I doubt that." Michael's gaze was hard. "You convinced her to do it, somehow."

"I? Why would I do something like that?"

"Precisely what I've been asking myself." Michael paced toward Edwin, whose eyes showed the beginnings of alarm. "Tell me the truth."

"Oh, Chloe's always been deucedly easy to tease," Edwin said carelessly, but his gaze was wary.

"To tease?" Michael's voice was quiet, and all the more deadly for it. "Was she teased into what she did?"

"Lord, I never forced her into it, Lyndon. She's an independent type."

Independent? Yes, to a point. "Did you goad her into it?" he asked again.

Perhaps Michael's urge to murder showed. Perhaps Hempstead finally read it in his eyes. Whatever it was, he grew serious very quickly. "We did tease her as children," he admitted. "But if you think I'd do something to put my prize blacks in danger—"

In one quick, fluid motion Michael was across the room, grabbing Edwin's neckcloth and lifting him in a remarkable display of strength. "Are you thinking to tease *me* now, Hempstead?"

"No, that was a bad jest!" Edwin squeaked. "Put me down, Lyndon, let's talk about this—"

"Damn you, you could have killed her! Did you think about that when you 'teased' her?" he demanded.

"Lord, Lyndon, I wouldn't deliberately do something to put Chloe into danger. Now put me down!"

"You damned well knew she would be in danger. Driving a phaeton in town, when she'd never done so before?"

"She could drive once," he said defensively. "I thought she still could."

"You knew it would be too much for her."

"Put me down, Lyndon. Let's talk about this."

"I should throw you out the window," Michael said dispassionately, and abruptly released him.

Edwin grunted as he landed on the floor. "Lord, Lyndon, you are strong," he complained, rubbing his throat. "Didn't know you could lift someone with one hand."

"Why the devil did you let her drive?"

Edwin looked away. "Bad judgment on my part," he muttered, and looked back at Michael. "For what it's worth, I've apologized to her."

"When?"

"This morning. I meant it, Lyndon."

"I hope you did—for your sake."

Edwin rubbed his throat again. "Credit me with some sense. I've grown up since those days when we were all together."

Michael looked at him, hard. "I hope so," he said, quiet again. "I will not look kindly on anyone who hurts her. And I'll have your word you'll not do something like that again."

"You have it, Lyndon," Edwin said.

Michael gazed at him a moment longer, then picked up his hat and turned away. He wasn't precisely satisfied at what he saw, but he had no other choice at the moment, save giving the man a good thrashing. "I hope I don't see you hanging about her."

"I don't plan to. Lyndon."

Michael turned. "What?"

Edwin's face was serious, in contrast to the flippant manner he'd used before. "I told you, that day in the park, that Chloe didn't ride. I lied."

Michael felt that urge to murder again, though he schooled his face to calmness. "Oh?"

"Truth is, she can't ride. She's scared of horses."

Michael went still. *Ah.* That explained a great deal. Of course she'd been frightened at her brush with death in the phaeton, but he'd seen another fear in her when he'd finally gotten her to the ground. "Why?"

"Don't know, really. Well, I do, but it's not logical. She fell when she was trying to learn."

"Oh?"

"Don't know why she couldn't learn." He frowned. "Her father taught all of us, and we managed well enough."

"Miss Russell is different from you."

"So she is. She—never mind," he said hastily, again reading something in Michael's eyes. "Probably she'd have been all right if her mother hadn't stepped in. You know what it's like when you fall off a horse, Lyndon. You don't get back on right away, you get afraid. That's what happened to her."

Again, it explained a lot. If Chloe had been afraid of horses since childhood, that fear had had ample time to grow. "Thank you for telling me this," he said curtly, and turned for the door again. This time he didn't allow Hempstead to distract him. A thought had occurred to him while he stood listening to Hempstead's excuses. He had an idea of what he needed to do.

"Lord Lyndon is here for you, Miss Russell," Horricks said from the doorway of the drawing room.

Chloe, book in hand, sat up quickly and patted at her hair. Should she see him? He'd not been pleased with her yesterday, both because of her foolishness and, she suspected, because he'd been forced to give up the race to Brighton. She wondered if he was going to cut up stiff at her now.

"Lord Lyndon? Oh, but this is beyond all things wonderful!" Helena exclaimed. "Oh, do show him up, Horricks. And put away that terrible book, Chloe. A man doesn't like an intelligent woman, and heaven knows you behave as if you have more brains than most of them—"

"Oh, leave off, Helena. I do grow tired of your scolding all the time."

"I don't scold! I simply point out what you've done wrong and how to correct it, and you simply won't attract him with a book in your hand—"

"I *am* intelligent, Helena. I've no intention of hiding it."

"Oh, dear. You'll do all you can to scotch this match, won't you?"

Not for the reasons you think. "If he is to marry me, he should see me as I am."

"Ahem." Horricks stood in the doorway again. "Lord Lyndon, ma'am."

"My lord." Helena held out her hand, smiling so graciously that it was hard to remember she'd been scolding just a moment ago. Chloe looked at her sourly.

"And Miss Russell." He was bowing over her hand, but his eyes were on hers. "How do you today?"

"I am well," she said, watching him with apprehension.

"I am glad to hear it." He sat on down on a chair upholstered in gold brocade, his gaze still on her. It was hard to gauge his mood, whether he was still angry or merely being polite. "You suffered no injuries from yesterday?"

"Only to my pride, sir." She smiled at him. "It isn't the first time."

"I am sorry, my lord, that such a thing happened," Helena began. "Our Chloe has always been prone to such mishaps. Oh, she was a clumsy girl, and she still is, do you know when she was being fitted for a new gown, she—"

"Yesterday's mishap, as you call it, could have ended in disaster. It had naught to do with clumsiness," he said, and there was such quiet steel in his voice that both Helena and Chloe stared at him. "Miss Russell."

Chloe swallowed. "Yes?"

"I came to ask if you would care to drive with me this afternoon."

"Drive?" she said, her heart sinking. "I—don't know if I should—"

"No harm will come to you. I promise." He was gazing at her again, and this time his eyes were soft, warm.

Something within Chloe relaxed. "If you will but wait until I get a shawl, I would be happy to, my lord."

Sometime later, Michael handed her into his curricle. She was still nervous, but, as he took the ribbons, she began to relax. There was no doubt that she was with someone who was skilled at handling a carriage. "Do you drive?" he asked.

"I did, once," she admitted. "But only a gig."

"Why did you stop?"

She considered how to answer that. "I wasn't very good."

"Driving can be difficult."

That wasn't what he had once told her. "Yes."

"Especially if you're afraid of horses."

Chloe looked at him in astonishment. "Whoever told you that?"

He flashed her a quick glance. "No one had to tell me. I saw it in your eyes yesterday."

"Yesterday I let the carriage get away from me."

"A phaeton can be tricky," he said prosaically. "But it was obvious you were afraid of handling the team."

She swallowed. "I was," she admitted in a small voice.

"Oh, my dear." He looked at her again, his eyes holding that warm expression again. "It must have been terrible for you."

His sympathy was her undoing. She looked away, her eyes moist. "If I but had more experience—"

"Town is not the place to learn. At least, Oxford Street certainly isn't."

"I learned that," she said ruefully, and frowned. When he had asked her to go driving with him, she had assumed he meant the park. Instead, he was heading deeper into Mayfair. "Where are we going?"

"The Grantham stables."

Six

"The Grantham stables—" Chloe began.

Michael held the ribbons lightly. "There's something there I'd like you to see."

She closed her eyes. Why, when he knew of her fears? "Why?" she asked again.

"Because I think you need to."

"My lord—"

He took the tight corner into an alley near Grantham House with easy competence. "No harm will come to you, Chloe. I promise you that."

She took a deep breath. What choice did she have but to trust him? At least he hadn't taken her in disgust. "Very well."

The stables were dim and had the distinct odor of horse. Chloe looked fearfully along the long cobblestoned floor, which had wooden stalls to either side. With his hand at her back, Michael ushered her inside. Most of the horses came to the doors of their stalls as Michael walked by, and one tossed his head and neighed, making Chloe shrink back against Michael. "Hush, there, you great Nuisance," Michael said in an affectionate voice.

"What did you call him?" Chloe asked in surprise, and wondered if Michael realized he'd drawn her back to him with his arm about her waist.

He pointed to the sign painted in white above the door.

"His name. Even as a foal he was a nuisance. It seemed a natural name for him."

"Oh," Chloe said, realizing for the first time that there was more to this business of keeping horses than she'd thought.

"Good bloodlines, though." He reached in to pat the horse's nose, still holding her firmly against him. "He wants a treat. A bad habit I have."

"Oh," Chloe said again, regretful that, now they were walking once more, he had loosened his grip on her. "You're not afraid of them at all."

"No. Now, there"—he indicated a horse as they passed—"is one to avoid. See how his eyes are rolling?"

"Yes, I do know what you mean."

"No one's been able to tame him. Not even I. We may have to put him down."

"But what a shame."

"Better that than that someone is hurt. And this one is Firefly." He stopped in front of yet another loose box, where a small bay mare whickered and came over to them. "The sweetest, gentlest mare we have. Hello, girl. Sorry, no treat today." He stroked the mare's nose. "Isn't she a beauty?"

"Even I have to admit that," Chloe said. "What is that white mark on her head?"

"It's called a blaze. She's one of the smallest horses we have, too. Perfect for you."

She shrank back against him. "M-me?"

"Yes." He looked down at her, and his smile faded. "You're pale. Chloe, did you think I meant you to ride?"

"I—don't know." She looked up at him, pleading with her eyes. "I do remember some of what I was taught. I think I could, if you were beside me—"

"No," he said, so firmly that she wanted to pull back, in fear of his anger at her ineptitude. She was surprised, then, when he pulled her close, one large, strong hand holding her head against his heart. Never in her life had she felt so safe, so protected. This was a man, she knew with sudden clarity, who would never hurt her or scorn her. It did not spring from love of her. It was in his character, bred into his very bones. In one sense, she was very lucky. In quite another, she wasn't. "I'd never ask such a thing of you."

She relaxed, wishing he would hold her like this forever. "Then?"

"If you ever wished to try again, I'd teach you on Firefly."

"Oh." She burrowed her head against him. "Maybe someday, Michael," she said, and then waited, aghast, to see his reaction at her use of his name.

"When you're ready," he said, showing no signs of annoyance. Instead, he stroked her back, making her want to shiver. "Chloe, you don't need to ride to hounds or any such thing if you don't wish. We seem to be dealing well enough together now."

She pulled back a little from him. "Common interests would help."

"They would," he agreed. "I believe we both would prefer country living, and less formality."

"Mercy, yes," she said fervently.

"There, that is one thing. As time passes I'm sure we'll find others."

"If nothing else, I could keep the accounts for your estate."

He looked startled. "I suppose you could."

"Do you disapprove?" she asked in a small voice.

"It is something a man should do, my dear."

"Why?" she challenged him. "Why should not a woman have as good a brain as a man, or better?"

"Most women I know have been pea gooses."

"Are you referring to your mother?"

"Lord, no!" he exclaimed, and gave her a rueful smile. "Very well, I'll concede that point. And you. But"—his smile widened—"every other woman is a pea goose."

She smiled back up at him. "Then most men must be peacocks."

That made him grin. "Am I?"

"Oh, no, of course not."

"I am glad of that," he said, and, to her regret, released her. "Shall we leave, my dear?"

She took a deep breath. Part of her did want to run from this place. But he had brought her here for a reason, and she was made of sterner stuff than he realized. "No."

He raised an eyebrow. "No?"

"We came here so I would learn not to be afraid of horses."

"And I frightened you more, instead." He traced a fingertip down her cheek, making her shiver again. "I wouldn't put you through that for the world, my dear."

Am I your dear? she wondered, feeling warmer and just a little nervous of his consideration, so rare had it been in her life. "Thank you, but I think this is something I need to do."

He frowned a little. "If you're quite certain."

"I am."

"Very well. Close your eyes."

"I can look at her, Michael."

"That's not the reason. Close your eyes and take a deep breath. Good. Now, relax." His breath was soft in her hair. "Imagine yourself in a safe place. Likely where you grew up."

Involuntarily Chloe thought of the Russell country house and nearly panicked. *A safe place, a safe place,* she thought frantically, anyplace where she had absolute safety, besides Michael's arms. Then she had it. Her studio.

"You're there?" he asked softly.

"Yes."

"Good. Now, imagine Firefly there. Very small, if you wish, perhaps no larger than a cat, but definitely a horse. Do you see her?"

This time she was slower in answering. The thought of a horse in her cramped studio was so incongruous that she nearly laughed aloud. A tiny horse, though, was manageable. "Yes."

"You're not afraid to touch a cat—"

"I like cats."

"Good. So you're not afraid to touch Firefly."

"This is strange."

"I know. Put your hand on her head. Let her grow larger and larger. Now she's full size. Are you still touching her?"

She took a moment to answer. "Her hair is coarse, but it feels like satin."

Behind her, he exhaled. "Does she frighten you?"

"No."

"Then open your eyes, Chloe."

Chloe blinked, just a bit surprised that she stood before Firefly's loose box in the stable block. Somehow the horse didn't look so large to her, or so frightening, though she still had no desire to ride. For the first time, she concentrated on the horse, rather than on old memories. Hesitantly she reached out to touch Firefly's nose. The horse, startled, tossed her head, making Chloe snatch her hand back. But then, when Firefly looked at her, her large, liquid brown eyes seeming only curious, she reached out again, this time with more firmness, and began to stroke the horse's nose. The feeling of the horsehair under her hand was indeed satiny and coarse.

"Well done, Chloe," Michael said quietly. "I didn't expect you to do so much today."

"How tall is she?" she asked, with real curiosity.

"About fourteen hands. A good height for you."

"She looks very large."

"That's because you're not used to horses. Next time we'll bring her a treat. A lump of sugar, or a carrot."

Chloe turned laughing eyes on him. "I don't think I'm quite ready to have those big teeth take a lump of sugar from me."

He smiled back. "Very well, a carrot. You'll relax more as time goes on, my dear."

That endearment again. "How did you learn to relax like that?"

Briefly his lips tightened. "The head groom taught me

when—when I was young. I've found 'tis helpful for facing my fears."

She looked up, curious as to what fears this large, supremely confident man could have, as he slipped his arm through hers and they began walking out of the stable block. "I nearly laughed when I thought of a horse in my studio."

"Your studio?" He looked down at her, surprised. "Not where you lived?"

"No. What of you?"

"Chimneys," he said promptly.

"It's a beautiful place, then?"

"I've always felt at peace there, even if the place is in shambles."

"We'll have to do something about that then, won't we?"

" 'We?' "

"Of course. I'm not helpless, Michael."

"I didn't think you were." He was quiet again. "Did Hempstead apologize to you for what he did?"

She looked up, startled at the change in subject. "Yes. Why did you ask?"

"Just curious. If he ever bothers you, I will handle him for you."

"Lyndon, I doubt that will be necessary."

"I liked it better when you used my name, Chloe."

So he had noticed, she thought. "I wouldn't have done so, except for the situation."

"I know, but I still liked it. Michael," he said again, placing his hand over hers, resting in the crook of his arm. It was warm and strong, and it sent that shiver of sensation through her. Though it wasn't unpleasant, it startled her so much that she pulled free.

He raised an eyebrow at her as they stepped out of the stable block into sunshine that was so strong that Chloe briefly closed her eyes. "Is all well?"

"Yes." She frowned up at him. "How do you do that?"

"What?"

"Raise one eyebrow. Do you practice in a mirror?"

He laughed. "No, Chloe."

"I tried, you know, but all I did was grimace."

He laughed again at the face she made. "No, my dear, I am certain I never did that."

"Oh." She pondered that. " 'Tis not fair, you realize, that you do such things so easily."

"But you have talents I do not."

"I suppose I do," she said as he helped her into his curricle. To her vast relief, she didn't catch the hem of her frock on the carriage step, as she'd feared she might, and fall back against him. That might actually not be so bad, she thought. She'd rather like to be in his arms again.

Michael's groom let go the horse's head and then jumped onto the back of the carriage, which was already moving. They were quiet as they left the mews, as Michael drove along Grosvenor Street, to South Audley Street, and then to Curzon Street. He pulled up in front of the Russell house, then came around the carriage to help Chloe down.

She placed a hand in his as she stepped down, and this time his fingers closed warmly over hers, as they never had before. Again she felt the warmth through the material of her gloves.

"I'll see you inside," he said, his hand once again at her back. She was growing accustomed to that shivery sensation his touch gave her, yet she was in something of a daze as Horricks, the Russell butler, opened the door for them and they stepped inside. "Good afternoon, Horricks," Michael said.

Horricks bowed. "My lord, Miss Russell. Mr. and Mrs. Russell have not yet returned from Richmond."

"Then I mustn't stay." Michael raised her hand to his lips, to her surprise turning her hand over. His mouth on her palm was warm and open, and the kiss went on for longer than was proper.

"Ahem," a voice said, and both of them, startled, looked at Horricks, who was standing very upright, yet had a gleam in his eyes. "I shall be in the kitchen should you need me, Miss Russell," he said.

"Yes, thank you, Horricks," Chloe said, her gaze held again by Michael's eyes.

"Of course we're only allowed ten minutes alone," he said.

"Of—of course, " she stammered. "I'm not sure wh-what anyone thinks we could do in ten minutes—"

He gazed down at her. "A man is permitted to take certain liberties with his fiancée."

Chloe swallowed. "Such as?"

"Such as a kiss."

"Oh?"

"Yes. Oh," he murmured, and, hands still at her waist, drew her against him.

She kissed with prim innocence, he thought with amusement and tenderness, as his parted lips slanted across hers, tightly pressed together. For all that, though, her mouth softened and she quivered in response under his hands. He was surprised, then, when she stiffened as he opened his mouth wider.

Reluctantly, he opened his eyes to see her staring at him, her brow furrowed in puzzlement. As he so often did when he was with her, he wanted to laugh. As always, he restrained himself. Too many people had laughed at her already. "What is it, Chloe?" he asked softly, resting his brow against hers.

She swallowed, hard. "I—well, it's not what I expected."

"Not like kissing your brother, is it?"

"Mercy, no!" she exclaimed, and this time he did chuckle. She looked startled for a moment, and then smiled, a trifle sheepishly. "Your pardon, Lyndon. I fear I am letting my emotions get the better of me."

Again he laughed. "You used my name in a stable, Chloe, and now you use my title?"

She played with the edges of his neckcloth, not looking at him. "Somehow it doesn't seem proper—"

"To do so now? When I'm kissing you?"

She laughed a little. " 'Tis silly of me, I know, but . . ."

"Chloe, will you still call me by my title on our wedding night?"

That brought her head up, her cheeks blazing with color. "I may call you by other things instead."

He threw his head back and laughed. "I never know what you're going to say," he said, hugging her to him.

"Does it bother you?" she asked anxiously.

"I rather like it. I like it that you show your feelings, too."

"Do you?" she said, looking up at him.

"Yes. Shall we try again?"

She drew in her breath. "You truly wish to?"

He frowned. "Of course I do. Why wouldn't I?"

"Because I—oh, it hardly signifies."

Someone had hurt her, he thought, gazing down at her. He wondered who. "Yes, dear, I do wish to," he said softly, and lowered his head again.

This time there was less innocence in her response, though she still kept her lips closed. She moved under his hands, so that he had no choice but to slide his arms about her, one at her waist, one at her shoulders. She had no choice but to move her hands to his shoulders, though she didn't yet go so far as to embrace him. She moved closer to him instead, making him repress the urge to catch her up and press her closer yet. Her response encouraged him, though, enough to slide his tongue against the closed seam of her mouth, teasing at it to open—and she stiffened again.

Repressing a sigh, he raised his head. "What is it now?"

"Why did you do that? With your tongue?"

"For you to part your lips, of course."

She frowned. "But why?"

"Because, my dear, 'tis very pleasurable."

"I don't know how it can be."

Again he felt the urge to laugh. "Shall I show you?"

"Well—"

"Open for me, Chloe," he whispered, and bent his head to hers again.

She hesitated for a moment at the touch of his tongue,

but then, relaxing, opened at last. She resisted when he pressed his tongue, more urgent now, against her teeth, and so he deliberately slowed his assault on her senses, deliberately forced himself to relax. It didn't matter that his body was clamoring to hurry things along. He made himself remember how new this was to her.

Pressing her lips open with his own again, he let his tongue sweep sensually around the soft inner flesh of her lips, and felt her jolt of response in the way she suddenly clutched his shoulders, in the way her body moved against his, innocently provocative. As if of their own volition, her teeth parted at last. He took quick advantage to slide his tongue within.

Instantly, she pulled back. This time, he did sigh. "Well?"

Her eyes were dark, fathomless. "Do people really kiss like that?"

He shook with silent laughter, in spite of his efforts to repress it. "I can't speak for anyone else, but . . ."

"Oh." She looked thoughtful. "It was—odd."

"But not unpleasant?"

"Oh, no. Not at all unpleasant."

"Shall we try again, then?"

"If you think we should."

Again he sighed. "It isn't just my decision, Chloe. I'll not force you into something you don't want."

"I know that," she whispered.

"Then?"

"I have this strange feeling inside that goes from—well, never mind," she said hastily. "It rather frightens me."

Ah. Her own desire was rising, whether she realized it or not. "Trust me, Chloe. Trust me," he said, and this time when he bent his head, her lips came up to meet his. He slid his tongue out again, pressing it against her teeth, and she opened to him at last.

Seven

Oh, dear heavens. She had never felt anything like this, Chloe thought, as his tongue explored the recesses of her mouth. She was almost passive in his arms, except that her lips moved against his in response. What he was doing was pleasurable, rather than disgusting, as she would have thought had someone told her about it. She wished she knew what was expected of her, though.

Then he stroked under her tongue, and that jolt of pleasure went through her again. He pressed her closer against him, and she wrapped her arms tight around him, wanting never to let him go. At her reaction, his hands rubbed almost frantically over her, down her back, to her waist, and up her sides. But when they began to move forward, he abruptly pulled away. She felt bereft, empty, wondering why he had stopped.

He rested his forehead against hers, his breathing as ragged as hers. "Dear God," he said.

"Why did you stop?" she asked.

He gave a little laugh. "Because if I didn't, I wouldn't have been able to."

"Oh," she said, understanding and yet not quite believing it. He wanted her? He could have any woman he wanted. Any young miss would certainly set her cap at him, even without his title, even without a fortune. Irrationally, her hopes rose. If he desired her, he had to feel something for her.

"I should go." He took her shoulders and set her away from him. "If I stay any longer, it will compromise you."

"Yes, our ten minutes must be up."

He chuckled. "They were up long ago, my dear."

"Oh." She let him go reluctantly. "I thought it wouldn't take more than ten minutes."

At that he roared with laughter. "Yes, my dear, it does."

"I meant—oh, you know what I meant." She looked up at him through her lashes. "Though I think we did fairly well in ten minutes."

He rested his forehead against hers again. "We did," he said, and kissed her again. "I must go."

Her lips clung to his. "Yes."

"I shouldn't"—he lowered his lips again—"keep my horses standing."

"No." She reached up to him this time.

"I don't want them to get cold."

"Mm, no," she murmured, kissing his jaw.

"Mm, no. Now, no more of that," he warned after a moment, though he had been the one to start the kissing again, and stepped back. "Behave yourself."

"Yes, Lyndon," she said with deceptive meekness.

"Lyndon, indeed." This time his kiss was a brief one of good-bye. It might have deepened into something more if they had not heard voices on the stairs.

"My brother and sister-in-law are home." Chloe gave Michael a wry look as she stepped away from him.

"So I hear." He bent his head, listening to Helena's chatter and Horricks's long-suffering replies. "Does she ever stop talking?"

"Rarely. Helena," she said, turning to greet her.

"Why, Lord Lyndon." Helena's sky blue eyes had widened. "But how very nice to see you again. Of course, we would, since you and Chloe are betrothed, and since I knew you were to go driving today, and did you have a nice ride? You do have a beautiful curricle, my lord, do you think you'll teach Chloe how to drive it?"

"Perhaps one day," he said politely, breaking in before

Helena could go on, and returning Chloe's wry smile. "I must go, my dear." He took Chloe's hand in his, quite as if they hadn't been embracing for the last several minutes, and bowed over it. "I fear I have appointments elsewhere."

"Of course, Lyndon," she said calmly, though her pulse sped up from just his touch.

"I will see you soon. Mrs. Russell, Chloe," he said, bowing to them, and left, leaving Chloe watching him go, her fingers to her lips, anxious and eager for her wedding day.

Michael drove home in something of a daze. Good God, that was something he hadn't expected. When he'd given in to the urge to kiss her, he'd thought it would be friendly and warm. He hadn't thought they would explore each other so thoroughly, that they would respond to each other as they had. It had been a long time since a simple kiss—kisses, he admitted to himself—had affected him so, if ever. Even now, as he drove along Grosvenor Street, he wanted her in his arms. Who would ever have thought she'd be such a sweet armful?

The truth was, since the day he'd first met her, he'd seen her as Miss Bumblebroth, slightly untidy, somewhat dowdy, and very clumsy. Once he'd come to know her, he'd tried to suppress the thoughts, but they'd been buried. Until this afternoon. Until a few moments spent in her arms had changed everything for him.

Suddenly her clumsiness didn't matter, and her lack of vanity had become an endearing trait. Certainly he didn't care that she was dowdy, not with what felt like a delectably curved figure under those all-encompassing folds of fabric. What mattered was that within she was a sweet, sometimes outrageous, sometimes surprising person. He liked her, enjoyed being with her, and now had discovered passion in her arms. Suddenly he had more hopes for the marriage than he had before.

Two acquaintances passing on horseback hailed him.

"Hallo, Lyndon," one of them said. "On your way to the park?"

Michael drew the curricle to a stop. "No, as it happens, I've other plans."

"Not stopping in to look at Danfield's grays, I hope? Had my eyes on that pair any time this age."

"I wasn't planning to, no."

"You've not a prayer of affording them, Freddie," the other man said. "Myself, I'd rather go to the park. Claudine is said to be planning to walk there today. The latest opera dancer," he explained, at Michael's look of incomprehension.

"Maybe that's why he's not going that way himself, Tony." Freddie grinned at him. "He can afford both Danfield's grays and Claudine now he's getting a rich wife. Eh, Lyndon?"

Both men laughed uproariously. Michael's smile felt stiff. No man cared to have his name bandied about quite that way on a street corner. "Quite," he said again, and nodded to the men. "Gentlemen, if you'll excuse me?"

"That's right, don't want to keep Claudine waiting," Tony called as Michael gave his team the office to start.

The devil! he thought, his jaw set. If anything could ruin his good mood, that encounter had done it. He might have popped the unfortunate Freddie on the mouth for the insult both to himself and to Chloe, except that it was bad *ton* to do so on the street. When he next saw them at Gentlemen Jackson's, it would go very hard for them.

And then what? He couldn't very well challenge any man who made a similar comment, when everyone must be saying the same thing. He liked Chloe. He wasn't going to deny that, or that it would make life with her that much easier. So would the unexpected passion he'd just discovered in her arms. Left to himself, though, he would not have chosen her for a bride. Not Miss Bumblebroth.

It was time he stopped air dreaming. It was time he stopped letting a few kisses blind him to the truth. The Granthams needed an infusion of cash. That he liked Chloe

had nothing to say to it. He was marrying for money. It
would be best if he didn't forget it.

Chloe rested her elbows on her dressing table and, prop-
ping her chin on her hands, stared glumly at her reflection.
"I am not exactly a blushing bride."

Helena fussed about behind her, tucking in an errant curl.
"Why you ever chose this color," she fretted. " 'Tis most
unsuitable for a wedding."

"Fiddle," Lady Grantham stood back, coolly supervising
the process of preparing Chloe for her wedding. "That
shade of aqua suits you exactly. Celeste does do lovely
work."

"Far too plain. Oh, dear, why you could not have asked
for just one rouleau about your hem—"

"Helena, I've lace and satin roses and even a flounce,
so I am certain no one will worry about the lack of more
decoration." She returned to studying her reflection. "I do
hope I'm not throwing out spots."

"Fiddle. All you need is a bit of color."

"Lady Grantham!" she exclaimed as the countess leaned
over to rub some rouge onto Chloe's cheeks, and caught up
a towel to rub the rouge off. "I don't paint my face."

"There." The countess smiled at her in the mirror. "Now
you look just as you should."

Chloe stared her reflection. "You did that on purpose."

"Of course I did. Pray don't expect me to countenance
any daughter-in-law of mine to wear paint."

Daughter-in-law! Chloe's nervousness abruptly returned.
"Pray tell me again why I am doing this."

The countess glanced covertly at Helena, who had gone
over to Patience and was fussing over the flowers Chloe
would carry. "Because you love my son," she said quietly.

Chloe's eyes swept upward in surprise. "Then you
know—does he?"

"No, the clunch. And pray do not tell him. Yet."

Chloe let out her breath in a rush. "Mercy. I'd no idea I was so obvious."

"About what?" Helena asked as she came up behind her again, then went on without waiting for an answer. "There is something I've meant to tell you about this age—"

"Oh, no," the countess said.

"Ma'am?" Helena stared at her blankly, making Chloe duck her head. The person who could stem the flow of Helena's speech was rare.

"Oh, the merest trifle. Do go on. I shan't stay to embarrass you."

Mystified, Chloe turned on the stool to watch the countess walk across the room to a window. "What on earth?"

Helena nodded approvingly. "It is just that I stand in the role of a mother to you, Chloe, though I suppose Lady Grantham could say the same. Though I wonder if she would care to speak so of her own son. I shouldn't, but then my Richard is only two, and so—"

"Helena," Chloe broke in rather desperately. "What are you talking about?"

Helena's gaze dropped to the circlet of flowers in her hands, as she began to turn it in her fingers. "Well, my dear, to put it bluntly—you do not mind if I am blunt about it? Lady Grantham is quite correct, it can be embarrassing, but I would be quite remiss if I didn't tell you about—oh, dear, how shall I put this, I'm sure I don't remember what my mother said, but then that was a different age—"

"Helena." Chloe looked up at her in dawning horror. "Are you talking about marital relations?"

"Exactly," the countess said from the window, and Chloe raised hands to cheeks that suddenly felt hot.

"Dear, dear." Helena's face was pink to the tip of her ears. " 'Tis not a thing to bruit about."

"Helena, you will mangle my headdress if you continue so."

"I beg your pardon?" She glanced down at the circlet of flowers, then laid it on the dressing table. "Oh. Well. It is like this. Men have certain needs—"

"Yes?" Chloe, intrigued by the brevity of Helena's speech as much as by anything else, prompted when Helena stopped.

"Well—and that is it."

"Hmph. Next she'll be telling you about the birds and the bees," the countess grumbled.

In spite of herself, Chloe wanted to howl with laughter. "So. Men have needs."

"Shh! Yes." Helena's whisper was piercing. "Women do not."

"We don't?"

"No. Perhaps the lower orders do. I do think that is how they have so many children, though I do wonder about the *demimondaines*—but I should never speak to you of such things!"

From the window came something that sounded like a snort. It made Chloe bite her lips and look away. "Are you saying Cyprians—"

"Hush, Chloe, how do you even know of such things?"

"Helena, I have been in town this age."

"Yes, but—oh, dear, what am I trying to say?"

"We have needs men don't," the countess prompted.

"Yes. No! Men have needs. Oh, help me," Helena implored her.

"My dear, I think you are doing quite well alone."

"But you know what 'tis like. Chloe should be prepared."

"Of course."

Helena looked at her, but when nothing more was forthcoming, took a deep breath. "Needs. Yes. No proper woman has them, but we must do what we have to, for our husbands. And in your case, for the succession. And that is how you have babies," she finished triumphantly.

Chloe ducked her head again. "Helena, even I know more than that."

"You do?"

"Yes. I was raised in the country, after all."

"Oh. Yes. Well, then. You know what happens." She

wrinkled her nose. "Though I have often wondered why the females squeal so."

Some evil genius possessed Chloe. "You do not squeal, then?"

From the window came another snort of laughter. Helena glanced desperately that way, and then plowed on. "Good heavens, no! How you can ask such a thing—Chloe, it is as graceless a thing as I have always expected from you."

Some of Chloe's glee faded. "Helena—"

"I must make certain all is ready below," she gasped, and fled.

Chloe stared after her and then raised the circlet, placing it on her hair. "Does it look all right?" she asked as Lady Grantham neared her again.

"Here, let me just straighten it and tuck some pins in. There." She stepped back. "You look charming, my dear. Helena is wrong, by the by."

"About my gracelessness? 'Tis very kind of you to say so, my lady, but—"

"Yes, yes, that too. But I wasn't speaking of that."

"Then?"

The countess bent low. "Even proper ladies squeal," she said confidentially.

"Lady Grantham!"

"And on their wedding nights, too," she added.

"Oh, mercy." Chloe raised her hands to her cheeks again. "I must needs survive preparing for my wedding first."

The countess chuckled, and Chloe looked up to see that her lips were tucked back in the gesture so characteristic of her, as if she were about to laugh at any moment. "I am so going to enjoy having you for a daughter."

"Why, thank you," Chloe said, more touched by this than by any compliment she could have received. "Lady Grantham—"

"I dislike hearing that from you. Please call me Mother."

Chloe caught her breath. "You wish me to?"

"I do."

"Oh." It had been so long since she'd had anyone who

would answer to that name. "I'd love to. Mother." She looked up at the countess. "Will you tell me, since my mother is gone and I certainly can't leave it to Helena—will you tell me what I am to do tonight?"

"Michael will show you, or he's not the man I think he is," she said serenely. "I hope he comes to his senses soon, too, and realizes what he has in you. No, don't get up yet." She set her hands on Chloe's shoulders, pressing her back onto the stool. "The earl and I wish you to have this."

For the first time, Chloe noticed that she held a long, narrow blue velvet box. She eyed it with a mixture of surprise and anticipation. "Ma'am, are you sure—"

"Oh, nonsense, they are merely the Grantham diamonds."

"Merely? Oh, my—oh, Mother," Chloe gasped, as the countess opened the box to reveal a suite of necklace, earbobs, tiara, and two bracelets, all of the finest stones, all set in a vine-like design of thin, glistening gold. For a moment Chloe viewed them through vision that, itself, glistened. "Oh, ma'am."

"The tiara is too heavy, of course, for everyday wear."

"Oh, then I shan't wear it when I paint."

"Pray don't be impertinent," Lady Grantham said, but her lips were tucked back again. "The earbobs will hurt after a time, I fear, but they do look very well on you. You have a lovely neck, dear, and lovely shoulders as well."

Chloe, eyes wide and wondering, reached up her fingers to touch the necklace. "I do?"

"Oh, without a doubt. We will not discuss your bosom, as I know it embarrasses you."

"After today, I'm not certain anything can embarrass me."

"After tonight, nothing will. There." She stepped back. "They suit you."

"Thank you." The woman who stared back at Chloe from her mirror seemed suddenly an attractive stranger. "Ma'am, how is it these weren't sold long since?" she blurted, and then clapped her hand over her mouth. "Oh, dear, I didn't mean—"

"Of course you did." Lady Grantham's eyes brimmed with laughter as she leaned closer. "I'll tell you a secret, shall I? It may overset you a trifle."

"Oh?"

"Yes. Most of the Grantham jewels are paste. Shall I tell you something else?"

"I'm not certain I wish to hear anything more about anything."

"I quite understand. If my mother-in-law had ever spoken to me as I just have, or given me a nightgown such as the one I'm giving you for tonight—well, that's neither here nor there. You may be comforted to know that everyone in the *ton* has done the same from time to time."

Chloe's head was spinning. Paste, nightgowns, that absurd discussion on marital relations—she didn't know what to think of any of it. "I'll redeem them for you, ma'am," she said finally, settling on the safest topic she could think of.

"Fiddle," Lady Grantham said, not quite meeting her gaze. "Help my son to find himself, and I'll ask for no more."

Chloe frowned. "I don't understand."

"You will, I fear. Now." Her tone became brisk. "I'll just leave you to finish your preparations."

"Thank you, ma'am," Chloe said finally. "For everything."

"Fiddle," Lady Grantham said, and went out.

Alone for the first time that morning, Chloe turned toward her pier glass, seeing again a stranger, and thinking again of all that had been said in the last few moments.

I wonder if I will squeal? she thought, and clapped her hand over her mouth as if she had said the words aloud. Perhaps the idea wasn't so preposterous as if seemed. Because, lord help her, she did love him. If only he loved her in return.

She stared at herself for another moment, and then, squaring her shoulders, picked up her gloves and went out.

Late evening, and Michael and his new bride were at last alone in their suite at a comfortable inn along the Dover road. Alone, Chloe thought as she brushed out her hair in the bedroom—except, of course for Patience, the innkeeper, the maid who had served them dinner, and any number of people. It would be worse when they reached Chimneys. Although she had grown up with servants all her life, it would be the first time she would have the charge of running a house herself. The thought frankly terrified her.

St. George's church on Hanover Square had been filled to bursting that morning. It could not be otherwise for the wedding of Viscount Lyndon, even if he were marrying someone entirely unsuitable for him. Holding tight to Stephen's arm with one hand and to the small nosegay of white roses in a silver holder that Michael had sent her, Chloe walked with deliberate slowness down the aisle, careful not to look to either side and see the faces of people who had once mocked her. Only as she neared the front of the church did she see Michael, his face serious, gazing at her.

Oh, mercy, but he was so handsome. He was attired as faultlessly as ever, in a coat of midnight blue worn over white satin knee breeches and a waistcoat of blue and silver brocade. His neckcloth, a marvel of simple perfection, was adorned by only a single sapphire and diamond stickpin. All this she took in in one quick glance she suspected would remain with her forever. She knew what she saw when she looked at him: the man she would love to the end of her days. What, she wondered, did he see when he looked at her?

Michael took her arm then and smiled down at her. Only the solid, reassuring bulk of his presence kept her from turning and bolting from the church. This was a terrible mistake, she thought, even as she mechanically spoke her vows. Marrying when there was love on only one side could not be right. But then he was bending to kiss her, a brief, but warm, kiss that made her insides spin, and the organist was playing the recessional. Panic welled up within her. Too late, too late. Now she'd landed herself in a real bumblebroth.

Michael bent to her. "You decided to chance a train?" he whispered, and she looked up swiftly to see his eyes twinkling at her. Suddenly, she relaxed. Mistake or no, this was Michael, who'd never seemed to regret his proposal.

"Mind you don't tread on it, or I won't answer for the consequences," she whispered back, and saw the gleam in his eyes become more pronounced as he pressed his lips tightly together.

"If you fall, I fall with you."

"Perhaps I should twitch it into your way."

His shoulders shook. "You are a minx."

"Yes, and who would have guessed it?"

"Lord, what have I sentenced myself to?" he asked in mock resignation.

She was suddenly glum. "A lifetime with Miss Bumble-broth."

"Lady Bumblebroth."

"Does that mean you're Lord Bumblebroth?"

"There are worse things." His hold on her arm had tightened. "We'll brush through it together, Chloe," he'd murmured, and for the life of her she hadn't known if he'd meant this day, or the rest of their lives.

Now it was evening, the long summer twilight having at last faded. She was just rising from the dressing table when there was a knock on the door leading from the private parlor. It made her spin around, her hand to her throat. Did she look all right? Should she have braided her hair as she usually did, or left it loose and wanton as it was now? Oh, what would he see when he looked at her, she wondered despairingly, and then had no more time for thought. Michael stepped into the room, and closed the door behind him.

Oh, mercy, she thought for the second time that day.
Chloe's mouth went dry as he crossed the room to her,
smiling. He wore a brocade dressing gown, and, from what
she could see, little else. At least, she couldn't see any sign
of a nightshirt above it. Only smooth masculine skin
showed, and the beginning of crisp, dark curls. What was
even more startling was that he was gazing at her with such
appreciation that she turned involuntarily, to see what he
was looking at.

"That is a vastly becoming nightgown, Chloe."

In spite of herself, she felt her cheeks turning pink. Her
lace nightgown was rather more revealing than she was accustomed to. "Oh. Thank you. It was a gift from—well,
never mind."

He crossed to her, standing so close that she could feel
his breath on her cheek. "Does it matter?"

"Well—no."

"Good." He smiled and held his hand out to her. "Come
here."

She regarded him for a moment, and then, head held
high, went into his arms. They closed around her, and she
was suddenly, achingly aware of him, of the scents of shav-
ing soap and brandy and something that was uniquely his
own, of the angles and planes of his body, so different from
her own. *I just may squeal,* she thought, and gave herself
up to his kiss.

Eight

The occupants of the traveling carriage emblazoned with the Grantham family crest appeared occupied with the view unfolding outside their windows. They had left the Dover road some time back, and were now driving on a secondary one, along cliffs above the sea. Chloe's thoughts, however, were neither on their journey nor their destination. She might not have squealed the night before, but the experience certainly had not been as fearsome as Helena would have had her think. In fact, she thought she might come to enjoy it. "It wasn't so bad," she said aloud.

"Hm?" Michael turned his head. "What is that you said?"

"Last night. It wasn't so bad."

"Not bad!" He stared at her. "I'll have you know I've never had any complaints before."

"And is that supposed to make me feel better?" She glared back at him, and for a moment the tension between them was almost palpable.

Michael was the first to break it, grinning wryly and shaking his head. "Who ever told me you were shy?"

"I always was." She rested her head on his shoulder. "I don't know why I feel so at ease with you."

"Should I be honored or insulted?"

"Oh, honored, by all means."

He laid his hand on hers and brought both to rest on his

thigh, making her senses jump. "I shall endeavor to do better tonight. Will that satisfy you?"

She looked up at him from under her lashes, the first time she had consciously flirted with him. "I suppose it must."

"Then I shall," he answered with the same mock gravity. "Ah."

"What is it?"

"We are nearing Sandgate. Chimneys isn't far distant, once we turn inland."

"The view is lovely here—mercy, what is that smell?"

Michael glanced out his window again. "Mud flats. We'll turn inland now."

Her handkerchief to her nose to shield her from the pungent smell, Chloe looked out to see a straggling line of houses and shops and taverns. A stone church of Norman design was set farther back from the road on a green. "Mud flats?"

"The sea front used to be closer, but now it's nearly a mile away. What's left are mud flats. Tidal beaches. 'Tis low tide."

"Oh." She didn't remove her handkerchief, though she assumed she would become accustomed to the sulfurous odor. "And I thought sea air was supposed to be so fresh."

He grinned. "It will be different at Chimneys."

"I would hope so! Are we nearly there?"

"Not much longer."

"I will be glad to be done traveling. Tell me about Chimneys."

"Chimneys? It's rather a small house. Last time I was there, it was in need of repair. I hate to think of what 'tis like now."

Chloe dismissed that with a wave of her hand. "No matter. I've nothing else to do with my time."

It was his turn to look at her from under his brow. "Nothing?"

She ducked her head, feeling her cheeks growing warm. "I cannot think of anything else."

"I can," he said, and slipped his arm about her shoulders. The kiss they shared was so achingly sweet that they were in danger of letting it become something more, until the carriage was jolted more than usual. Chloe clutched at Michael's chest, rather an interesting state of affairs, she thought, except that he was looking outside again as they began to roll downward. "We're here."

The moment of closeness had passed. Inwardly she sighed, though she knew this was neither the time nor the place to succumb to desire. "Where is the house?"

"Ahead. We just passed the gatehouse. This drive is terrible," he added, as they hit another rut.

Another thing to be fixed. Suddenly she was depressed. It was one thing to know she had been married for money, another to experience it firsthand. She turned to look out again, and so was the first to see the house come into view. She tried to raise one eyebrow, much as she had seen him do, and turned to him. "A small house?"

"Yes," he said absently.

"By your standards."

He looked startled. "By my standards? I am not sure I understand you."

"Grantham must be a great pile," she said, thinking of the family's main seat in Buckinghamshire.

"One of the showplaces of the country, or it once was," he agreed, and then grinned. "Chimneys is small in comparison. Not above fifteen bedchambers."

"Oh, indeed. Quite manageable. And you tell me it needs work? Michael!"

"I've every dependence on you." He rose from his seat as the carriage came to a stop. "I sent Caswell ahead," he said, referring to their butler. "He and Mrs. Barrie between them should have hired enough staff."

"I hope so," she muttered, and pasted on a smile as she placed her hand on his, to step down. Already she'd work ahead of her. She was no longer plain Miss Russell, but Viscountess Lyndon, and therein lay a world of difference.

The daylight had faded again before Chloe finally had

a chance to be alone. Candles softly lit her bedchamber, disguising the water spots on the faded wallpaper, high up on the wall, as well as the shabbiness of the brocade bed hangings. Still, the room was of decent size, the chimney fortunately drew well, and, best yet, it faced east and thus was scented by fresh sea air.

The house, a solid Jacobean manor of gray stone, was indeed in need of work. She'd seen that in the dull, dreary dining room, which was furnished mostly in shades of brown and tarnished gold, in the frayed carpeting, and in the endless oak paneling, which, though it shone with care, showed scrapes and scratches in too many places.

Oddly enough, though, she felt more invigorated than she had in many a long day. Closeted though she had been for the past few years in either the library or her study, she had been brought up to run a house such as this. It was a task she could accomplish, and accomplish well.

There was a tap on the door leading from her dressing room, and then Michael strolled in, wearing, again, only a dressing gown. Chloe watched him through her mirror, all her senses suddenly, vividly alive, though she kept her face schooled to calmness. "Well, my dear." He set his hands on her shoulders. "Have I set you too much of a task?"

"You, or the house?"

He let out a crack of laughter. "I never know what you're going to say," he complained.

"Good." She rose and saw his eyes widen just a trifle, as well they might. She was, after all, wearing the lace nightgown again, which he had seemed to like very well last night. "I like it here, Michael," she said as his arms closed about her.

"Do you, indeed," he murmured, his gaze slipping first to her mouth, and then lower. She had the distinct impression he was no longer thinking of the house.

"Yes." She reached up to kiss him on his neck, and felt him stiffen in surprise. "I could stay here forever."

"Ah. At Chimneys?"

She leaned back from his embrace. His eyes drifted lower again. "Why, wherever else would I mean?"

"Perhaps here?" he said, and abruptly brought her back against him.

This time she gasped. "Ye-es. Here, too."

"Ah, good." He bent to kiss her, and then straightened. "Come with me."

"Yes," she said again, and let him lead her away from the dressing table.

And that night, Chloe squealed.

"Is it always so clear here?" Chloe asked. She and Michael were standing at the top of the rise near where their drive met the road, he with his arms wrapped around her waist, she standing with her back to his chest. It was a vastly improper posture for a viscount and his viscountess, but they were more than that. The devil of it was, though, that Michael had no idea what.

"No, of course not." He rested his chin on the top of her head. "Not this close to the sea."

She sighed. "Fog, I suppose. The view was so beautiful yesterday," she said, almost dreamily. "I'd like to paint it."

"Mm? With the color as it was, and the sun on the water? How would you be certain of it looking the same?"

"Oh, I wouldn't." She turned her head to look up at him. "I was thinking of something more dramatic. A storm." She frowned. "You are sure those small boats we saw yesterday weren't smugglers?"

"Not by day. Though family legend has it that the cellars here were once used by them."

"Surely not!" She paused. "Now, as well?"

"No." His mouth straightened into a grim line. "Not when too many good men are fighting and dying on the Peninsula. Boney will have no gold because of me." He paused. "It does explain the excellent quality of our brandy."

"I wouldn't know." She frowned, an expression he now

found so delightful that he wanted to kiss her. Each of her expressions made him want to kiss her. What the devil was wrong with him? "I'd like to go back there, to sketch it," she said wistfully.

He rested his chin on her head again. What had her life been like that she sounded as if such a simple request would be refused? "Of course. We'll ride there."

"Ride?" She turned her head sharply toward him. "Michael, you know I can't ride."

"I know," he said calmly. "However, I had Firefly brought here for your use."

"You didn't!"

"I always meant for her to be your mount."

"And just how am I to learn?"

"I'll teach you. Far better for you to learn here than in town."

"Michael." Something in her voice made him look down, to see that she had closed her eyes. "Don't you know by now how terrible I am at such things?"

"You did grow up in the country, did you not?"

"Yes, and there I learned . . ."

"What?" he said, when she didn't go on.

"Nothing. It hardly signifies."

"Then 'tis the only type of horseback riding you can't do?"

Her head whipped around. "Michael! Such a thing to say."

He grinned down at her. Her face was very red. "I know. I don't find horses as interesting just now, though," he said, gazing with frank approval at her bosom.

"No?" She looked up at him, and then, following the line of his vision, ducked her head. He suspected, though, that this time the color in her cheeks came as much from pleasure as from embarrassment.

"I haven't heard any complaints from you."

"I've none to make," she said, and abruptly pulled away. His arms felt surprisingly empty without her in them. "Will you be busy with Mr. Pennyworth again?"

"Yes, I fear so." He tucked her hand into the crook of his arm. "There's so much I want to do here, Chloe. I've a lot of work ahead of me. Just as you do down there."

They turned to look down at the house with its many chimneys, which had given the estate its name. "So I do," she said, sighing. "I gather you won't be thinking about establishing the stud yet."

"No, not yet. Pennyworth has some sound ideas on estate management. He simply needed permission."

"But you weren't here to implement them."

"I didn't pay much attention to the reports." He tightened his hold on her. "The land must be brought into good heart, and the tenants' houses need work." He frowned. "I'm not at all pleased with the rents they've had to pay."

Chloe glanced at him. "I know nothing about that, but they seemed rather high to me."

His lips tightened. It was not always comfortable having a wife who could read account books. "Too high, I think, for what they receive in return." He paused. "They're angry at me."

"But, Michael, you had nothing to do with it."

"This is traditionally the heir's estate," he reminded her. "They've no idea why I've not seen to their welfare."

"You hadn't the money."

His laugh was bitter. "Chloe, what we in the *ton* consider to be poor means untold riches to them."

"We must do something for them."

"We?"

"Yes." Chloe returned his gaze steadily. This was her task as much as his. "We. Surely I could bring them food and medicines. I've the money."

"Ah, the money." So he was right. This was where the discussion had been heading. "I wondered when we would come to that."

" 'Twould be foolish not to use it." She fell into step beside him, though this time he didn't take her hand. "I'm viscountess now." She shivered, though she smiled.

"What is it?"

"It sounds so strange. Viscountess."

"Lady Lyndon." He smiled at her. "I like it."

She returned the smile. "So do I. So." Her tone became brisk. "When do I meet the tenants?"

Inwardly he sighed for another lost moment of closeness. "I'd rather you didn't. You wouldn't like what you see."

"I'm not particularly missish, Michael."

"I realize that." He patted her hand. "But this would be too much."

"You forget I lived on an estate. I dealt with the tenants there."

He stared at her and then turned away, rubbing at his forehead. She longed to reach up and soothe away the headache she was certain was gathering there. She didn't, though. She didn't yet know how he would take such a wifely gesture. "You're a stubborn wench."

She gave a surprised laugh. "Michael!"

He grinned back at her. "You are, my dear."

She went still. Was she his dear? "Stubborn or no, I want to help. And pray don't tell me I shouldn't," she challenged, as he opened his mouth to protest. "I am your wife, am I not? That means, I believe, being your partner."

"I don't think you quite realize what you've taken on. We're likely to have visitors very soon."

"Visitors?"

"Yes. Do you not think that people about here are curious about us? Depend upon it, someone will call within the next day or two."

"So soon?" she said in dismay.

"Yes."

"Then I'd best see to the house."

"I wish you would. It needs your touch."

Briefly she smiled down at the house, already feeling so much more her home than the Russell house in London ever had, no matter its shabbiness. "I'm not a dab hand at such things, but I daresay I could learn." She turned to him. "And I'd like to help with the tenants, too. Please."

He looked at her dubiously. "I don't know, Chloe. With

conditions as they are, there's likely illness there. I'd not
see you sick."

A warm glow spread through her. She could not remember anyone being so protective of her in a very long time.
"I have the constitution of a horse," she declared, and then
bit her tongue.

His eyes twinkled at her. "But not the constitution to
ride one?"

"No, well . . ."

He grinned, and suddenly hugged her to him. "Never
mind, Chloe. I would like it above all things if you would
ride with me, but only when you're ready."

Ready? "Maybe someday, Michael."

He smiled down at her, and took her hand. "Someday,"
he agreed. "Come. It must be nearly time for nuncheon."

"Likely so," she agreed, and, sighing within, walked back
to the house with him, wondering if she would ever be the
wife he wanted. Wondering if he would love her if she were.

It took only a few days for Chloe to find life at Chimneys
far more fulfilling, and far busier, than life in London ever
had been. There was simply too much for her to do here
for her to live in seclusion in a library or studio. She still
pored over her own account books at night, as well as those
pertaining to the household; she still planned her investments and wrote to her man of affairs; she still planned her
paintings. Yet she enjoyed her work at Chimneys so much
more.

While Michael labored with Pennyworth both to restore
the land and to provide better lives for the tenants, Chloe
had gathered together an army of maids and kitchen help.
She concentrated on the most promising of the tenant girls,
who were thrilled at the prospect of working at the big
house and earning a living. At the same time, she scoured
the neighboring towns for more experienced help, so that
Chimneys at last had a decent cook, who produced the plain
fare both she and Michael preferred. The new maids labored

alongside Chloe to restore each room to its former glory, something that wasn't yet possible without the purchase of new carpeting and drapes, or the furniture being reupholstered.

Until then, however, carpets were taken out and beaten until not a speck of dust remained in them, curtains and drapes were brought down, shaken, and, in some cases laundered, and sheets were inventoried, a tedious but necessary job that fell to Chloe's lot. Some of the less acceptable pieces she relegated to the attic so that the good ones showed to greater advantage.

She needed, as well, to consider restoring the gardens, both kitchen and decorative, and to see to various repairs, inside and out. At night, she fell into bed exhausted, but she wouldn't have traded a moment of it, especially since Michael was beside her. He, and Chimneys, were hers.

She was in the drawing room two days later, standing on a ladder to help a maid take down the truly dreadful draperies in there, when Caswell came in. "There is a visitor for you, my lady," he said, proffering her a silver salver bearing a card.

Chloe turned, startled. "What? A visitor for me? Are you sure, Caswell?"

"Quite certain, ma'am. A Mrs. Darnley."

"Oh, she's a lovely person," the maid said. The staff already knew they didn't have to stand on ceremony with their new mistress, unless there was company.

"And I'm all over dust," Chloe said. "Oh, dear, did you put her in the salon, Caswell?"

Caswell coughed. "Yes, my lady, but—"

"Afternoon, afternoon," a booming female voice said, and in walked the largest woman Chloe had ever seen. She was as wide as she was tall, making her resemble nothing so much as a child's ball. "I'm intruding, am I? Sorry, sorry. Should have known better, but I'm nosy, don't you know. Just wanted to meet you and welcome you to the neighborhood, Lady Lyndon."

"Oh, dear, and I'm all over dust," Chloe said, smiling

as she crossed the room to the woman. Unorthodox she might be, but there was something immensely likable about her: her broad smile, perhaps, or her eyes, which were unexpectedly kind. "Though I've looked worse than this."

"Haven't we all. Hm. Looks like you're finally doing something about this old pile."

"Yes, it is in terrible shape," Chloe said ruefully, looking about the room. "I fear I've a lot of work ahead."

"Wallpaper." Mrs. Darnley nodded wisely. "Nasty job, that. All over plaster dust."

"I can't say I've ever done that, myself. Although I might." Chloe looked back at the walls. " 'Tis my house," she said softly.

"And about time there were people here again. Any other visitors yet?"

"No, you are the first. Oh, but where are my manners?" Chloe crossed the room. "Do please sit down. Caswell, will you please bring tea?"

"It is on the way, ma'am."

"Cream cakes?" Mrs. Darnley said, a gleam in her eyes. Caswell bowed. "And macaroons, too."

"Oh, splendid. I imagine you've never seen anyone as fat as me," she went on, as Caswell left the room. "Don't mince words. Fat is what I am. You can't imagine what a tremendous relief it is."

"Is it?" Chloe said. Her head was spinning from the events of the last few moments, from Mrs. Darnley's unexpected entrance to Caswell's uncanny knowledge about the tea tray.

"Yes, yes. I eat whatever I please, don't you see. Of course, when Mr. Darnley was alive, I did my best to reduce. Not that it ever worked. Bless him, he always said it didn't matter. Blast the man for dying."

"Is it a recent bereavement, ma'am? Thank you, Caswell."

"Lovely. Ladies in waiting, too, I see," Mrs. Darnley said, beaming as she looked at the tea tray. "No, nigh on ten years, and I still miss him, the old fool. Now, I don't believe there's anyone else in the neighborhood I could say that to. Mrs. Harlow, that's the vicar's wife, and a sour old thing she is, would be shocked."

Chloe poured out the tea and handed Mrs. Darnley a cup. "But I understand what you mean, ma'am. I think I'd feel the same . . ."

Mrs. Darnley's eyes were unexpectedly shrewd. "Not one of those arranged marriages, then?"

She paused. "In a manner of speaking, but Lyndon and I would not have married had we not wished to."

"That's the best way. You must think me terribly prying. Mr. Darnley did. He'd say, 'Emmie, now just you keep your nose out from where it doesn't belong.' He was right, but how do you get to know people if you don't ask?"

"Indeed," Chloe murmured, feeling a great gust of amusement welling up inside her.

"Now, everyone talks and everyone wants to know about everyone else. I'm just more open about it. Think I don't know about what people say about me? Fat and nosy." She looked critically at Chloe. "Now you, dearie, you have a lovely figure."

Chloe flushed and ducked her head. Just so had Michael said last night, and again this morning . . . "Thank you, ma'am."

"Newlyweds," Mrs. Darnley said knowingly, and Chloe's flush deepened. "Don't understand why you hide in that frock."

"This? 'Tis one of my oldest, ma'am. I knew I would be doing heavy work today. I do apologize for my appearance."

"No, no, my fault. Mr. Darnley always said I went where I had no right. True enough, too. Poor man, he put up with a lot from me."

"But is that not the way of most marriages, ma'am?" Chloe said, handing the tray of cakes to her guest again. Already most of them were gone.

"Lovely," Mrs. Darnley said again, wiping her fingers on a napkin before taking another cake. "So you know that already, do you? Just you remember it. Takes two to make a marriage, two to break it."

"Did you break something again, Chloe?" Michael said, coming into the room, and then stopped, blinking.

Nine

Chloe felt another gust of laughter inside. She could just imagine how they must look to him, she in her old dusty dress, and a beaming Mrs. Darnley.

She smiled. "Lyndon." He, too, was dressed roughly. At Chimneys he favored loose linen shirts, leather breeches, and a worn tweed coat. For all his protestations that he was no farmer, he looked like one, except for his athletic, aristocratic bearing. "I must introduce you to one of our neighbors. Lord Lyndon, this is Mrs. Darnley."

"Ma'am," he said, bowing.

"My lord. Can't say as I've ever had anyone bow to me before. Nice manners, my lord."

Michael looked at Chloe in blank incomprehension, as well he might. "Thank you," he said, and sank into an armchair. "Is there tea left?"

Chloe's head was bent as she reached over to lay a hand on the teapot. If she looked at him another moment, she suspected her laughter would burst out of control. "I fear 'tis gone cold. I'll just ring for Caswell—"

"I saw him just now in the hall."

"Here, ma'am." Caswell came in bearing another tray, on which rested several substantial sandwiches, as well as more cakes. Mrs. Darnley looked at those avariciously.

"Thank you, Caswell. How does he do that?" she asked Michael.

"Dashed if I know. I appreciate it, though."

"Don't stand on ceremony, my lord. Eat," Mrs. Darnley urged. "And while you're about it, would you hand me the cakes, please? Are you Church of England?"

Michael blinked and looked at Chloe, who turned away, biting her lips. "Yes, Mrs. Darnley, we are."

"Thought so. Of course Mrs. Harlow—that's the vicar's wife, she'll be calling any day—will ask. Now if you'd said you were Methodist, that would be another matter."

That did it. Chloe put her hand over her eyes, lowered her head, and began to shake. "Chloe?" Michael asked, his voice filled with concern. "Is aught wrong?"

"No, no." She raised a face streaming with tears of laughter to him. "No, 'tis just—"

"I tend to have that effect on people," Mrs. Darnley said to a clearly bewildered Michael. "A good cook, ma'am," she added to Chloe.

"Chloe," Michael began, as she continued laughing.

"I'm—I'm sorry," she gasped. "I'm trying to stop, but—"

"Like laughing in church," Mrs. Darnley agreed. "You know you shouldn't, but you can't stop."

"Yes." Chloe wiped her streaming eyes. "Oh, but I am sorry, ma'am. You've been so very kind."

"Nonsense, nonsense. Wanted to welcome you to the neighborhood." Her eyes gleamed again. "Wanted to be the first. But don't worry," she added quickly. "I'm not one to gossip. Mr. Darnley was proud of that. Well." She rose. "I'll just take myself off. I can see you want to be alone."

"No, don't be silly—"

"Pish tosh. You'll be seeing me soon enough. I turn up everywhere. My lord," she said, as Michael bowed again. "And my lady."

"Caswell will see you out—oh, there you are, Caswell."

"If you'll follow me, ma'am."

"Thank you kindly for the tea. A good cook, ma'am," Mrs. Darnley added, and then was gone.

Michael stared after her, and then sat again. "What in the world was that?"

"One of our neighbors. Oh, I do hope the rest of them aren't like her. I think I'd die of laughter."

Caswell walked back into the room at that moment. "There is nothing else you wish, is there, my lord?"

Michael, still bemused, shook his head. "No, Caswell."

Caswell bowed. "Very good, my lord."

"Caswell," Chloe called.

The butler returned. "Yes, my lady?"

"How is it you know what we want before we do?"

"I listen," he said simply, and, bowing, left the room.

Chloe stared after him. "I feel as if I've landed in Bedlam. A very pleasant Bedlam, but a madhouse, all the same."

Michael sank lower in his chair. "When I warned you we'd have visitors, I never imagined—that."

"Who could imagine her? Oh, dear."

"What?"

"Now we have Mrs. Harlow to meet."

"Heaven help us," Michael groaned, and reached over for the remaining cream cake.

The Reverend and Mrs. Harlow arrived the following day. Mrs. Harlow was indeed dour of face; the vicar, genial and gentle, had a long-suffering look. Forewarned by Mrs. Darnley's visit, Chloe was not only dressed more carefully, but was prepared for the question about her religion. The answer seemed to disappoint Mrs. Harlow, who clearly had wound herself up for a lecture. Though why a peer's son would be anything other than Church of England was mystifying, Chloe thought. If the rest of the neighbors were as eccentric as their first visitors, she hardly knew how she would survive.

Fortunately the squire, Sir Horace Mayfield, until their arrival the most senior of the neighborhood's gentry, was blessedly as they had expected him to be. He was interested in farming, horses, and his dogs, not necessarily in that order. He also served as one of the local magistrates, and was eager to abdicate that position to Viscount Lyndon. Michael politely declined, with the excuse that he would be in London much of the year, much to the squire's disappointment.

While he was dealing with the squire, Chloe was having a difficult time of it with Mrs. Mayfield. In the ordinary way of things she was likely a pleasant person, but she had four daughters of marriageable age, and was disgruntled that Michael had married elsewhere. "We will bring them for a visit one day, if we may," she said, accepting another cup of tea from Chloe. "They are quite accomplished. We made certain they have had the best of everything. Of course they had a governess from London, as well as a dancing master. They do exquisite watercolors, and we have found them to be much in demand to play the pianoforte or to sing."

"I am sure they are as skilled as a young lady should be," Chloe said politely, feeling, for the first time since her marriage, inadequate. She glanced over at Michael, but he was absorbed in a discussion of horses and their bloodlines with the squire. That conversation could go on all afternoon.

"Will you, Lady Lyndon?" Mrs. Mayfield was saying, and Chloe came out of her trance.

"I do beg your pardon." She took a sip of her tea. "I fear I didn't hear you."

"The monthly assemblies in Dover. You will be attending, of course."

Assemblies? As in dancing and socializing? Panic washed over her, yet what could she say? She and Michael now comprised the leading family in the neighborhood. "Of course," she answered, throwing another longing look at Michael. Thickheaded male. Why did he not know when she needed him?

"An assembly, Michael," she repeated, when Sir Horace and his wife had left. "And we have to go."

"Of course we do," Michael said absently. "Sir Horace seems not to have much imagination, but he does have some sound ideas on horses—"

"Oh, hang the bloody horses!" Chloe exclaimed, causing

him to blink at her. "An assembly, Michael! You know how I do at entertainments of that sort."

"I thought you'd got over that."

"Well, I haven't," she said crossly.

"It's time you did. When is the next one?"

"In two weeks. Oh, Michael—"

"You'll do fine. You'll be the only one there wearing a London gown."

"I doubt that," she said gloomily, imitating his slouched posture in her chair. "Sir Horace has four daughters. Mrs. Mayfield has high hopes for each of them, including you."

"The devil she has! But I'm already married."

"And a good thing for you, else you might have been snared by one of them."

"I managed to escape the snares, as you call them, of the young ladies in London. Except for one."

Chloe looked up. "Who?" she demanded, startled by the flare of jealousy within her.

"You, Chloe."

"Bosh. I didn't use any snares."

"Exactly."

She frowned at him. "I beg your pardon?"

"You didn't try to. A snare in itself, my dear."

"But—"

"You were simply yourself. Very unusual." He bent to kiss her. "I need to go back out. I am meeting Pennyworth at the field where we're growing corn to convince him to let it lie fallow next year."

" 'Tis your land, Michael."

"After all these years, I don't think he believes it." He kissed her cheek again and then was gone, leaving her to ponder all the thoughts whirling through her head. Eccentric, demanding neighbors, an omniscient butler, and, lord help her, monthly assemblies. Who had ever said life in the country was quiet?

And yet, she thought, rising and looking about the shabby drawing room with fondness, when all was said and done, Chimneys was her house. When all was said and done, she was the one with Michael. She wouldn't have it any other way.

The weather had turned misty and cool, with a damp breeze blowing off the Channel. Today the rain streamed down, not in torrents, but steadily, with no sign of abating. Hands tucked into the pockets of his tweed coat, donned more for warmth than for style, Michael gazed out at the fog-shrouded landscape, and then turned away from the leaded window. Channel storms could last for days, he knew from experience.

Now that Chimneys was his, he chafed at anything that kept him within. He never would have expected it, but he liked being here. He liked learning about his estate and the best ways to improve it. He liked meeting with the people who lived on it, and the people in the neighborhood, who, if less polished than those in town, were certainly more individual. Oddly enough, he didn't miss sport as much as he'd expected, except for riding. Some days, he wished he could jump astride Thor and go for a mad gallop across the Downs to the cliffs with Chloe by his side.

At the thought, he turned to look at her, sitting engrossed at the large library table. Her fingers were stained from the pen she held, and her fine hair was coming loose from the knot at the back of her neck, which had been neat not so long ago. Not that she would notice. There seemed not to be a shred of vanity in his Chloe, he thought, fondness welling up within in him. If he found being at Chimneys to be fulfilling, his life with Chloe promised even more, something he could never have imagined only a few short weeks ago. He could wish she were a little less busy, a little less involved in the running of the house or the estate than she was, but then, wasn't that what he'd wanted?

As if she felt his gaze on her, Chloe looked up and smiled. "You're wishing to be outside."

He sprawled into a chair across from her, drumming his fingers on the table. "How well you know me."

Chloe peered down at the papers lying before her, and then moved one aside. "It doesn't take long acquaintance to know that."

"What is that you are writing?"

"Lists of all that needs to be done inside the house. I haven't even begun to plan the gardens." She frowned at the next list. "We may have to send to London for some things. Fabric swatches and wallpaper samples and such."

"I know." He leaned back, his gaze still on her. "We haven't yet had that ride to the sea, Chloe."

"Mm, no."

"I haven't taught you to drive yet, either."

"There's time."

He frowned. "Not as much as I'd like, once the weather clears. 'Twould be better for you to learn how to drive in the country than in town. As you discovered."

She twined a strand of hair about her finger, inadvertently brushing ink across her face. "Mm."

Smiling, he touched her cheek. "You've ink there."

She looked up. "I don't, do I?"

"I fear so."

"You needn't look so amused. It will be ever so difficult to wash off."

"You never seemed to mind before."

She waved that off. "Paint is different."

"Of course. Turpentine is much to be preferred to soap."

"Michael, do go away if you intend only to vex me. I'm far too busy."

"As I once was told, there's time."

"I know, but there's so much I wish to do. 'Tis such a wonderful house."

"You needn't work so hard, you know. We do have servants."

"Oh, but Michael, I've never had a place of my own before. I so wish restore it."

"There's time," he repeated. He stirred restlessly, and then rose. "You haven't seen the rest of the house, have you?"

She looked up. "Mrs. Barrie showed me when first we came here."

"From what you said, though, just the main rooms."

"I suppose. The State rooms, and of course I'm familiar with the rooms we use. The kitchens and still rooms and dairy, as well."

"The bedchambers," he interjected, grinning.

"As you say," she said, appearing not one whit discomposed, except that her color was high.

"But not the nurseries, or the music room, or the ballroom."

She brushed back her hair again. "Oh, drat, why did you not tell me my hair is coming loose?"

He smiled lazily at her. "I rather like it. It suits you, somehow."

She pulled a face. "Well, I don't. Sometimes I despair . . ."

"What?"

" 'Tis nothing."

"Of yourself?" He frowned as he laid his hand on hers, all pretense of detachment gone. "Don't, Chloe. Don't let them do that to you."

She looked up again, her brow puckered. "Who?"

"Anyone who has ever made mock of you."

Again she made a face. "There have been too many."

"There should never have been any."

"But, Michael, I truly am untidy and clumsy and—"

"And unique."

"A fine way of calling me an antidote."

"Chloe!" He forced her chin up with his fingers. "Do you truly believe I'd do such a thing? Or that I'd choose you as my bride?"

She held his gaze. "We both know I wasn't your choice."

"No one forced me to offer for you," he said quietly, and this time she was the first to look away.

"No," she said after a moment. "I suppose not."

He studied her, frowning, and then tugged at her hand,

pulling her to her feet. "Come. I believe we both need to escape our megrims."

"Where are we going?" she asked as she followed him into the oak-paneled hall.

"To tour the rest of the house. I'm curious to see it myself. It was once the family seat, you know," he said, as they climbed first the principal staircase and then narrower ones, until they reached the attics. "Charles II gave the land to one of my ancestors and created him viscount for standing with him during the Civil War. The earldom with the rest of the properties came during the Rebellion."

He told her more history of the family as they explored the house. Chloe had already seen the State Rooms on the first floor: the Gold Drawing Room; the bedroom where, family legend had it, Charles II had once slept; and the gallery, with its paintings of the family going back several hundred years. The only portrait that interested her was a Gainsborough of Michael and his family, with the earl looking very much as Michael did now. There, he told her, he and his cousins had played at being knights and had staged wonderful tournaments, using sticks for lances and swords.

In the attics, they had donned old, perhaps priceless, clothes for their playacting, while on the nursery floor they had slept, ate, and learned their various lessons. It was at the rooms on this floor that Chloe looked most wistfully. Though she had been married only a few weeks, she had already had evidence she was not carrying Michael's child, filling her with fierce pain and longing. Someday, though, she thought as she looked at the night nursery with its cot, its bulky shape now shrouded with a holland cover, and at the day nursery with its scarred desk, her children would live in these rooms. The thought made her stomach feel hollow.

"There is a room along there," Michael said, pointing down the hall as they left the day nursery, "for a governess, when our daughters are old enough."

"We'll teach them not to torment the poor woman," she said.

He grinned at her. "Did you torment yours?"

"Mercilessly. At least, Helena did."

"Why not you?"

"I always behaved myself. Almost always," she amended. "Ever practical, after all."

The look he sent her as they paced along the corridor back to the stairs was quizzical. "Why?"

She ducked her head. "It seemed to be what was expected of me." She hadn't been pretty, like Helena, or a boy, like Stephen or Edwin. She had no grace, no talent that anyone could discern, no social skills. At least, so everyone had said. She had learned quickly how to behave. "I think my mother would have been attentive, had she lived," she went on, as they turned down the corridor toward the stairs. "My father, though, didn't seem to know I was there."

"Life's not easy for a child even when one's parents are alive," he said quietly.

"Your mother is a lovely woman."

"So she is. But my father's not changed much. He ever did prefer to stay in town." He paused at the bottom of the stairs. "You've seen this floor, of course."

She barely glanced down either of the hallways leading off the top of the main staircase, not the one where their suite of rooms was located, or the one leading to the guest chambers. "Yes. I plan to have some of the rooms aired and cleaned, should we have guests."

"Which we very well might, should we not return to town."

They were walking downstairs again. "Why wouldn't we? Though I believe we're both happy enough here."

He nodded. "I believe we are. All that remains now are the music room and the ballroom," he added. "Unless you'd prefer to leave those until another day."

"No, I might as well see them all now." Unexpectedly she had a vision of herself and Michael standing at the top of the stairs greeting guests for a ball. He would look splendid, as usual. She wouldn't, but she wouldn't be untidy, either. "Michael, we should have a ball," she blurted out.

He looked at her oddly. "A ball? Chloe, I don't think the ballroom's been touched for years."

" 'Twas just a thought."

"Or an excuse to return to London to see a modiste?" he teased.

"No, you know I do not care for fripperies."

"I wish you did," he said, suddenly serious, as he reached past her to open a door. "You have a lovely figure, Chloe. You shouldn't hide it."

Color burned in her cheeks. Lovely? When they were alone together, Michael sometimes said some unexpectedly appreciative things. In this setting, the compliment seemed more real, and it both embarrassed and thrilled her. Maybe, she thought suddenly, she would send to her mother-in-law to buy her more gowns. Gowns, she thought with another thrill, with more daring necklines. Maybe it was time to stop thinking of herself as plain and graceless. "Yes, well, we'll see," she said vaguely. "What is this room—oh."

"The music room," he said. "This part of the house was added years after the rest."

"Oh, but it's beautiful." She wandered in, gazing up at a ceiling that, unexpectedly, was carved and gilded and painted in glorious designs. Underneath her feet was a parquet floor in need of refinishing, but still beautiful. The furniture consisted of a harp, a pianoforte, a harpsichord, a spinet, and several chairs. "The sound is superb. We could have a wonderful musical evening here."

He was staring at her. "I had the distinct impression you didn't like to entertain."

"I didn't think so, either, but I never had my own house before. Or a room like this. Oh, Michael, that ceiling."

He looked up. "Angelica Kauffman's work. Of course, none of the instruments have been played in years. The pianoforte should be tuned, at least."

"Of course, though I don't play."

"Were you not taught?"

"Yes, but I'm only indifferent at it. I fear I'm sadly lacking in feminine accomplishments."

"Yet you paint."

"Not in watercolors or on china. Those are acceptable pursuits for a lady, are they not?" She wrinkled her nose. "Not oils, I am told, especially when one goes about with paint smudging one's face."

He grinned. "I rather like those smudges. The ballroom is through here." He placed his hand under her elbow, leading her across the room to a set of double doors. In spite of herself, Chloe shivered at his touch. She was so very sensitive to him. Why did he not feel it, too?

"If we entertain many guests, these doors can be opened to make one large room."

Chloe followed him into the gloomy room, hearing her footsteps echoing on the wood floor. It wasn't nearly so impressive as the music room, she was thinking, when Michael pulled back the draperies from one of the long windows that marched along the walls to either side. The outside light, dim though it might be, made her blink, even as it illuminated everything within—the ceilings that were carved and gilded and painted as in the music room, the parquet floor, the ivory and gilt walls. "Oh!" she exclaimed involuntarily. "Oh, Michael, 'tis magnificent."

He grinned as he returned to her. "It is, isn't it? There used to be some grand balls here. I was sometimes allowed to watch from the gallery up there."

She glanced up to where a minstrel's gallery jutted out from one wall. "Is that where the orchestra would be?"

"Sometimes, or on a dais in here."

Chloe followed the careless flick of his hand, and then gasped again. They weren't alone—but no. What she had taken to be other people were actually their own reflections in one of the long gilt-framed mirrors hanging on the opposite wall.

"Oh," she said again, and glanced up at the crystal chandelier high above, only the tip of which showed in the mirrors. It was an enormous globe, tapering down to one large oval luster, and it was badly in need of polishing. So was the floor. "The draperies are old," she said, as if to herself. "They'll have to go. Do all the windows reach to the floor?"

"Yes. Those, there, lead out to a terrace overlooking the drive. The morning room is just below it. The others"—he pointed toward the other side—"look over the garden."

"It would be lovely to have a ball here," she said again. "When all the work is done."

"Of course," he said, entering into the spirit of things. "When we have a house party, and with all our neighbors present. You and I will, of course, lead out the first dance. Should it be a waltz, do you think?"

"A—a waltz?"

"Yes. I know 'tis not done in London, but I hear it's all the crack in Vienna."

"Michael!" She eluded him when he would have caught her about the waist. "Surely people don't dance like that."

"I see nothing wrong in allowing it at a house party."

"Oh." The elation that had begun to drain from her at the mention of dancing was now completely gone. A house party would, of necessity, be made up of people of the *ton,* those who knew her from her come-out and likely remembered only her disastrous missteps. "I hadn't really thought that far ahead."

"Why not? I was thinking we could ask Sherbourne and his wife, among others. I've friends you've yet to meet."

"Who will know me as Miss Bumblebroth."

"No, as my bride." His voice was cool. "No one would be unkind to you, Chloe. I'd see to that."

Perhaps, but she knew what they would be thinking. "Michael, you know I don't know how to dance."

"Chloe, why do you always so belittle yourself?"

" 'Tis true. You saw that at our engagement ball. I trip all over my feet, and the harder I try, the worse it gets."

He studied her, a frown on his face. "Then there's only one thing we can do," he said finally.

"We'll forget we ever discussed holding a ball?"

"No. I'll teach you to dance, of course."

Ten

Chloe stared at his outstretched hand in horror. Mercy, he really meant it. "Michael, I can't—"

"Of course you can." He caught at her hand, his grin too firm for her to escape. "Nothing could be easier."

"For you, perhaps."

"We won't start with the waltz," he went on. "That can be difficult to learn. A country dance, then."

"And a country dance *isn't* difficult? Michael—"

"Relax, Chloe. This is the sort of thing one never forgets, like riding a horse."

She looked at him at that. "Very well. But if I tread on your feet, pray don't hold me responsible."

He laughed. "I am held to be rather good at this, Chloe."

"I don't doubt it," she muttered.

"We'll start with just the one figure. I bow, you curtsy."

He executed a flawless bow, and then straightened. Taking a deep breath, biting her lip, Chloe dipped low, her skirts held to either side. To her astonishment, she managed it without falling. A trifle stiff, it was true, a trifle off-balance, but still a credible effort.

"There. Easy enough, is it not?" His eyes laughed at her. "And you were worried."

"Yes, well—"

"Now we come together, like so, our hands high—dash it, Chloe!" This, as she stepped squarely on his foot.

"I told you," she said almost defiantly as she pulled back. "Did I hurt you?"

"Not in these boots, no."

"I'm wearing half boots, Michael,"

"There's no harm done."

"But I'm no lightweight."

"Nonsense. I've carried you, remember?"

Chloe's face flamed at that memory. "Yes, well—"

"We'll try it again. Do relax, Chloe, and follow my lead." They came back together, and this time she succeeded. "There, that's not so hard, is it? Now we release each other."

"Why?"

"Chloe, have you not done this dance before?"

"Not often, no."

"We'll have other partners," he explained patiently. "You'll both take a hop and then a skip. Like so."

She bit her lip as she watched him. If she tried that, she would surely fall. If she didn't try, he would surely insist. "A hop. Like this?" She jumped up on both feet and landed with her hands outstretched, to prevent overbalancing.

He frowned. "No, on one foot, your left. You really do mean you don't know how to do this?"

"I could never learn," she said simply and, concentrating, tried again. Hop, hop, skip—mercy, she had done it! She turned on him a smile of such dazzling joy that he blinked. "I know that was stiff, but I'm sure with practice I'll manage."

He returned her smile. "Don't forget, you'll have a partner to help you. Like so."

His arm slipped about her waist, firm, supportive. She relaxed against him. Hop—a beat behind him, but still successful—hop—*oh, again!*—skip, and as she landed, his foot came down on hers. "Oh, ow!" she exclaimed, pulling back and hopping about the ballroom on her good foot.

"Chloe!" He caught her by the shoulders, steadying her. "Oh, my dear, I am so sorry. Are you hurt?"

"Of course I'm hurt," she grumbled, and then looked up at him. "No, not really. 'Twas my fault."

"I stepped on you," he pointed out.

"But I wasn't in time with you." She leaned back against him. "It was just a surprise." She sighed. "I told you I couldn't do this."

"Ah, Chloe," he said, and, to her utter surprise, turned her in his arms and drew her close. She was shivering, she noted with detachment. "If you would but relax, all would be well."

"I can't. I've tried, I really have."

"Don't try so hard," he murmured, holding her closer.

Chloe nestled her head against his shoulder. They so rarely embraced or kissed during the day. But then, their marriage wasn't a love match. "I don't know what else to do."

He pulled back, his face serious. "Trust me, Chloe."

It seemed to mean so much to him, Chloe thought. It couldn't be easy to be so athletic and to be married to someone who wasn't. Yet he treated her so well, better than anyone else ever had. For that alone, she was grateful to him, wanted to do as he asked, if only she could.

Held safe against him, she felt a great upswelling of love for him. If he didn't love her, he surely cared about her, didn't he? "I do trust you, Michael," Chloe said softly. "In everything."

He looked startled at that, and then smiled. "I don't think I could ask for anything more," he said, and bent his head to kiss her.

Little by little, Michael's efforts to improve the estate were beginning to show results. Small ones, to be sure, but significant ones. New drains for all of the tenants had been dug, some new houses were being built, and the rents had been reduced. That was one problem well in train. Another was his decision to leave a field which had not been yielding well to lie fallow. Pennyworth had other suggestions, but he agreed with Michael that not everything could be done at once. The orchards needed new trees, and there was livestock to be considered. Michael had never before known farming was so complicated or so absorbing. Chimneys was his. The advances that had already been made satisfied him to the soul.

Chloe appeared to be thriving, too, he thought as he went in after a morning spent surveying his land. The house already was far more presentable. Its floors shone, the carpets were clean, rooms that had been gloomy no longer were. She had even had the chandelier in the ballroom cleaned, though he wasn't sure why. The house was not yet in shape for entertaining.

He found her in the library, which she had appropriated as her office, frowning down at some papers. As usual, her hair was coming loose. Michael regarded her with amusement and unexpected desire. He longed to bury his face in that silky hair, to press kisses on the nape of her neck, to turn her in his arms and kiss her and caress her until they both were mindless. Lord, but she stirred him in a way no other woman ever had, something that sometimes puzzled him. He had not married for love; he didn't expect to find it with her. She was no conventional beauty, though that had ceased to matter. He didn't see just her surface anymore, but the innate woman, who had been hurt by life and yet managed to live it on her own terms.

She looked up at his entrance and smiled. "I didn't expect to see you so soon. I thought your business with Pennyworth would last longer."

He bent to kiss her cheek and then sprawled into a chair. "Not an aptly named man. He has more plans than I do."

She smiled. "So he does."

"What do you smile at?" he asked suspiciously.

"You. Your friends in town would hardly recognize you. You were so hey-go-mad for sport, and now you're a farmer."

"Not racing my curricle across plowed fields."

She laughed at that memory. "No, not at all."

He leaned forward. "What is that you're studying?"

"This? Oh, a letter from my man of affairs, with some

investments for me to consider. I'm not sure I agree with him. He's a dear, but too conservative sometimes."

"Has it occurred to you, Chloe, that sometimes it feels as if all we do is work?"

She laid down her pen. "Yes, now that you say it. And here we are, the idle rich."

He decided not to take offense at the mention of money. "I do miss sports," he confided. "As you must miss painting."

"Mm. I think we should indulge ourselves once in a while."

"So do I. Chloe."

She looked up from her papers, which had already caught her attention again. "Mm?"

"I've an idea. Let me try to teach you to ride."

"No."

"No?" he said, annoyed. "Just like that?"

"Just like that."

"I thought you'd got over your fear of horses."

She laid down the pen again and looked at him seriously. "Not enough, Michael. Please, could we let this rest?"

He stirred in his chair. "I'd like to be riding about the estate and the neighborhood with you."

"I know."

"Let me teach you."

"Why can't you accept me as I am? You're forever pinching at me to do things I can't. Dancing, riding, driving. And that damned assembly is in four days. Don't laugh at me."

"Not at you. Your language, my dear."

"It seems appropriate."

"I think you underestimate yourself."

"Michael, do go away."

He was silent for so long that at last Chloe looked at him. He was gazing at her, his face serious. "What?" she asked, still annoyed.

"Who did this to you?"

"Whatever in the world are you talking about?"

"Who made you so unsure of yourself?"

"I'm not," she protested.

"You manage well at many things, Chloe, but not at anything physical."

"You knew when you married me that I'm clumsy."

"This goes beyond that, Chloe."

"Go away," she said again.

"Someone hurt you."

She looked swiftly up at him. "Don't be silly."

"Do you know, I just thought of something."

"What?"

"Have you noticed you're not clumsy with me?"

"Not clumsy! Michael, I bump into things. I fall all over my feet. I drop things. All the time."

"Not here."

She gave him a startled look, and then considered his words. "No, not as often," she conceded. "I wonder why?"

"I'm not sure."

This time she pushed the papers away. "I think I know."

"What?"

"I'm at ease with you."

"Are you?"

"Yes. I think 'tis because you don't take my clumsiness seriously. Teasing me about my train on our wedding day."

"It was worth it, to see you blush."

She threw a wadded-up paper at him. "You're horrid."

"Yes, I know." He grinned at her. "But you know, I think you're right, Chloe. It doesn't bother me."

"Why is it so important to everyone else, then? I hate being known as Miss Bumblebroth."

"If I ever find out who first called you it, I will call him out and run him through," he said conversationally.

She laughed, making him blink in surprise. "Michael, you're quite bloodthirsty, aren't you?"

He didn't smile. "Where you're concerned, yes."

"Oh," she said, and, rising, went to sit on the arm of his chair. "You're sweet."

"Sweet!"

"Yes." She bent to kiss his forehead. "Sweet."

"I'll give you sweet," he growled, and hauled her down onto his lap.

The syllabub, the fruits, and the nuts had been removed from the table in the breakfast room, where Chloe and Michael took most of their meals. Nuncheon was over. They had chatted lightly about their morning, content simply to be together. Michael looked so much different now than he had in town, she thought affectionately as she watched him cracking open a walnut between his lean, brown fingers. Fingers that touched her with such gentleness and tenderness . . .

She shivered, and determinedly turned her mind to other subjects. He was leaning back in his chair, rather than sitting completely straight, and his gaze was open, not opaque, as it had often been in town. He looked younger, more at ease, certainly more in command than he had. And far more attractive. No matter what his motive had been in marrying her, he treated her well. She was very lucky.

As if feeling her gaze on him, he looked up. "What are you doing this afternoon?"

She made a face. "Inventorying the linen."

"On a fine day like today? 'Tis a shame to waste it, tucked away in a closet."

She sighed. "I wish I could leave it until a rainy day, but it really must be done. Some night you'll likely put your foot through one of the sheets, so old are they."

He chuckled. "And how will that happen, unless I am extraordinarily active in my sleep, or—"

"Michael!" she exclaimed, her face going red, and tilted her head to the side. He glanced over at the footman who stood against the wall, and his smile widened. Chloe didn't dare look at the man at all, though from the corner of her eye she could see that his lips twitched. "What are you going to do? Ride about the estate?"

"I'd thought perhaps we could drive to the sea. You've mentioned sketching it a few times."

"So I have." She gazed into space, thinking about the morning's discussion. He was right. She had been hurt. Still, it was time she put the past behind her. "Michael."

He looked up from cracking another walnut. "Mm?"

"Why do you not give me a driving lesson?"

He raised his eyebrow. "Excuse me? Did you not say you didn't wish me to—ah, let me see if I can find the right words—pinch at you about such things?"

"I know, but I did know how to handle a gig at one time. I could probably learn again. Especially if I ever again have to drive a phaeton in town."

He snorted, absently flipping the walnut into the air and catching it, again and again. If she were to try that, she thought enviously, she would drop it every time. "That's a crackbrained notion if ever I've heard one, Chloe."

"So it is. I'm serious, Michael. I want to try again."

At that, he looked at her. "You do?"

"Yes."

He shrugged as they rose. "All right. But please don't land us in a ditch somewhere."

She made a face at him behind his back, and the footman, who'd remained so admirably straight of face, grinned. "He has no faith in me," she complained to the footman.

Michael turned. "I don't believe I trust you, Chloe."

She gave him a serene, innocent smile. "And then I promise you'll have your ride to the sea."

"Huh," he said, but he went to call for the gig.

A little while later, Chloe was less sure of herself. The gig, a light vehicle with a narrow back and small handrails on either side, stood before her, with a small, dappled gray horse harnessed to it. Michael had told her that Peter, the horse, was a quiet, placid beast, no longer young. It was true that Peter did stand still, she thought, even when she climbed into the gig, shifting its weight.

Michael handed her the reins. "You don't expect me to start off immediately, do you?" she said, clutching the leather so spasmodically that Peter turned to look at her reproachfully. The movement so startled her that she dropped the reins. In response Peter stepped forward a few paces, making her clutch at the side of the gig.

Michael uttered an oath and swept up the reins in one fluid, competent movement. "You haven't changed your mind already, Chloe, have you?"

"No."

"Then do be careful. If you do such a thing, Peter will believe he's in charge."

"You told me he was placid."

"So he is, but even the dullest horse will take advantage of you should you let him. Here, try again."

"I cannot do this," she said, and to her surprise her voice was thin with anxiety.

"Easy, Chloe." His smile was reassuring. "I hardly expect you to qualify for the Four in Hand Club."

She shuddered. "Heaven help me. Those Belcher kerchiefs you wear are quite off-putting."

He grinned. "Let's see what you remember about the reins. Hold them in your—"

"Yes, I know, in my left hand, with the riding crop in my right, and I use my right hand only for turning."

He was staring at her. "Very good. I didn't think you knew that much."

"Why not?"

"When you were in Hempstead's phaeton, you used both hands."

"I was holding on for dear life. Pull on the right side for a right turn, on the left for a left."

"Yes. Don't saw at his mouth," he added hastily, as Chloe, her brow furrowed in concentration, pulled back hard on the right rein. "Ease up."

She relaxed her grip. "Sorry. I forgot. I think I'm more nervous than I realized."

"It's as well that Peter's mouth isn't particularly tender."

"I'll be careful," she said, and dropped the reins. "Oh, drat!" This time she was the one to catch them up, instinctively pulling back and bringing the gig to a stop. "I didn't mean to drop them!"

He nodded, and she could swear it was approvingly. "Perhaps, but you knew how to stop."

"I gave him the signal to start, didn't I?"

"Or to go faster."

"Well, I don't want that! Oh, dear. This is difficult."

"You're doing well. You know how to stop, how to turn, and how to go faster."

She smiled at him, and he blinked. "I do, don't I?"

"Yes."

"Oh, good," she said in delight. "Then should I start?"

"Mayhap we should leave that for another day."

"Michael, I do have an idea of what I'm doing."

"I don't know, Chloe."

"And you'll be with me to help, should anything go wrong."

"You sound a little too confident." He pursed his lips as he studied her. "No, it won't do."

"But you said yourself I'm doing well."

"So I did." He looked at her dubiously. "I'm not sure."

"So now you think I shouldn't learn?"

"Huh. Very well, then. Slap the reins on his back."

"I remember," she said, and did so. The gig surged forward, jolting them both back.

"Lightly, Chloe! Pull back. No, not right! Back!"

The gig shuddered to a stop. Shaken, Chloe clutched the reins in a death grip, only half noticing that Peter gave her a reproachful look. "Oh, dear."

"Quite," Michael said. She glanced quickly at him, to see that he appeared as shaken as she felt.

"I think I was wrong about learning how to do this."

He arched an eyebrow at her. "Giving up so early?"

"You sound just like Edwin."

He blinked at that. "Hempstead? Is that how he goaded you into driving?"

"No," she said shortly. "I can't do this."

"Yes, you can, Chloe. You can," he added, when she looked doubtfully at him. "You need to keep trying."

"There speaks a man who succeeds at all he does."

"Do you think I did well my first time trying something?" he said, sharply. "No one does."

"I am certain you were more confident."

"That's all you need, Chloe. Confidence."

"I'm scared, Michael," she confessed.

"Easy, Chloe." He laid his hand atop hers, and somehow she felt his strength flowing into her. "Give me the reins. Mayhap you'd do better if I show you what to do, rather than just tell you." Whistling softly, he set Peter into motion far more gently, and with far more capability, than she had. "I doubt you could handle the drive, with the way it curves, but once we have straight going it will be your turn."

"Very well." She concentrated on watching what he did as he guided the gig along the curved drive leading up the hill, and then took a tight right turn around hedgerows onto the narrow lane. His touch was so relaxed, so confident. She doubted she would ever drive with such ease.

Once they were in the lane, straight and smooth and with no obstacles, he stopped the gig and handed the reins to her. "All right, your turn. Remember now, start slowly and easily."

"I'll remember." Shoulders stiff, teeth set, she tentatively slapped the reins onto Peter's back. To her surprised delight, the horse started off. "Mercy! I did it."

"Good for you. Now, drop your hands just a little."

This time she bit her lips for good measure, but she did as he said. The gig sprang forward, and, as she had in the drive, she pulled back hard on the reins. "Oh, dear."

"Don't worry about it," he said soothingly. "Try again, and don't be so frightened this time."

She took a deep breath. "If you're sure." Carefully she set Peter into motion; carefully she dropped her hands, though she had to will herself to calmness when the horse broke into a trot. Beside her, Michael said nothing. She dared not look at him for his reaction.

Somewhat more confident, she pulled back very slightly, and in response Peter slowed to a walk again. Why, that had been easy! Why had this frightened her so?

"Good," Michael said quietly. "Pull up, now."

"Why? I thought I was doing well."

"You are. We've someone coming toward us." Before she could protest, he took the reins from her hand and pulled the gig to the side. "Good afternoon, Reverend."

"Good afternoon, Lord Lyndon, Lady Lyndon." The vicar nodded his head in greeting as he pulled his gig up next to them. "Are you learning how to drive again, ma'am?"

Chloe's face flamed. "Yes, Reverend."

"Good. You'll be glad to finally drive yourself around the estate."

"Yes, Reverend," she said, wondering why she could not seem to say anything else."

"Good, good. You'll excuse me, sir? I'm off to visit Mrs. Marsland."

"Don't tell me," Michael began.

"Yes, sir." The vicar's face grew almost mischievous. "She believes she's dying. Again."

"Good gad, she believed it last I was here, five years ago."

"Doubtless she'll believe it five years from now. I must be off. She'll be turning Catholic and calling for the last rites if I'm not there soon."

"What would Mrs. Harlow say to that?" Chloe said, and then clapped her hand over her mouth. "Oh, dear."

The vicar looked briefly startled, while beside her she could feel Michael shaking. Then the vicar smiled, that gleam in his eyes again. "I dread to think."

"Oh, dear, I do apologize."

The vicar waved that off. "I will tell Mrs. Marsland you wish her well."

"Oh, I do," Chloe said fervently.

"I must go. If you'll excuse me, my lord?"

"Of course," Michael said, his face admirably controlled.

"Oh, dear," Chloe said again. "I fear I'm not a very good viscountess."

"Bosh, dear." He grinned at her. "To borrow your own word. People in the neighborhood love you."

"They do?" she said doubtfully.

"They do. They like plain speaking."

"I don't know where I get it from. I was so mealy-mouthed as a child."

"You have been outrageous since the day we met."

"That was different."

"But it charmed me."

She blinked at him. "Oh." She paused. "Michael, does everyone here know I have no athletic skills?"

"Talk spreads in a neighborhood such as this."

" 'Twas quite embarrassing."

"Quite."

"You needn't laugh," she said, at the look in his eyes.

"On the contrary, my dear."

"Hmph." She sat beside him in silence for a time. "Are you going to let me drive again?"

"What? Oh, sorry. I forgot." He pulled to a stop and transferred the reins to her hands. "Here."

"Thank you." With a little more confidence, she let Peter go, slowly at first, and then faster, all the time keeping in control. But this was marvelous! The sun was shining, the air was balmy, and the lane ahead was straight and clear. She dropped her hands a little more, and Peter sped up.

"Slow down a little, Chloe," Michael said.

"I can handle it."

He shook his head. "Better to go slowly for now."

She sighed. He was right, of course, but oh, it had been so exhilarating to drive like that, feeling the wind on her face and knowing she was the one in control. It was the first time she could remember mastering something physical.

With supreme confidence, she pulled back on the reins, careful not to saw at Peter's mouth, and the gig slowed. It was so well done, she thought afterward, that everything should have gone fine. At that moment, though, a rabbit bolted out from under the hedgerows. Perhaps Peter sensed her inexperience or wanted in some dim way to repay her for the treatment he'd earlier received. Whatever the reason, he took exception to this, and danced across the road, jouncing them both against the side of the gig.

Chloe let out an exclamation of surprise and pulled back on the reins. Without realizing it, though, she had tightened up on the right side. The gig careened madly across the lane, brushing hard against the hedgerows as she desperately pulled back.

"Chloe, give them to me!" Michael yelled, reaching out to grab the reins from her. At that moment one of the wheels hit a rock, and, for one of the few times in his life, Michael lost his balance, catching only the left rein. The increased pressure sent Peter across the lane again, his speed increased, in spite of the efforts both Chloe and Michael made. Again they scraped along the hedges, making Michael swear as branches hit him again and again. "Damn! Oh, hell—"

"What?" Chloe, still clinging to the other rein, gasped. Not far ahead the hedgerows ended. To either side of the lane the land sloped down into grassy fields. Were they to go down either slope, they stood a fair chance of being overturned.

"Chloe, let go of the rein. Let go!"

Looking down, she realized he now had both reins in his hand, though she still kept a tight grip on hers. Letting out her breath in relief, she released her grip.

It proved to be a mistake. Neither of them had realized how hard she'd been pulling back, with the result that now the pressure on the left rein was stronger. Peter pulled farther left, and though Michael pulled back as hard as he could, what happened next was inevitable. Peter was already veering off the lane toward the field. "Hold on!" Michael yelled, as the gig, jouncing off the lane's smooth surface, followed.

Chloe's grip on the side of the gig was already tight. Oh, dear God, the gig had taken so sharp a turn that it had tilted, putting Michael in danger of falling out. Not caring about herself, she caught at his arm and squeezed her eyes shut. He exclaimed in surprise and tried to pull free, making her grasp that much tighter. If they were going to come to grief, she did not want to save herself at his expense.

It was the shift in weight caused by her action that saved them. With Michael pulled over to her side, the gig remained upright, though it continued to jolt and bounce down the slope. At last the land leveled off, and Peter ran on for a few hundred yards or so, until, for no reason either of them could say, he came to an abrupt halt.

For a long moment there was silence. Chloe cautiously opened her eyes. They were in the middle of the field, alive and unhurt. Beside her Michael reached over and pried her fingers off his arm, and then let go of the reins. Peter, until then contentedly munching grass, turned to look at them, one ear twitching back, for all the world as if he were asking a question. Michael stared at the horse balefully. Peter tossed his head, as if in challenge. "A placid horse, indeed," Chloe said aloud, without quite meaning to.

Michael raised his head, looked at Peter, looked at her, and then, blowing out his breath, reached for the reins. "I think that's the end of the driving lesson for today."

Eleven

The morning post, already sorted, lay in a neat pile at Michael's place at the table the following day. He flipped through it as Caswell poured him coffee, and then served Chloe her customary breakfast of tea and toast. Chloe had a letter from Helena, much crossed and misspelled, filled with gossip about people she knew only slightly. She was trying to decipher a particularly convoluted passage when Michael let out an exclamation.

"What is it?" she asked, glad of the excuse to put Helena's letter down.

"Sherbourne and his wife intend to pay us a visit. In two days' time, according to this."

Chloe smiled at his tone as she spread jam on her toast. "Oh, how dreadful of them."

He glared at her. "I don't want them here."

"But, Michael, they're your friends."

"Dash it, not yet."

"I know there's always something to do around a farm—"

"That has nothing to say to it," he said, the expression in his eyes so warm that she had to look away.

"Oh," she said inadequately, understanding without words.

"Yes, oh."

She sighed. She wanted to be alone with him, too. This was, after all, their honeymoon. Until now, though, she hadn't known that it meant as much to him as to her. "I suppose something like this was bound to happen sooner or later."

"Not yet. 'Tis too soon."

"Michael, we've been here almost two months."

He looked startled. "That long?"

"Yes."

"It doesn't seem it."

"No," she said softly. "It doesn't."

For a moment their gazes caught and held. "I shall write and tell them this is not a good time for a visit."

She laid down her toast. "You'll do no such thing! They'd think us terribly rag-mannered."

"I don't particularly care for that."

"I do. Oh, dear, what bedchambers are clean? I'll have to set Mrs. Barrie on that. I do hope they like plain cooking, too. I doubt our cook is up to fancy sauces and such."

"Chloe—"

"Perhaps we can have a dinner party for them. Oh, I'd love to entertain here, wouldn't you?"

"No."

"Thank heavens there'll be that assembly in Dover. And the area is pretty for riding."

He arched an eyebrow at that. "Are you planning to take anyone for a drive?"

She ignored him. "Oh, and I didn't inventory the sheets yesterday! Oh, there are so many things to see to."

He caught at her wrist as she rose. "Chloe, none of this must be done at this moment."

"Oh, but—oh, Michael, I've never had a home where I can entertain!"

His face softened, his hold on her wrist becoming a caress. "I see," he said. He turned to the footman. "You may leave us."

"Yes, my lord," the footman said, and, expression wooden, left the room.

Chloe stared after him. "What was that about?"

"This," Michael said, and, tugging at her wrist, pulled her down into his lap.

"Michael!"

He bent his head and kissed her so thoroughly that, when he stopped, she had completely forgotten what they had been discussing. "I don't want to share you, Chloe," he said, brushing his chin across the top of her hair.

"Nor I you." She raised her head, and they kissed again. "But it was bound to happen sometime."

"Yes. Just not yet."

"I'm surprised your parents haven't come down here."

"Sometimes my mother has more tact than you'd expect."

"Mm." She laid her head on his shoulder. "I suppose. Why are they coming here? Does it say?"

"No. Sherbourne does mention that his brother was injured on the Peninsula and is being invalided out of the army."

She sat up. "Oh, how terrible for him! I'm so glad you're not a second son and so didn't go into the army."

There was a strange look on his face, but it was gone before she could ask about it. "You're set on this? On allowing them to come?"

"I don't know how we could refuse. Besides, by the time a letter reached them, they may very well have started off."

"There is that. Yes, Caswell, what is it?" he said, appearing not at all concerned at having been caught with his wife in his lap.

"Excuse me, my lord, my lady." He bowed, and Chloe thought she caught a gleam of amusement in his eyes. "Mr. Pennyworth is here to see you, my lord."

"He would be," Michael muttered, and at last released her. She rose with a great show of smoothing down her skirts, looking anywhere but at Caswell. "I suppose I must see him."

"Of course you must." She sighed. "I'm like to be so busy all day, I don't know when we'll see each other."

"At nuncheon," he said, kissing her briefly.

"Yes."

His fingers stroked lightly down her cheek. "Until then, my dear."

"Yes," she said, and stared after him, knowing she looked like a ninny, but not caring.

Caswell cleared his throat. "Excuse me, my lady."

Chloe looked up. "Yes, Caswell?"

"I was once newly married myself, ma'am."

Chloe smiled at this bit of information. "Thank you, Caswell. That is nice to know."

"Yes, my lady. Do you require anything more?"

Only my husband, she thought. "No, Caswell, thank you," she said, and walked out of the room to inform Mrs. Barrie of the upcoming visit.

Viscount Sherbourne and his wife arrived two days later, accompanied by a baggage coach and, surprisingly, another traveling carriage. As they had recently been wed, Chloe had assigned the Blue Chamber to them, since it had an adjoining dressing room and a sitting room. She doubted very much that a second bedroom would be needed. Judging by Sherbourne's face as he handed his bride down, she was right.

What startled both her and Michael, making them exchange glances, was the sight of Lord Adam Burnet, swinging himself down from a horse following the carriages. Even more unexpected, he strode toward the second coach without acknowledging his hosts, to help down a little brown wren of a woman. He, too, wore a tender expression as he took the woman's arm and led her toward the house.

"Sherbourne. Good to see you again," Michael said, as Lady Sherbourne and Chloe exchanged embraces.

"Good to see you," Sherbourne said, and gestured toward Lord Adam. "As you can see, we brought extra guests along."

"We're so glad," Chloe said, wondering all the while where she was to put them, with so few of the guest chambers even cleaned. "As you can see, we've plenty of room."

"You must be wishing me to the devil," Lord Adam said wryly. "I'd like you to meet someone. Lord Lyndon, Lady Lyndon, this is Miss Elizabeth Collier."

"How nice to meet you," Chloe said, holding out her hand to the woman, who until then had held back. Though her simply styled hair and eyes were both ordinary shades of brown, her face was oval in shape, her brows finely arched, her nose straight and small. She was classically pretty, but she became beautiful when she gazed up at Adam. "Welcome to Chimneys."

"Thank you, Lady Lyndon," Miss Collier said shyly. "I hope you aren't bothered overmuch that I'm here."

"Not at all." Chloe walked inside with her. "I do hope you don't mind waiting until chambers are prepared for you."

"Oh, dear." She glanced back at Adam. "I told you we'd be putting them out."

"Don't be foolish. Chimneys, I fear, needs work, but of course there's room for you."

"The entire estate needs work," Michael put in. "I'll show you about tomorrow, if you wish."

"In the meantime, I'll ring for refreshments. I presume tea will be all right? Unless the gentlemen would prefer something stronger." She smiled over at Michael. "I have it on good authority that we've a particularly fine brandy."

"Thank you," Lord Adam said, taking Miss Collier's arm again as they climbed the stairs to the drawing room. "I hate to sit down in all my dirt, but . . ."

"Pray don't refine upon it. Oh, Caswell." Chloe looked up from her chair, which had recently been reupholstered in cream and red striped satin, at the butler. "We'd like tea, please. And tell Mrs. Barrie to make up two more bedrooms."

"She is doing so already, ma'am," Caswell said, and left the room.

"I'm sure you're wondering why we've intruded like this," Lady Sherbourne began, removing her bonnet and shawl and handing them to a hovering footman.

"Mercy, Ariel, 'tis no intrusion," Chloe interrupted her.

"I know 'tis your honeymoon, but we do have reasons."

"Yes." Sherbourne was standing near the fireplace, his elbow comfortably propped on the mantel. "I believe I wrote that my brother Charles has been invalided out of the war?"

Michael nodded. "Yes. I'm sorry to hear it."

"He won't admit it, but it's been beastly for him."

"Quite."

"I've an estate in Sussex I thought I'd let him manage, once his injuries are healed. Thank you," Sherbourne added to Caswell, who stood before him proffering brandy. "We are on our way to inspect it first."

"Of course," Michael said dryly. "We are, after all, on the direct road to Sussex."

"Oh, of course ordinarily we'd take the Brighton road," Lady Sherbourne put in, "but we wished to see how you go on." She turned to Chloe. "Marriage seems to agree with you."

Chloe looked at her hands, at the stitchery she was attempting in her tambour frame, at the threadbare carpet—anywhere but at Lady Sherbourne. "Thank you."

"Of course, we've been rather busy," Michael put in, rescuing her from her embarrassment.

"Yes." Chloe looked up at last. "I've done little painting or studying of ven—the various books I like to read, and Lyndon's been all about the estate. Is your brother progressing, Lord Sherbourne?"

"To an extent. He's rather low in his mind."

"Quite," Michael said. "Work will be good for him. You're wise to give him management of an estate."

"There's another reason," Lord Adam said. He was sunk low in his chair, legs outstretched comfortably before him and crossed at the ankles. His eyes had a heavy-lidded look, and he appeared thoroughly lazy.

Michael took a sip of his brandy. "I don't imagine you'd put yourself through the rigors of travel for no reason, Adam."

"Yes, dear boy, travel can be so fatiguing. But"—he reached over to the chair next to his to take Miss Collier's hand—"Miss Collier and I are engaged."

"But how wonderful!" Chloe exclaimed, smiling at the other woman. "I do wish you happy."

"Thank you," Miss Collier murmured. In contrast to her fiancé, she sat so straight her back didn't touch the chair, and, until Lord Adam reached for her, her hands had been folded primly in her lap. "I believe I'm very lucky."

"No, my dear." Lord Adam brought her hand to his lips for a brief kiss. "I am the one who is lucky."

Michael gave him a searching look. "You said not a word of this in town. Though I did notice you seemed preoccupied."

Lord Adam glanced at his fiancée. "Nothing was settled. Now I have a special license, but she wishes to wait."

"I wanted to tell my family first," Miss Collier said. "They're in Hampshire. That took time."

"Then to Tunbridge Wells, of all places," Lord Adam grumbled, sinking lower in his chair.

"My old governess is there," she explained.

"We might as well have had the banns called."

"We came along partly for propriety's sake," Lady Sherbourne said.

"Tunbridge Wells isn't so very far from here," Chloe said. "I'm glad you came to visit."

"Thank you. Of course, we wouldn't so impose on you without a reason." She glanced at Lord Adam. "We'd like to invite you to the wedding."

"Of course! We'd be happy to come," Chloe said, without looking at Michael.

"We're rather late for St. George's," Lord Adam drawled. "Not that I mind. We intend to have a smaller affair. In town, though, of course. My family is there."

This time, Chloe did exchange a startled look with Michael. To return to London? In spite of her love for Chimneys, she was unexpectedly excited by the thought. "Michael?" she said, deferring to him.

"Of course." His eyes gleamed. The thought of returning to his former pursuits must please him. "Matters are well in train here, with the crops and the tenants."

"Can you manage from a distance?" Chloe asked.

"I imagine so. Pennyworth is competent."

"Then it's settled," Lord Adam said with crisp finality. "You'll come to town."

"We'll be so happy to have you." Miss Collier's face was so aglow as she looked at Lord Adam that Chloe felt a brief stab of envy. They were so obviously in love, just as she and Michael so obviously weren't. No. Just as Michael wasn't.

She reached over to lay her hand on Miss Collier's. "I do hope we'll become friends," she said warmly.

Miss Collier's smile was shy. "I'd like that," she said.

"So would I. Yes, Caswell?" she said, as the butler appeared in the doorway.

"Excuse me for intruding, my lord, my lady." He bowed to Michael. "Mrs. Barrie has informed me that the two additional bedrooms are ready."

"Thank you, Caswell. Please extend to her my thanks. A good housekeeper is worth her weight in gold," she commented to Miss Collier as they rose. "Which rooms, Caswell?"

He cleared his throat. "The Rose Chamber in the south corner, ma'am, for Miss Collier, and the Green Room on the north side of the house for Lord Adam."

"Thank you," Chloe said again. "I fear the house is not in the best repair," she added to Miss Collier, as they walked along, "but these rooms should at least be presentable."

"And far away from each other," Lord Adam muttered.

"Not as far as you might think." Michael grinned at the two women, who had turned to glance back. Much to Chloe's surprise, he winked at her, making her blush in confusion. He was so rarely playful, and he rarely jested. Perhaps he did so only among friends. It was a depressing thought.

"Do you mind very much?" Michael asked a little while later, after they had seen their guests comfortably settled and were walking arm in arm down the stairs to the drawing room.

"Returning to London? Not at all." She paused. "Do you?"

"Lord, no. I'll be glad to go back."

"Your father's son, after all."

"Yes," he said moodily. "More than I'd expected."

"Whyever do you say that?"

He frowned. "I'm not sure. I like being here at Chimneys, but I like town as well. Yet . . ."

A footman was holding open the door to the drawing room for them. "What is it?"

As Sherbourne had done, Michael leaned against the mantelpiece, staring broodingly down into the hearth, as if there were a fire there rather than a vase of dried flowers. "I envy you."

Chloe looked up in surprise from trying to untangle, again, her embroidery silks. "Mercy! Why?"

He sat on the footstool near her, taking her hand. As always, his touch sent a little frisson of excitement through her. "You have a purpose to your life."

Carefully she anchored her needle in her embroidery. "So do you."

"What, driving or boxing or shooting wafers at Manton's? Bah." He waved them off. "What do they matter? At least you spend your time profitably. When you're not busy with your investments, you paint."

She looked down at his hand, still holding hers. "But I wish I didn't stumble for no reason or lose my balance or knock into things," she said in a low voice. "I wish I could do the things you do, to share them with you." She paused. "I wish I weren't Miss Bumblebroth."

He caressed her cheek with the back of his fingers. " 'Tis a cruel name."

She didn't meet his eyes. "I know, but I earned it."

"No. No." He pressed his lips against her hand in a

warm, openmouthed kiss that nearly made her moan. "What you did hurt you alone. You never caused pain to anyone or started a true scandal. Whoever gave you the name deserves scorn, not you."

She looked at his bent head. What would he do if she told him? She dreaded to think. Yet, as his mouth moved to the inside of her wrist and then to the soft, sensitive flesh of her arm, the thought faded. There was only here and now, and what was between them. "Lord Lyndon, I do believe you are trying to seduce me."

He gave her the same mischievous grin he'd earlier shared with Lord Adam. "You only believe it? Then I must not be trying hard enough." Both his hands slid up her arms to her shoulders. "Mayhap I should be a trifle more forward."

"Mayhap you should," she said, and let him slip his arms about her waist, let him pull her forward. Mercy, 'twas only the middle of the afternoon. Not that she had any intention of denying him, though. After he had kissed her, once and again and yet again, she rose as he tugged her to her feet. He didn't love her; that, she knew too well. Yet there was one place where she felt truly close to him. This afternoon, after seeing two couples who were in love, she wanted to be there with him. Head resting on his shoulder, she went upstairs to her room with him.

"This will be a good way for you to meet our neighbors," Michael said to the Sherbournes and their other guests, as they entered the assembly room at Dover.

Chloe turned. "Just do be prepared for the vicar's wife to ask about your religion."

Lady Sherbourne looked startled. "Good heavens, why?"

"We've no idea. Oh, and the squire's daughters are like to swarm around you," she added to Lord Adam. "There are four of them, none married."

Lord Adam toyed with his quizzing glass. "I shall dampen their pretensions."

"And I shall tell each one to go to the devil," Miss Collier said fiercely, startling Chloe.

Lord Adam smiled at her. "No pistols tonight, my love."

"Not yet, at least."

Chloe exchanged a startled look with Michael. *Mercy!* Did Elizabeth know how to shoot?

Lord Sherbourne was surveying the room. "Not a sad crush."

"No, thank heavens." Chloe had been looking about the room as well. It was handsomely proportioned, simply plastered in white, with pilasters at each corner and long windows along the side. No one was present who intimidated her; she saw mostly acquaintances and friends from the neighborhood. "I do hate to sound conceited," she murmured to Michael, "but I suspect we are the fashion leaders here."

His eyes gleamed. "We are. We are the leading family in the neighborhood, my dear, and you are its ranking lady."

"Mercy! I'd not thought of that. Does that mean everyone will be looking to me to set the style?"

"Yes."

Her laugh rang out. She was only marginally aware that several people turned to look at her, smiling. "Heaven help them. I am hardly fashionable."

"No one else has a gown from Celeste," he reminded her.

"Or a coat from Weston, except for Sherbourne and Lord Adam," she said, looking up at him with a proprietary air. His coat of midnight blue superfine, worn over fawn pantaloons and a waistcoat of swirling golden brocade, fit well across his broad shoulders. It complemented her own simply cut, unadorned gown of bronze satin. With it she wore topazes at her throat and ears. Patience had managed to fasten her hair into a Psyche knot, which Chloe suspected was coming loose already. For once, though, she knew she looked well enough.

"I like that gown," he said. "It brings out the gold in your hair."

She looked up at him, startled. "My hair is brown."

"With gold in it." He bent to her. "I should know," he said in a low whisper that sent shivers along her spine. She ducked her head, wondering if her face was as red as it felt.

"Good evening, my lord, my lady," a voice said.

Chloe looked up to see the vicar. *Oh, it would be!* she thought, listening to Michael greet the man. "It is pleasant to see you again, Reverend. And Mrs. Harlow," she added to the vicar's wife, who looked Chloe up and down, looked away, and then sniffed, making Chloe feel like a fallen woman. Irrationally she wanted to laugh.

"May I say you're in looks tonight, ma'am," the vicar said.

At his words his wife sniffed again, and Chloe was hard put to it to keep her countenance. "Thank you, Reverend. A lovely evening."

"Indeed, indeed. I'm sure I speak for the entire neighborhood when I say how pleasant it is to have you here."

Michael bowed. "Yes, we show great condescension."

The vicar's eyes twinkled. "Indeed you do, and your London guests. I have been meaning to tell you, sir, that lowering your tenants' rents was a generous gesture."

"Thank you, Reverend. Of course Sir Horace and I disagree on the subject," he said, indicating the squire.

"Oh, indeed, I am not surprised. I fear he has more in common with Master James than with you. Not that Master James wouldn't have been a good manager of Chimneys, of course."

"Quite," Michael said in a clipped voice, making Chloe look up to see that his face was tight. "I believe the music is starting. If you will excuse us, Reverend?"

"Of course," he said, and moved away with Mrs. Harlow, who had yet to say a word to Chloe, beside him.

Chloe let Michael lead her farther into the room, where sets were already forming. "Oh, dear. 'Tis a country dance."

He smiled down at her. "This is one we've practiced, dear."

"The one where I fell all over your feet? Oh, of course. I did that with all of them."

"I have great confidence in you."

They joined other people to make up a set, ending any chance of further conversation. Chloe bit her lip as the dance started and tried to concentrate, but within a few moments her mind wandered. Who was James? She thought she knew the answer, though she was surprised that Michael had never told her about him. What bothered her most was the look on Michael's face merely at hearing his name.

So preoccupied was she that she went through the dance without thinking, and so made no missteps. "You did that well," Michael said, when they stood together again during the interval. "The lessons were well worth it."

She looked up at him blankly. "Lessons? Oh, dancing."

"Yes, my dear, what did you think?"

"I suppose I did dance well."

His gaze was searching. "Why do I suspect that you are thinking of other things?"

"Actually, I was. Michael, who is James?"

His face tightened again. "My brother."

"I didn't know you had a brother," she said in surprise, in spite of her earlier conclusion.

"I did. He died."

Chloe ignored his icy tone. "I'm sorry. Was it recent?"

"No. Sixteen years ago." He paused. "I was twelve."

"Oh, Michael, it must have been terribly difficult for you."

"He should have been the heir. Even the vicar believes James would have done a better job—"

"Michael, he didn't say that!"

"—and Sir Horace certainly believes it."

"Sir Horace is a pompous ass."

"Chloe!" He looked down at her in laughing surprise. "My dear, your language."

"I reserve it, sir, for people who deserve it."

He was shaking his head, but, to her relief, he was smiling again. "Then I must be careful not to annoy you."

"Oh, you're not in any danger, sir. Yet," she added.

"Danger? Are you in danger, Lyndon?" the squire said as he joined them.

Chloe's eyes met her husband's, brimming with laughter. "No, Sir Horace," Michael said. "We weren't talking about anything in particular."

"Oh. I see." He chuckled. "Just a jest, eh? Would you do me the honor of standing up with me for this dance, Lady Lyndon?" he swept on, before Chloe could do so much as greet him. He was pompous, she thought as he led her onto the floor for a Roger de Coverley, a dance she disliked, but his behavior was courtly and kind. He was simply self-involved, as were his wife and daughters. A heavyset man, he was a veritable sight in his bright green coat, worn over a waistcoat striped in yellow and cerise. At least Mrs. Mayfield, his wife, had more sense of style, though her clothes had obviously come from a provincial dressmaker, and—

Appalled, Chloe caught the trend of her thoughts. It wasn't so long ago that people had said similar things about her. Just because she was now a viscountess didn't mean she should be puffed up in her own consequence.

Something snapped in Chloe then. That she was unable to do the things that nearly everyone else could didn't mean she should have been given a cruel nickname. It certainly didn't mean she should take that name and apply it to herself. No longer would she take her trivial missteps or mistakes so seriously.

At that moment, in the middle of a step, she somehow managed to land wrong and lost her balance, stumbling against the man who was passing to her side. Fortunately it was Michael, who looked briefly startled at the unexpected impact, and then, with a quick grin, set her on her feet. She smiled back at him, and then applied herself to the dance more vigorously. Mercy, but this was fun! She knew more of the steps than she'd realized. Even when she didn't, it didn't matter. She was enjoying herself.

"You look to be enjoying the dancing," Michael said a

while later, when the musicians had taken a break and she was standing with him, drinking lemonade."

"Oh, I am." She took another sip. "My, this is good. 'Tis hot in here, isn't it? I never realized dancing was so easy," she went on.

He raised an eyebrow. "Excuse me? Did I hear aright?"

"Dancing is easy," she repeated. "As long as I don't care whether I do it right or not."

"Well." His smile was slow. "I do believe you've discovered something, my dear."

"I have, haven't I? You told me so often to relax."

"And you finally have."

"And I finally have," she agreed. "I do wish I hadn't worn this gown, though."

"Why?"

"Satin is heavy to wear on a warm night like this. I should have chosen my green silk, or the figured muslin."

He gave her a long, measuring look that encompassed her from top to toe. "I'm glad you didn't."

She looked at him in astonishment. "First Mrs. Harlow, and now you! What is wrong with this gown?"

"Nothing that I can see," he said, grinning. "It fits you extremely well."

She raised her fan and plied it vigorously. "People will think, thank heavens, that I'm flushed from the heat."

"Are you blushing from embarrassment, or . . ."

"Or," she said frankly.

He laughed. "Chloe, you are a treasure."

She looked up at him, startled, but before she could ask what he meant, the music began again and another partner claimed her hand. Was she, indeed, a treasure?

By the time the evening ended, Chloe was still flushed, not only from the heat but also from laughter. Her mind was awhirl with so many thoughts as they were driven home through the dark Kentish night after the assembly that she couldn't seem to settle on any one thing—the dancing, the music, the conversation, the people. Especially the people, who seemed so much more alive than those in London society. They might lack polished manners, but then, what they said or did was more real. She could trust that what someone said was a true expression of his thoughts, whether compliments or criticisms. Those fortunately had been few tonight. Oh, Sir Horace had been outspoken in his disapproval of Michael's management of Chimneys, and the vicar had ventured a very mild opinion on Michael's brother—

Abruptly Chloe's head cleared. In her enjoyment of the evening, she had forgotten that brief, critical conversation. "Michael?" she said softly.

"What is it?" he said, after a moment.

"Were you sleeping?"

"Just dozing, I think. We don't keep town hours anymore, Chloe." She thought he smiled at her. "You certainly seemed to have enough energy."

"I still do." She rested her head against his shoulder and laced her fingers through his.

"For?" he said, letting his voice trail off suggestively.

"For," she agreed, and heard him chuckle. She suddenly remembered what he had said just tonight. She was a treasure. It was hard to believe, when in many ways they knew so little about each other.

Her smile faded. "Michael, why didn't you tell me about your brother?"

"It didn't seem that important," he said, his voice tight. "Why do you bring him up?"

"It matters to me that you didn't think to tell me. He was part of your life."

"Long ago."

"He must have been young when he died."

"Leave it, Chloe."

She considered that for a moment. He sounded weary. "I suppose I should, shouldn't I?"

"Yes." He paused. "No. You deserve to hear about it."

She twisted her head to look up at him. "I believe I do."

"You should know what kind of man you married."

"What kind of man—Michael, what are you talking about?"

"I'm not who I seem." He paused again. "You see, I killed my brother."

Twelve

Chloe stared at him in shock. "How could you have? You were only a boy."

"True, but I did it." Michael leaned back against the squabs, his arms crossed over his chest. "I've been reminded of it all my life."

"Your father?" she whispered.

"My father," he agreed. "James was exactly the son he wanted."

"But that's not fair! You were a child—"

"I still should have known better."

Chloe fell still, aching for him. "How did he die?"

He took a deep breath. "It was a boating accident."

"Here?"

"No, at Grantham. There's a decent sized lake there. A real one, spring-fed and deep." He kept his head averted. "James was six years older than I. He had his own life. He'd just finished his first year at Oxford. He was my idol." He turned to her at last. "He didn't care for sport, yet he taught me how to ride, how to box—although I had more skilled teachers at that later—and how to handle a boat."

"How did it happen?"

He took a deep breath. "We were out in a punt. It was a hot day, and we were being silly, splashing each other with the oars. One time I did it, the boat rocked, and it seemed great fun. I did it again. James told me to stop—I didn't know at the time that we were over the deepest part of the lake—but I didn't listen. What twelve-year-old boy does?" He paused. "Finally, I rocked it so hard it overbalanced. I don't think I would have fallen in. I had a good grip on the railing. But James grabbed for me. The boat tipped over. We both fell in."

Chloe resisted the urge to put her hand on his arm. "But surely you could swim, with a lake on the estate."

"I could. I was always restless, Chloe. I wanted only to indulge in sport. James didn't."

Chloe stared at him in horror. "Michael, are you saying he couldn't swim?"

"Of course I sank," he went on, as if she hadn't spoken. "But when I came back up, I thought it was famous. I started laughing and yelling for James." He swallowed, hard. "Chloe, he didn't come up."

"Oh, Michael—"

"I couldn't find him. I panicked. I called for him, then dived, called for him and dived. Finally when I came up, he was there. I was so relieved. But he was flailing and splashing," he went on, overriding her when she started to speak. "I struck out for him, but he went under again." Again he paused. "It's odd, how one's mind can detach itself when something serious is happening. I knew what I had to do, but I seemed to be watching myself do it. I dived, and I couldn't find him. No, don't look at me like that." He pushed away the hand she had tried to set on his arm. "I don't deserve any sympathy."

"But you tried, Michael."

"It wasn't enough."

"You were just a boy—"

"I should have known better." His eyes were closed. "By then, there were servants running toward us. One of them grabbed me. I kept struggling and hitting him, but he never let me go. And when he did drag me out of the water, I tried to go back in again."

"Oh, Michael."

"My parents had been visiting, but they were there by then," he said dully. "My mother was kneeling beside me.

My father was watching. There was no expression on his face. I didn't understand that for a long time."

Again he paused, and Chloe had the tactfulness not to break in.

"They finally brought him in. He was pale, and so still, Chloe. Both my parents were beside him. My mother hugged him and cried. My father bent down, touched his hair, and said, 'My son.' Then he looked at me, said nothing, and walked away."

Chloe was biting back tears. If she showed any sympathy, though, she sensed he would break down. She wondered if he ever had cried for his brother. "Oh, Michael, how awful."

"Yes." His voice sounded normal. "Nothing was the same after that. We had been a happy family, Chloe. We still are, in most ways. My mother had more children. I realize now she and my father were both hoping for another son. It must have been disappointing when they had only girls."

"Michael, your parents love your sisters."

"I'm not saying they don't. But they wanted another son. Not to secure the succession, but to have one."

"Perhaps it's as well they didn't."

He frowned at her. "What do you mean?"

"He could never have been another James, the poor boy."

"No one could be. Well?" He glanced over at her. "Now you know."

He still hadn't healed from it, Chloe thought. "We go through some terrible things in life, don't we?"

"Yes. Some you pay for the rest of your life."

"But, Michael, there's happiness, too." She reached out her hand to him. "There's happiness."

He looked at her hand, then slowly took it, holding on as if to a lifeline. "Yes. There is, isn't there?"

Michael paced the hall of their London town house, wondering when Chloe was going to come down. It was past time they were leaving. What the devil was she doing? She never had been one to primp or preen, or to keep him waiting. Admirable, but on tonight of all nights, she was late, for the engagement ball of Lord Adam Burnet and Miss Elizabeth Collier.

It felt strange being back in London, though just a few weeks ago he would have told anyone who asked that this was where he belonged. He was no longer so sure of that, however, not when he had found life at Chimneys so unexpectedly fulfilling. Not when he felt caught between two worlds. He still enjoyed athletics, but they left a gnawing, unfulfilled space within him. That empty pit had always been there. He simply hadn't noticed it until now.

There was something else about London he disliked, much to his surprise. It took him away from Chloe. While they hadn't spent all their time together at Chimneys, they'd had a common purpose that pulled them closer. London only pulled them apart. He was busy with his pursuits; so was she, painting and involving herself with her investments, sometimes going into the City to speak with her man of affairs. In addition, she now had a circle of friends, not only the Sherbournes, Lord Adam and his fiancée, but a court of lonely, isolated men whom she'd singled out at balls and routs before their wedding. The odd thing was that both her activities and his left him lonely and isolated, too. He wanted to be with her. Lord help him, he wanted his wife.

At the thought, he rubbed his hand over his face. That was something else he wouldn't have believed in the past. He'd expected that he'd see little of her, never taking into account the fact that he might like her. He liked her bluntness, the fact that he never quite knew what she was going to say. He liked it that she honestly didn't care about her appearance. He liked the way he could talk to her. He liked best, though, the way she felt in his arms. That surprised him most of all.

At that moment he heard her voice, accompanied by the sound of her light footsteps as she ran downstairs. His

Chloe was more graceful than she knew. "Yes, Patience, I know. I'll fix it downstairs," she said, sounding so impatient that he grinned. Something was apparently amiss with her ensemble. It wasn't unusual.

"Oh, Michael," she said, a bit out of breath as she ran down the main staircase to the hall. "I am so sorry I'm late. My hair—what do you stare at?"

Michael had gone completely still. *My God, but she's beautiful.* Why had he not noticed it before? Suddenly, achingly beautiful. Not because of her stylish gown of red watered silk, not because of the garnets at her throat. No. It came from her.

Of course, being Chloe, she had just a hint of untidiness about her. There was a wisp of hair out of place, as well as the twist in her glove that caused it to wrinkle. None of that mattered to him, as it apparently didn't matter to her. She was beautiful. "You look—quite nice."

"Thank you. I hate it when you do that."

"When I do what?"

"Go all still and inscrutable."

"Do I do that?" he said, surprised.

"Yes. You're doing it again," she pointed out, and frowned as she adjusted the wrinkle in her glove. "Dash it, I can't get this to fit right. Oh, well, I suppose it doesn't really matter."

"Why not?"

"Because we're late."

He bit back a smile. She had answered with a perfunctory breeziness that told him, again, that her appearance mattered little to her. If that trait had amused him before, now he found it endearing. How easily he could have ended up with some spoiled society darling, or with some dewy-eyed ingenue, both of whom would likely have cared far more for their clothes than for anything else, himself included.

"Here, 'twill take just a moment," he said, reaching for her hand.

"I should have let Patience fix it, after all," she grumbled.

"Let me see what I can do." His fingers felt unexpectedly stiff and overly large as he fumbled with the tiny pearl buttons of her glove.

"You are altogether too good at that."

"At what?" Lord help him, but just the simple act of unbuttoning her glove was doing things to him. Things that made him want to stay home with her, alone.

"Unfastening women's clothes."

He chuckled as he smoothed her glove. "All in the past, my dear."

Her eyes were unexpectedly vulnerable as she looked up at him. "Do you keep a mistress?"

"Good God!" He stared at her, aware of a smothered sound that sounded suspiciously like a laugh behind him. One of the footmen, he'd guess. "I most certainly do not."

"But gentlemen do keep them."

"This gentleman does not."

"I'll wager you did at one time."

"Chloe, this is neither the time nor the place to discuss this." He shook his head, amazed. "I cannot believe the things you say sometimes."

"I know, but—"

He bent his head close to hers. "Why would I want a mistress, when I have you?"

That made her head jerk back, made her look up at him with eyes that were unexpectedly huge. For long, long moments their gazes held, until the sound of someone shuffling his feet broke the spell. *That damned footman,* he thought, and returned his attention to the glove. Only a small amount of flesh showed now, soft, white. On impulse he pressed his lips to it, feeling and tasting the warm texture of her.

"Michael," she gasped.

He straightened, quickly fastening the last few buttons. "There," he said, his voice husky. His pulse had sped up; his breathing was shallow. "That should be fine."

"What?" she said, still looking at him.

"Your glove."

"My—oh, yes," she said, looking down at it without, he thought, much comprehension. "Thank you."

"My pleasure." Her shawl had dropped to the floor at some point, he noticed, and bent to pick it up. "I like this gown," he said, as he draped the shawl about her shoulders.

"Do you? You don't think the color a bit brazen?"

"Red suits you. You should have the Grantham rubies."

She fussed with her shawl for longer than seemed necessary, apparently needing the chance to compose herself. "I cannot very well take them from your mother."

"You know she's not one to adorn herself."

"Bosh. Every woman likes jewels."

And he had never bought her any—with her money. He tested the thought in his mind, and found to his surprise that it didn't matter anymore. It was simply part of their lives. He would, he thought, shower her with all the luxuries she either had not been allowed, or had not allowed herself.

"Come, my dear." He held out his arm. "I imagine the carriage has been waiting a time."

"I imagine so, too." She set her hand on his arm, smiling as they walked to the door. His Chloe, he thought again. How very lucky he was that she was his wife.

"What do you smile at?" she asked, as Caswell opened the door of the house and they stepped out into the street.

"Just that I'm happy to be here."

The answer irrationally disappointed her. At Chimneys they had been so very close. There had been times, even here in London, when he looked at her as if he loved her. In some ways, she thought perhaps he did. She could never quite forget, though, the reason they had married. "You're enjoying being back in town, then."

"Quite." He handed her into the carriage after the footman had let down the step. "You seem to be, too."

"Ye-es."

"You don't sound so certain."

"Oh, I'm glad to be back to painting." She smoothed out her skirts as he settled beside her in the carriage. "I'm glad to do more with my investments." She paused. "I just wish we didn't have to go to these dos."

Michael rapped on the roof of the carriage with his fist. It started off with a jerk that briefly tossed her against him. "Even for something like tonight?"

"Oh, of course tonight is different. Still," she said, sounding wistful, "I'd rather be home."

"Going over your investments?" he said, sounding irritated.

"Unfair of you, Michael! You know I don't let them intrude upon you."

"Not usually, no."

"Not ever! As to that, you've become so involved in sport again I hardly see you."

"There are ways to change that, Chloe."

"That you know as well as I have been impossible. We've not been back long enough, for one thing."

"I've accepted your life—"

"Oh, have you."

"Why have you not accepted mine?"

She turned her head, her lips pursed. "I have, for you, but you know how hopeless I am at such things."

He reached over for her hand. "It wasn't your fault a rabbit dashed into the lane in front of Peter."

"I daresay if I'd more experience, though, I would have controlled him."

"As you said. More experience. You're right, of course. There's not been time for you to learn here in town."

"No, there hasn't." She was suddenly annoyed, and for no reason she could guess. "I would learn if I could, but I never see you. You take your meals at White's, except for dinner," she rushed on, before he could speak, "you ride with friends, you go to Gentleman Jackson's. Why can you not once be home to accompany me to a showing at the Royal Academy?"

His look was startled. "I didn't know you'd wish me to."

"Well, I do," she said, feeling thoroughly disgruntled.

He was quiet for a time, and then rumbled with laughter. "Whyever are we quarreling?"

"I don't know." She turned back to him. "Except that I wish we didn't have to go to these dos."

"Quite. So we're back where we started."

"I suppose we are."

"You did well in Dover, Chloe. Why do you not think you'll do well here?"

"No one in Dover knew about the things I've done." She paused. "No one knew me as Miss Bumblebroth."

"Oh, bosh," he said, smiling at her.

"I beg your pardon?"

"As you told me, you stopped caring if you did things right or not."

"So I did, but that was then—"

His breath was warm through the palm of her glove as he raised her hand. "And I have every confidence in you to-night."

She only wished she did. It was not going to be easy being among the *ton* again, after two blessed months away from them. *Oh, bosh,* she told herself. For tonight at least, she was not going to let these people worry her.

They were greeted at the top of the stairs in Ware House, the town house belonging to the Duke of Ware, Lord Adam's father, by Elizabeth and Lord Adam. Elizabeth glowed in a gown of oyster white satin embroidered with gold thread, and with a filet of gold and pearls on her hair. Already relations between Chloe and Michael's friends had grown so relaxed that, in private at least, they used each other's Christian names. Chloe greeted them and then, on Michael's arm, walked into the ballroom, already a whirl of color and sound and motion. So many people had attended that the room, large though it was, was warm and stuffy. The sight made her check. Then, holding tightly to Michael's arm, she walked into the room. Thank heavens she had him. It might not have been the done thing for married couples to be forever in each others' pockets, but, to her astonishment, she didn't give a fig what the *ton* thought. Not about her relationship with Michael.

The thought made her relax, so that she could ignore the smirks hidden behind feminine and masculine hands alike, as well as those that weren't hidden at all. Smiling dazzlingly up at Michael, she took to the floor, dancing quite creditably and laughing at her mistakes. There were fewer smirks now. The dance gave the lie to the prevailing opinion that she and Michael were ill suited to each other. Matters changed even further after she had stood up with Lord Sherbourne and after Lord Adam had bowed over her hand. The men she had befriended before her marriage, shy Mr. Wentworth and the lonely Lord Farrow, solicited her hand, while she sat out a dance with Sir Roland Parker, because of his deafness. Though she couldn't precisely say she was a success, she had very few dances left open. Her confidence, returned to her by the people near Chimneys and, more importantly, by Michael, buoyed her up.

It was during the interval before one of these dances that, flushed and warm from dancing, she sensed someone approaching her. Turning her head, she saw her cousin Edwin. The very sight of him sent a shock through her.

"Hallo, cuz." Edwin flicked her cheek carelessly with his finger, and she drew back. "Married life must suit you."

She watched him warily. "Thank you."

"I never would have expected it," he went on, "but you look well. That is a remarkable gown you are wearing."

"In what way?"

"Pax, cousin. I mean no disrespect. It is quite stylish, and the color suits you. Lyndon must be pleased."

"I believe so."

His eyes lingered briefly on her bosom, exposed by the deep cut of her gown. "You actually have a figure. I didn't know that."

She bristled. "Of course I do, I—" She stopped herself. He had always done this to her, put her on the defensive. He could behave as he wished, but she didn't have to react. "And so do you," she said sweetly.

He looked startled. "Excuse me?"

"You are rather good-looking, when you let yourself be."

"When I let myself!" He stared at her. "I'll have you know most women find me attractive."

"But of course. Isn't that what I just said?"

He studied her as warily as she had ever looked at him. "You've changed."

She gave him a brilliant smile. "Yes, I have, haven't I?"

"You've been out of town. Where had you that gown?"

"Oh, I found a marvelous dressmaker near Chimneys," she said dismissively, not mentioning that Michael's mother had had this made up for her. "Lyndon's estate, you know."

"And I haven't an estate. Is that what you're saying?"

"Why, Edwin, I said nothing of the kind."

He looked away, appearing so thoroughly confused that she wanted to laugh. "You've changed. At least, you haven't landed yourself in any bumblebroths lately."

The reference to the hated nickname was almost her undoing. "No, I haven't."

"So that still bothers you." He looked back at her, a gleam in his eyes.

"Certainly. I'll not deny it."

"Other people might call you by it."

"Is that a threat, Edwin?"

"Of course not."

"You do know that if Lyndon learns you are the one who first used that name, he will likely call you out."

Edwin laughed. "Over you? I doubt that. Besides, I never did quite say it. I simply said much the same as I did just now."

She gazed at him with remarkable steadiness. "It was more than that, and you know it."

His eyes mocked her. "Do I? But I did not come to quarrel."

"No, simply to insult me. Now that you have, I think you can leave me in peace."

His eyes were puzzled again. "You've changed," he repeated. "I'm impressed."

"I rather thought you were annoyed."

He ignored it. "You appear to be making Lyndon a creditable wife."

Chloe glanced across the room, to where Michael was standing with a group of friends, athletes all, and smiled. Remarkable that he belonged to her. "How kind of you to say so."

"Yet still you do not trust me."

"No, I don't. As you yourself said, Edwin, old habits."

He ran his hand over his hair. "I'm trying to change, Chloe," he said, very quietly.

He seemed sincere. At least, his eyes looked so, and Chloe, who never had been one to hurt or insult people, felt a pang of remorse. "I believe you."

"Do you? That does relieve me." He studied her critically. "Your hair is coming loose again."

"Oh, drat." She put her hand up to find that strands had, indeed, fallen free. "It ever will happen."

"You should consider cropping it."

"I'm not sure Lyndon would like it."

"Lyndon deserves a fashionable wife."

That arrowed deep, though she had somehow been immune to his prior attempts at insult. "He seems not to mind."

"Not now," Edwin said, his smile superior. He glanced over as the orchestra began playing again. "A contredanse."

Her eyes laughed up at him. "Do you truly wish me to fall all over your feet, Edwin?"

"I am persuaded you will."

"Oh, without a doubt," she said airily, and set her hand on his arm. For the first time she could remember, she had bested Edwin in an argument, and all because she'd refused to fight on his terms. Remarkable. Yet she wasn't completely satisfied, not when he had managed to nettle her. She was well aware that the strands that earlier had been becomingly curled were now straight, due to the heat and the humidity of the room, as they ever would. *Oh, drat.* Old habits, as Edwin had said. Let him find the right weakness, and she was uncertain again, doubting herself again.

Her hair was fine, she told herself stoutly. Michael didn't seem to mind it in the least.

Edwin returned her to her seat when the dance was over, bowed, and left her, instead of staying with her until her next partner arrived. It didn't take Chloe long to learn the reason for his discourteous behavior. "Was Hempstead bothering you?" Michael demanded as he approached her.

She rose, smiling. "Oh, no. Of course he tried—"

"He'll pay for that," he growled.

"But he didn't succeed, Michael."

The furrows in Michael's brow deepened. "Why not?"

"I didn't let him. You were right. Being in Dover helped me."

He studied her a moment longer, and then nodded. "Good. But if he or anyone else ever offers you insult, you've only to tell me."

"Why?"

"Because I'll settle with him."

"You are bloodthirsty," she said, though his words had sent a warm glow through her.

"As I said. Only for you."

The wonder of it made her smile genuinely dazzling. "You, sir, are inordinately condescending."

He looked startled for a moment, and then smiled. "And you, madam, are inordinately impertinent."

"So I am." She continued to gaze at him, as he did at her, and she wondered if perhaps they would leave the ball early tonight.

"Impertinence is damaging to my self-esteem."

"I fear 'tis something you'll have to live with, sir."

His smile grew wider. "Will I?"

"Yes."

"I'd not have it any other way," he said, and held his hand out to her. "My dance, I believe."

"Michael, would you do me a favor?"

"What?"

"Would you dance with Miss Darcy?"

"Who?"

"She's sitting with the chaperones."

He glanced over with her at the girl, who was making her come-out this year. Her gown was not in the first stare of fashion, nor did it suit her plump figure. "Why?"

"Because she's a wallflower."

"That gown is at least a season old. She has only a small dowry, does she not?"

"Oh, money! That ever is important, isn't it? The poor girl hasn't taken. She'll go home unwed and will likely end up a poor relation."

He frowned. "I doubt that dancing with me will help."

"Because you're stylish and respected, Michael. If you take notice of her, so will others."

"Why does this matter to you?"

"Because I was a wallflower once."

He looked down at her, and his face softened. "Oh, very well. I'll do it for you."

"Thank you. And do please look as if you're enjoying it."

"I will try," he said, and walked away.

At loose ends, Chloe looked around and saw Lord Farrow. A thought grew in her mind and wouldn't be dismissed. Before she could stop herself, she went over to him and took his arm.

"Been meddling, have you?" Michael said a little later.

"A bit."

"Introducing all those people to each other. Mr. Wentworth to Miss Darcy, Lord Farrow to Lady Sarah Pemberton—"

"They seem to be getting on well enough."

"And making me dance with all those wallflowers."

"But look, they all have other partners now."

"As long as I may have the supper dance with you."

"Oh, of course, sir." She let him catch her up in the music, wondering if her smile looked as idiotic as it felt. How very lucky she was to have him. He cared for her just as she was, she thought, and almost unconsciously touched her hair.

Thirteen

Patience came into Chloe's room the following morning with her chocolate, and promptly dropped the tray. "Oh, my lady!" she said with dismay.

Chloe turned on the stool from her dressing table. "I think I need a hairdresser, Patience."

"My lady, whatever possessed you to cut your hair?"

"I thought it would curl," she said defensively.

"But you know your hair has always been straight."

"I know." Chloe lifted the straight, lank strands of very short hair, and grimaced. Not exactly the soft, springy curls she had envisioned. "Remarkably foolish of me."

"Has Lord Lyndon seen it?"

"No." She glanced at an enameled clock set on a cherry wood table. "He's not at home, is he?"

"No, my lady, he went out about the usual time."

She nodded. "So I thought." By this time of day, Michael had gone riding; he had probably stopped into Gentleman Jackson's saloon, and perhaps had shot wafers at Manton's, or crossed swords with some other buck at Signor Gianni's salon. If there were anything she knew about Michael, it was that he needed always to be active. That she was different rarely seemed to bother him, yet she had gone and done—this.

Sometime later, the hairdresser stepped back, laying down comb and scissors. He had evened out the straggling strands, shaped her hair into a more flattering style, and used the curling tongs so that she did, indeed, have the curls she had dreamed about. Nothing, however, could hide the fact that she'd made a disastrous mistake. "It doesn't look very good, does it?" she said in a very small voice.

The hairdresser smiled sadly. "My apologies, madam, but—"

"It's not your fault, monsieur. I was foolish." She surveyed her hair from every angle. There was no disputing that it didn't suit her. Her face was just a little too round for the style to be flattering. "Oh, dear."

"You made a mistake, right enough," Patience said, "but it will grow back."

"Yes, but in how long?"

"Quicker than you think, I'll warrant. In the meantime I can thread it through with ribbons, or perhaps jewels."

Chloe made a face at herself in the mirror, and saw the other two exchange startled glances. "I've no doubt you'll succeed admirably, Patience," she said. "And, monsieur, you did a creditable job." Not that he'd had much to work with.

"Merci, madame." The hairdresser was packing his tools into his case. "When your hair needs attention, call for me. I can arrange it so that it grows out more evenly."

"Thank you." She rose, mustering up a smile. "You are to be commended, monsieur. Patience, you may go."

"Yes, ma'am," Patience said, and left the room to show the hairdresser out.

Chloe looked at herself in the mirror and sighed. This was a true bumblebroth. The *ton* would laugh and whisper behind her back when they saw her. More to the point was what Michael would say. She dreaded finding out.

Some time later, wearing a new gown of aqua watered silk with a silver net overdress, and with ribbon threaded through her curls, she entered the drawing room. Michael turned to greet her, his smile quickly dying when he saw her. "What the hell have you done to your hair?" he demanded.

Chloe winced. "You don't have to swear, Michael."

He walked all about her, his scrutiny so intense that she could feel it, even when he was behind her. "Good God."

"I think Monsieur Gaudreau did a creditable job."

"Who is Monsieur Gaudreau?"

"The hairdresser I sent for after I cut it."

"Do you mean it looked worse?"

"Yes."

He swore again. "Why did you do it?"

"To be fashionable."

"Fashionable!"

"Cropped hair is the style," she said defensively.

He closed his eyes. "Chloe, don't you know how much I liked to run my fingers through it?"

Her eyes widened. "Do you mean when—"

"Yes, I mean when."

"Oh." There was only one time during the day when he saw her with her hair down. "Patience has assured me it will grow out," she offered.

"Oh? When?"

"Well, it may take some time."

"Chloe." He shook his head. "Why must you always do such things?"

It was the first time he had come even remotely close to criticizing her. "I'm sorry! I thought it would please you." She lowered her head. "I try so hard."

"Ah, Chloe." He reached out, curling his hand about her neck, and slipped his fingers into her curls. "It isn't so bad. See? I can still put my fingers into it." His voice lowered. "And 'tis as silky and soft as ever."

"You like my hair? As it was?" she asked.

"As it is," he corrected. "Whether long or cropped."

"Oh." For a long moment their gazes held, and then he bent to drop a kiss on her nose. It was not what she had expected. "I—we are to go to the Nelsons later."

"Since we accepted their invitation, 'tis the only polite thing to do." His smile was slow. "However, I can think of something better."

" 'Twill be so crowded, I doubt they'll miss us," she said, huskily, looping her arms about his neck. "Annabelle Nelson will try to squeeze four hundred or so people into a few rooms."

"Far too crowded, when they have such a small house."

"Though sometimes, two people are enough."

"Just the right number," he agreed.

"We've been gadding about since we returned to London."

"It would be good to have a quiet evening for once."

"Yes." Their gazes were still locked. "Do you think I should let down my hair?"

Michael gave a surprised bark of laughter. "It depends on how you mean that, my dear."

"Oh, in the very best way." She was smiling up at him as his head bent again, definitely not for a brief peck on her nose this time, when there was a knock on the door.

"Damn," Michael said, forgetting himself again as he straightened. "Enter."

"Excuse me, my lord, my lady." Caswell stood in the doorway. "Ma'am, I fear there is a problem in the kitchen."

"Oh, dear." Chloe stepped away from Michael. "What is it?"

"The chef is upset because the soup is spoiled."

"Is that all?"

"Yes, madam."

"Very well. I'll see what I can do to settle him down."

"Fire the chef and hire a cook," Michael growled.

"If I don't do something, dinner is likely to be inedible."

Michael glanced at Caswell and apparently clamped down on what he'd been about to say. Chloe ducked her head again. Given the direction of their conversation, she could guess that just now dinner was the farthest thing from his mind. "All right. But mind you don't take too long."

"I'll be back as soon as I can," she promised, and left the room, Caswell closing the door behind her.

Left alone, Michael poured himself a generous glass of brandy and stared thoughtfully at the door. So. She'd cropped her hair. Who, he wondered, had put her up to that? Chloe had never before cared two figs about being fash-

ionable. After a brief while, it had become one of the things
he liked about her. Not for the world would he change that;
he very much liked her just as she was. The notion was
still strange to him. After all, they had not married for love.

The door opened and Chloe came in. "Whew!" she said
inelegantly. "I'm coming to believe you're right, Michael.
We should simply hire a cook. Thank you." This, as he
handed her a glass of sherry. "I know his sauces are divine,
but he throws a tantrum every other week. Is it worth it to
have him in the kitchen simply to be *au courant?*"

"By all means, my dear, do what you think best."

"A good, plain cook," she went on. "Perhaps there's one
available who doesn't disdain sauces for when we entertain.
I take it we will be entertaining?"

"Do you wish to?"

"I would, rather. We've never done anything of the sort,
not even at Chimneys."

"It's your decision. I know you dislike being in company."

"Bosh, not with friends. Besides, I need to show everyone my hair." She gave him the dazzling smile that never
failed to captivate him. "Perhaps I'll set a new style. The
bumblebroth."

He laughed at that. Now that was more like his Chloe,
outspoken, blunt. "Hm. My Chloe, fashion's darling."

Chloe went still, her goblet held partway to her mouth.
Now what was that all about, he wondered. "Yes," she said,
taking a sip of sherry at last, though her eyes were still
startled. "That would be a change."

"Yes. I—"

Michael's sentence was interrupted by the sound of the
dinner bell. "The chef must have rescued the soup."

"Let us hope so. If he believes he hasn't, heaven knows
what he'll do this time."

"And that might ruin tonight."

She laid her hand along his arm for him to escort her
into the dining room, and smiled dazzlingly again. "We
can't have that," she said in a husky voice.

"No," he agreed, returning her intense gaze. "Nothing must happen to do that."

As it happened, nothing did.

Some of Chloe's admirers came to call the following day, bearing flowers and compliments on her cropped hair. If most of the compliments rang hollow, Chloe paid them no mind. She was aware of only two things: Edwin, lounging in a chair across from her, and the night before. Of the two, the time she had spent with Michael took precedence. *My Chloe.* The thought of his calling her that still warmed her. Was she his Chloe? She knew now that he called her his dear almost absentmindedly, but this was different. This was far more personal, and thus more important. Was he coming to care for her, at least a little?

"Well, cuz," Edwin said after the others were gone, claiming the familiarity of kinship to stay past the allotted half hour for a morning call. "I see you did crop your hair."

Chloe, arranging some of her flowers in a vase, grimaced. "I know, don't tell me. I must look a perfect quiz."

"Chloe, you wound me. Would I say a thing like that?"

"Yes."

He laughed. "I wasn't sure what to think last evening when I realized how much you've changed, but now I know."

"Oh?"

"I like you. Yes, that is it. I like you."

"How very condescending of you."

"Yes, isn't it?"

His grin was so enthusiastic that it was contagious, and she grinned back. "Who would think it, for two old enemies."

"I was never your enemy, Chloe."

Her smile faded. "Odd. I've a different memory."

"Surely that's in the past. We were children then."

Not always. He had been an adult during one of their

worst times together. The worst time for her, that is. "Perhaps," she said, noncommittally.

His eyes narrowed, a trait she remembered from long ago. "Chloe, you sound as if you don't trust me."

"Have I reason to?"

He didn't answer right away. "No, I suppose you don't. I'm sorry for it."

"You almost sound sincere, Edwin."

"Because I am." His gaze seemed to bore through her. "I admire what you've done, Chloe. You've taken on the *ton* and managed to succeed, in spite of everything."

He couldn't know how little she cared anymore about what the *ton* thought of her. "Mm-hm."

"Cutting your hair like that—that was brave."

"And fashionable, Edwin?"

"Not exactly, but you tried."

"Not for the reasons you might think."

"Oh, you have no idea of what I think."

That put paid to her amusement. No, she didn't. It made him far more dangerous than he had been as a child, when his scorn for her had been obvious. "Edwin, I think it's best if we see each other as little as possible," she said crisply.

"But why?" He leaned forward. "We've grown up, Chloe. The past is past. In fact, I do believe I like you."

She regarded him steadily. "Under other circumstances, I might like you, too."

"Circumstances being our childhood."

"You taunted me unceasingly."

"True," he conceded. "I was young then, Chloe. I'm different now."

"Are you? The last time I saw you, you criticized my hair."

"Did I?"

"Surely you remember."

"If I was so ungallant—"

"You often have been."

"I don't remember it."

"So do you think this is flattering?" she asked, tugging one of her curls out. "It will be straight again before the evening, since 'tis so damp outside."

He twisted to look out the window. "So it is, dash it."

"Why?"

"I'd hoped to take you driving in the park."

"At the fashionable hour, or are you afraid to be seen with me then?"

"Cry pax, cuz. We never have been together but that we must be at each other's throats."

"I don't believe it was my fault, most of the time."

He smiled, and this time it wasn't a nice one. "If you could but have seen yourself—"

"Edwin." Her voice was quiet. "I believe I must ask you to leave."

He looked startled, and then pursed his lips. "That was unkind of me, wasn't it?"

"Quite." She rose. "Now, if you'll excuse me, I really must go. It will be time for luncheon soon."

Edwin rose as well. "I meant what I said, Chloe. I really would like to take you driving in the park today. For no particular reason," he said, quickly. "Simply because we are cousins who never knew each other well."

There were a number of things she could say to that, but, oddly enough, he seemed sincere. "Very well," she said slowly. "A drive it will be."

"You're going driving with whom?" Michael asked, startled.

"With Edwin," she repeated.

Michael frowned. "Why him, of all people?"

"He asked." Chloe turned from the mirror in her room, where she was adjusting the ribbon of her bonnet so that it was tied fetchingly under her left ear. His wife, it seemed, had a bit more vanity in her than she cared to admit.

"Chloe, what is between you two?"

Her eyes caught his in the mirror. "Why, nothing. Why would you think there was?"

"There's always tension between you when you're together."

She shrugged. "It was difficult between us when we were young."

If he weren't mistaken, there was strain in her voice. "How difficult?"

"Nothing so very much. He teased me, but then everyone did."

"Because you were supposed to be clumsy."

"I was—am—clumsy, Michael."

"Not with me."

"No, thank heavens." She paused, looking thoughtfully at her reflection. "Not at *ton* affairs anymore, either. I think because they don't matter to me very much."

"They don't matter to most people who have a brain."

That made her laugh. "True. Neither does driving the park in the afternoon."

"Then why do it?" he repeated.

She tilted her head. "I think because I've done it so rarely."

"All you had to do was ask."

"Michael, do I hear some jealousy in your voice?"

"No," he denied, more vehemently than necessary.

She walked over to him and stroked her fingers along his forehead. It touched him in a startling way for so innocent a touch. "Don't frown so. You'll have the headache."

His head was not the part of his body that ached, he thought wryly, and brought her hand to his mouth. "Can I not convince you to stay home?"

"And do what?"

"I'm sure we could think of something," he said, looking up from her hand.

"Michael! In the middle of the afternoon?" She blushed, a reaction he always enjoyed teasing from her. " 'Tis scandalous."

"True. That's what makes it more—enjoyable." He held his arms out to her. "Come here."

She stepped close to him with no hesitation. He was just about to draw her near when there was a knock on her door. "I—yes, what is it?" she called, and Michael turned away, cursing inwardly.

A footman stood at the door. "My apologies, my lady, but Caswell sent me to tell you that Mr. Hempstead is here."

"Thank you, John." She smiled briefly at the footman and then turned back to Michael. "I'm sorry, Michael."

"No more than I am," he said.

He didn't realize how much of his frustration showed in his voice until Chloe reached up to stroke his forehead again. "I am sorry, Michael. It's just that he's family."

"Oh? And what am I?"

"Family," she said. "My husband. This isn't fair to you, I know, but I did promise."

"We promised the Nelsons last night, as I recall."

"This is different. It's one person, rather than several hundred." She held her hand out to him. "Michael, it will only be for an hour or so."

"I may not be home then."

"Michael!" She drew back, surprised. "Are you so very angry at me?"

He sighed, his annoyance fading. She almost looked frightened, though since they'd married he'd given her no reason to be afraid of him. "No. I cannot say I like Hempstead, but I realize you need to have your own life."

"I'd rather be with you, if 'tis any comfort."

"I know." He pulled her back to him. She came willingly into his arms, resting her head on his chest without any apparent concern about crushing her bonnet. His sense of humor reasserted itself. Had he thought before that his Chloe was vain? "No, I'm glad for you, my dear, that you're finally able to get about in society, without being embarrassed."

"Without making a fool of myself, you mean," she said wryly, as she pulled away from him.

"You were never the fool." His voice was quiet. "The people who laughed at you were."

She reached up on her toes to kiss him, a brief caress that unexpectedly turned into something more. "Wait for me," she said, breathlessly. "I promise I'll not be above an hour."

"I'll be counting the minutes," he promised with mock ardor, and, on a laugh, she left the room.

The door closed gently behind her. She really was gone, he thought, his smile fading as quickly as it had come. *Damn!* Catching up a pillow from the comfortable chintz armchair, he flung it across the room with all of his considerable strength. Edwin Hempstead, of all people. *Damn!*

The park was crowded when Edwin turned his phaeton onto the carriage way, at such an angle that Chloe held tightly to the seat to prevent herself from falling out. Already today she had made one faux pas, stepping on her carriage dress of tan twill trimmed with green braid. She hadn't done anything like that in quite some time. "I'm surprised there are so many people here, in such weather."

"No one misses the promenade unless 'tis actually raining," Edwin said.

"I've been known to."

"But you've never considered yourself fashionable before."

"I don't particularly consider myself fashionable now." For a brief moment she regretted the conversation with Michael and what she had given up for this drive, which meant virtually nothing to her. Why in the world had she chosen Edwin and a ride on a damp, misty day, when she could have been with her husband in—well, never mind, she thought, ducking her head to hide the flush she was certain must be there. It was foolish of her to have done so, when she'd seen at various affairs that so many other women wished for Lord Lyndon's attention. At least, she thought they did, judging by the way they had looked at him, by the way they had placed their elegantly gloved hands on his arm, holding tighter than propriety allowed. Perhaps she was the one who should be jealous.

That was it, of course, she thought, belatedly realizing the reason behind Michael's behavior. He was jealous. Over her? *Oh, my.* Or was it simply because she was out with Edwin? She frowned. For the life of her, she didn't know.

Edwin chose that moment to look over at her. "Is something amiss?" he asked.

"Hm? Oh, no, nothing. A slight headache."

"You should have told me. I would have insisted we remain at home."

"We?"

"I mean that I would have kept you company, of course. I imagine Lyndon is out at his club this time of day."

Not for the world would she admit to him just where Michael was. "He did have luncheon there. He's a member of White's."

"I know." His voice darkened. "Even though he used to be penniless."

She looked up at him in astonishment. "What does that have to say to anything?"

"Nothing of import," he said innocently.

She looked away, so furious that she wanted to be let down that minute. Oh, she knew what he'd meant by that comment. "I suppose you're a member."

His face darkened. "Not everyone who applies gets in."

She frowned in surprise. He'd been blackballed from joining? But why? It was a disturbing thought. Still annoyed, she glanced at a couple who were riding together in the opposite direction, their gazes locked on each other. The man wasn't above average in appearance, yet the woman, garbed in a severely, but beautifully, cut riding habit of burgundy merino, looked at him almost worshipfully. He, in turn, appeared totally besotted. What would it be like, she wondered enviously, to be with a man who loved her as much as she loved him? What would it be like if Michael returned her feelings? she wondered, and sighed.

"What is it?" Edwin asked.

"Hm? Oh, not so very much. I was watching that woman over there, and thinking of how well she rides," she said, on the spur of the moment.

Edwin followed her gaze. "So she does." He looked back down at her. "Chloe, never tell me you still don't ride."

"No."

"With Lyndon as a husband?"

"No, I fear not."

"I'm surprised, considering his interests."

"I still fear horses, and he's been kind enough not to press me." She paused to wave at Lady Sherbourne, though in the crush of people there was no chance for more. "I'm sorry for it, actually, as he bought me a mount. A sweet goer, he said."

"Lyndon wouldn't choose any but the best."

"Oh, no. He knows so very much about sports."

"Bought with your money, I suppose."

"Oh, give over, Edwin. I am tired of dealing with these little barbs of yours."

To his credit, he had the grace to look shamefaced. "That wasn't well done of me, was it?" he asked. "My apologies, Chloe. It's hard to break old habits."

"You could at least try."

"I will," he said, nodding. "Ah, I dislike it when traffic becomes as slow as this."

"To see and be seen. Should I remove my bonnet and show everyone my hair?"

He laughed. "You're a treasure, Chloe. How is it I never knew it before?"

She didn't answer right away. "Perhaps because I didn't know it myself."

He was still smiling. "Are you saying Lyndon's made you realize it?"

"I believe he has," she said stiffly. What was between her and Michael was too private to share.

"Certainly no one else did. No, that wasn't an insult. He must be a perceptive man."

More than you know. Certainly Michael had never taken her mistakes and turned them against her. That was all her problems ever had been, mistakes. Yet everyone had caught her at them and teased her about them unmercifully, Edwin most of all. What in the world was she doing with him, when she could be with Michael? "I wish you would take me home."

Edwin looked at her, astonished. "Have I done aught wrong?"

"We've nothing to say to each other, Edwin. I don't know why we should try."

"Because we've changed—"

"But that is it. I don't think you have."

"But—"

"I suspect you're as cruel as ever you were."

"I was cruel, wasn't I?" he said, after a moment.

"Yes."

"Why didn't you say something?"

"Would you have listened? I doubt it," she went on, before he could answer. "Certainly it was great sport to make me cry."

He winced. "I hate to admit it, but it was."

"I believe you'll pardon me if I don't wish to subject myself to that again."

"Chloe, I must beg your pardon. I was young. I didn't know better."

"I don't think that would stop you now."

"Do you plan to keep insulting me?" he snapped.

"Ah." She smiled humorlessly. " 'Tis different when you're the one receiving the hurts."

"Damn it!" he exclaimed, staring ahead. "I believe I begin to agree with you. We should stop seeing each other."

She paused. In spite of the past, in spite of her distrust of him now, he was family. She was bound to see him again through the years. "I'm sorry it has to be this way."

"So am I." He glanced over at her, and slowly smiled. "Do you know, Chloe, you've become a dashed attractive woman?"

"Bosh."

"I mean it. Out of the common way. You've your own style."

"Bosh," she said again.

He grinned. "Another woman would be simpering at what I said. You say what you think."

Thank God for Michael, she thought. He'd helped her find that freedom. "It's about time I did, rather than feeling hurt and trying to hide it."

"I've had a thought. About how I could make up the past to you."

"What?" she said warily, in spite of herself.

"I'll teach you how to ride."

Fourteen

"I beg your pardon?" Chloe said in astonishment.

"Admit it, Chloe. Whatever my faults, I ride well."

"So you do, but Edwin, really!"

"Are you sure?" he said softly. "Wouldn't you like to ride with Lyndon?"

Above all things. "I doubt you're the best teacher for me."

"Think, Chloe, what a pleasant surprise 'twould be for him."

"Think of how he'll react when he learns who taught me. I think he'd challenge you to a round of fisticuffs, if nothing else." She considered his offer for a moment, and then shook her head. "No, Edwin. Not even to please Lyndon."

"You're a fool." His voice was crisp. "He's not trying to teach you."

"Perhaps, but I do know how to drive." *In a way.*

That earned her his startled attention. "Good gad, you surely don't!"

"Nothing so dashing as your rig," she went on, "nor do I drive as you do." *And thank heavens for that.*

"I'll be dashed." He shook his head. "And you dance, as well. Chloe, what other hidden talents do you possess?"

She smiled. "You'd be surprised."

"Perhaps 'tis just as well. You aren't precisely the most graceful person I've met."

"You aren't precisely the nicest I've met," she retorted.

"Very sharp-tongued. You've changed."

" 'Tis about time."

"I'm not so certain."

"It means you can't tease me anymore, can you?"

"Hmph." He drove for a moment in silence. "You've developed a sense of style, Chloe. I hadn't realized. That gown is well made, but the color is a bit too dark for you."

Her jaw set, too. "How kind of you."

Apparently he caught the irony in her tone. "I am only thinking of your good."

"Oh, really."

"Yes. My apologies," he said. "You have a nicer figure than you have let anyone see, and an erect carriage."

Chloe examined that for any criticisms, and found none. She *had* hidden her shape, along with everything else about her. "Thank you, Edwin."

"Mayhap you could ride," he went on thoughtfully. " 'Tis a pity you fear horses."

"Yes." *And you.* Yet, no matter how she felt, she couldn't give in. "No, Edwin. I don't want to be with you."

"So you wish to remain Miss Bumblebroth?"

"Is that a threat?" she said, as she had the night before.

"Take it as you will. Remember our childhood," he added.

Her hands clutched spasmodically on her skirt. "And you say you like me," she said bitterly.

"I do. I'd like to spend more time with you."

She looked up at him. "I don't understand you at all."

He smiled. "You don't need to. Simply remember. I always get what I want."

She stared ahead, her mind whirling. If she gave in, she would be safe—for a time. Oh, but she didn't want to be under his power anymore. "No," she said, her voice shakier than she would have liked. "I won't change my mind."

Again he looked at her. "So be it, then."

She didn't answer. What he would do, besides encourage everyone to use that hateful name again, she didn't know.

She had never known what he would do. She wasn't alone this time, though. This time she had Michael. *Oh, Michael,* she thought. Thank God she would be with him soon.

Michael was just coming down the stairs when Chloe came in. He'd been anticipating her return for the past hour, but one look at her face dampened his ardor. She was pale, and her eyes looked haunted. "What is it?" he asked sharply, going to her with his hands outstretched.

Chloe's expression was guarded. "Nothing."

"Nothing?" He felt suddenly, irrationally angry. It was obvious she hadn't enjoyed her drive with Hempstead, but he doubted she'd tell him why. She never did. Why had she accepted his invitation? *He* wanted to be the one driving her, perhaps showing her how he could drive to an inch, as if they were courting and not a married couple of nearly two months. He didn't want her strolling in the park with one of her lonely or eccentric admirers. He didn't want her shopping or visiting with her newfound friends, the young ladies who were otherwise beneath people's notice because they were poor or on the shelf or unattractive. Not that he begrudged her such pleasures. Rather, he was proud of her for noticing such people and for being kind to them. Sometimes, though, as today, he wanted her to himself.

"What did he do?" he asked, more gently.

To his dismay, tears filled her eyes. "I—nothing. Oh, nothing. I don't know how to say it."

In spite of Caswell's presence, in spite of the footmen standing at attention in the hall, he gathered her close. "Let's go into the salon, shall we?"

She had clutched at his coat, hiding her face against his chest, but she nodded. "All right."

His arm about her waist, he led her down the hall to the salon, which each preferred to the less intimate drawing room when they were alone. He settled her in a comfortable brocade armchair, and then handed her a glass filled with a small amount of brandy. "Here. Drink this. 'Twill do you good."

She eyed the glass with misgiving. "I've never had it."

"Drink it back. It will help." Still doubtful, she drank it and then choked, her eyes watering. He waited, hunched on the sofa across from her, until at last she raised her head and wiped her eyes. "Better?"

"A bit."

"Do you feel ready to talk?"

She looked anywhere but at him. " 'Tis so little a thing."

"You seem afraid of him." He reached over for her hands. "My dear, your hands are like ice."

She pulled her hands free and stroked them down his face. "I feel better now, Michael." Now her hands slipped down his neck. "The brandy helped." Along his shoulders. "What of our afternoon together?"

She was caressing his chest, making him shudder in response. Almost against his will, he slid his arms about her waist and drew her near, his head lowering, until he glanced into her eyes. Their expression was stark, still haunted, rather than soft with desire.

It was enough to cool his passion. Something was very wrong. He had the right, the duty, the desire to protect her. "It will have to wait," he said firmly, pulling her clinging hands from his neck. "I think this is more important, though I don't know why you won't talk to me about him."

She averted her head. "Because it doesn't matter."

He knew he wasn't particularly perceptive, but even he knew why she had tried to inflame him. "It does, if it bothers you so. Tell me, Chloe," he urged. "Let me help you."

"I'm not sure you can, but . . ."

"Let me try."

"I—I don't know what he's going to do."

"Do?" he said sharply. "Did he threaten you?"

"Not exactly, but . . ."

"I shall kill him."

She looked up, astonished. "A bit extreme, don't you think?"

"Not where you're concerned, no."

"Michael, you're hurting me."

He looked down at her hands and loosened his grip. "I'm sorry, my dear. But I can't have him hurting you."

"Do you care that much, then?" she asked, softly.

"Yes, damn it, I care. I'll have no man insult my wife."

"Oh," she said, and looked away. "Your wife."

"Yes. What did you think?"

"Nothing," she said, and seemed to come to a decision of her own. "He didn't really threaten anything. 'Tis just that I don't trust him." She paused. "I don't know what he'll do."

"Chloe—"

"You may as well sit back." She sighed. " 'Tis a long story."

He stayed where he was, holding her hands. "What is?"

"My childhood. He teased me when I was young. Everyone did. Oh, don't look at me like that," she said, irritated. "It was long ago, and I brought much of it on myself."

"For God's sake, Chloe!"

"You've seen for yourself how clumsy I am."

"I thought you didn't believe that anymore." He looked at her, hard. "Does Hempstead say you are?"

"No. Memories, I suppose." She glanced away. " 'Tis such a little thing. I'm not sure you'll understand."

Michael touched her cheek lightly. "Tell me, dear," he said, and, though he didn't know why, she broke down. Swiftly, though she waved him away, he gathered her into his arms, rocking her while she clutched the lapels of his coat. "Ah, Chloe, was it so very bad?"

She pulled back a little, wiping at her eyes with her fingers. "I daresay you won't think so—"

"Not if it hurts you so."

"Oh, please let me get my handkerchief."

"Here." He reached into his pocket and pulled out his own, freshly pressed and larger than hers. "I've a feeling you'll need this more."

Chloe mopped at her face. "I never cry."

"No? Why not?"

She crumpled the handkerchief into a ball. "It does no good."

He settled her against him on the couch. "Better?"

"Yes." She leaned against his shoulder. "Do you remember when I told you that my father tried to teach me to ride?"

"Yes," he said grimly.

"That was the start of it."

"The start of the teasing?"

"No, the worst of it. They always had teased me a little. Helena and Edwin were already living with us. Their father had run off with Helena's governess." She blew her nose again. "He was, I gather, an out-and-out bounder."

"Hm. So that's how Hempstead came by it."

"He was the oldest," Chloe went on, as if Michael hadn't spoken. "He was the leader of us all."

Ah. He understood that. "Because his father had left."

Chloe looked up at him, startled. "I don't understand."

He smiled down at her a little. "When some men don't feel particularly strong, they try to prove themselves."

"But he doesn't act weak."

"In your opinion," he said dryly. "Anyone who torments a little girl—how much younger than he are you?"

"Five years."

"Anyone who torments a child that much younger is weak."

"Oh." She took a moment to consider that. "I don't know much about men, I suppose."

He grinned down at her. "You do well enough."

She rubbed her head against his shoulder. "I try."

For a moment all he could think of was her, and how she felt in his arms. "Witch. Don't try to distract me again."

"I take it very unkindly of you to make me tell this," she said severely. "When being here like this . . ."

His arms tightened about her. "I know."

"I don't want to remember it, Michael."

"Do you ever truly forget?" he asked.

"No," she said slowly. "I suppose 'tis too upsetting."

"Worse than casting up your accounts at a *ton* ball?"

Chloe pulled back and glared up at him. "It was hot and crowded and I'd been ill!"

"That's my Chloe. Be angry with me. Though I was only funning you."

"Oh." She frowned, clearly puzzled. "Well, no, I suppose that was the outside of enough. I—"

"Enter," Michael called, at a knock on the door.

Caswell stepped in. "Excuse me, my lord, my lady. Lord Sherbourne has called for you, sir."

Michael looked down at Chloe, who had pulled away at the sound of the knock, and then turned to the butler. "Pray make my apologies to him, Caswell. I cannot see him just now."

"Very good, my lord," Caswell said, and went out.

"Won't he be annoyed?" Chloe asked.

"Sherbourne? Yes, I imagine so. 'Tis not my concern."

"You're surprising me today, Michael."

"Because I care about you more than I do about others? That shouldn't come as such a shock."

She looked up at him, her expression soft. "Do you care?"

"Of course I do. 'Tis why I worry about Hempstead."

She sighed. "Oh, him."

"Yes, him. I'd call him out—"

"Michael."

"—but I'd like to know why I would do so."

"It's not worth a challenge."

"I'll decide that, my dear."

She sighed. "Oh, very well. As I said, it started when I tried to learn to ride. You see, Edwin hadn't paid me much mind until then, while I . . ."

"What?"

"I adored him. He was so much older and he seemed so self-assured, where I never was, and he was so handsome."

"Huh."

"I thought he was. I was only five, remember."

"I hope you've learned."

"Oh, yes. No one could be as handsome as you."

For a moment he was startled, and then he let out a laugh. "I truly never do know what to expect with you."

"Good." She snuggled against him. "God—forgive me if I swear, but this seems to call for it—God, I'm so angry!"

Again he was startled. "Why?"

"Because I didn't deserve it! That horrible riding lesson. My father never understood me from the first. They were all bruising riders, you know, even my mother. I once heard him tell her that if he didn't know better, he would have thought she'd played him false."

"About you?"

"About me."

"This does call for swearing," he said grimly.

"I so wanted to keep up with the others, but they were older than I, and stronger, and I couldn't. For the most part, Edwin ignored me, until that riding lesson."

"What happened?" he asked quietly.

"I was so scared of horses, and yet they fascinated me, too." She looked up at him. "Does that make sense?"

He didn't answer right away. "I'm fascinated by the water." He raised her hand to his mouth. "Life wounds us all, Chloe. It doesn't have to take something big to do so."

"I know. I'm glad you realize that." She sighed. "He'd bought a pony for me. I think if I'd been left alone, I would have wanted to learn, but he had so very little patience. He expected me to be like the others."

Michael straightened, appalled. "He put you up on the pony without preparing you?"

"Yes. I was terrified."

"But surely he used a leading string."

"Oh, yes, of course, but, oh, Michael." Her eyes were bleak. "As soon as I had some control, he set me on my own in a paddock, and the pony threw me. It had been raining. I landed in mud."

"Ah, Chloe."

"It was all over me." She swallowed and pulled away.

"Papa yelled at me. He called me clumsy and stupid. He said I could have hurt the pony, and he went over to check its legs."

"Not you?" Michael asked incredulously.

"No. I got up, but it was slippery. I fell again. Everyone was there, Michael. The others, the grooms—and they all laughed at me." She leaned forward, her elbows on her knees, her head in her hands. "Papa was out of all reason cross with me. He demanded I get onto the pony again."

He ached for her. "Did you?"

"No. Mama was there by that time. One of the grooms had gone for her. She stood up to my father and took me away."

"Good."

"She was the only one who could put my father in his place. And she managed the others—"

"You always call them that."

"Who?"

"Your brother and your cousins."

"That is what they are, aren't they?"

"This is different. As if you're apart from them."

"I suppose I am," she said slowly, as if examining that for the first time.

"God, Chloe, I'd go mad if I had to live with Helena."

She laughed. "Yes, I can't quite understand what Stephen ever saw in her. But then, he has little imagination, and he does have his mistresses—oh!" She clamped her hand over her mouth. "I'm not supposed to know about them, am I?"

He was grinning. "Chloe, you are a treasure."

She ducked her head. "Thank you."

"It's amazing," he said thoughtfully, "that after all you went through, you are as independent and brave as you are."

"Thank you," she said again, sounding astonished. "Do you know, I think that in some way it made me stronger. But I cannot abide teasing. I really can't."

"I understand that." He stroked his fingers across the nape of her neck. "Is that it?"

She looked fixedly at a painting hanging across the room,

though he suspected she didn't really see it. "No. They teased me terribly. They knew they could make me cry, you see. And it was such a little thing that hurt me," she said, as she had before. "I'm not certain you'll understand why it bothered me so. No one else ever did."

"Not many people try." He was holding her hand now, stroking his thumb across her palm, in an odd way taking solace from giving her solace. "When I went down to Oxford for the entrance examination, I visited a friend who happened to live in the same house James had lived in." He paused. He could still remember the pain of it as if it had happened yesterday. "I passed his lodgings, Chloe."

"Oh, Michael—"

"I knew he was gone, it had been almost seven years, but being there . . . God help me, but when I went into his lodgings I thought he'd be there. And he wasn't."

"Oh, Michael." She kissed his cheek. "I am so sorry."

"It made me realize, for the first time, that he was gone. I don't think I'd quite accepted it before. My parents don't know about this, by the by."

"They won't hear of it from me."

"Thank you. It helped that I lived in a different house."

"And you turned to sport," she said softly.

He looked at her with arched brows. "I've always enjoyed athletics," he said defensively.

"But were you so involved before his death?"

"Were you so involved in your painting as a child?"

"Eventually, yes," she said, to his relief letting the subject of his past go. It was unsettling, what she had just said. "My past sounds so insignificant in comparison."

"Yet it marked you, Chloe." He paused. "Should I plant Hempstead a facer for whatever happened?"

She laughed. "Mercy, no. It doesn't warrant that. Most of it was just childhood things. Children can be cruel."

"Was he?"

"They all were. They called me names. Clumsy Chloe. They set traps for me so I'd fall, or they'd treat me nicely and then run away—childhood cruelty, but it hurt."

Damn him. There was little doubt in his mind who had been behind everything. "Were they all Hempstead's ideas?"

"He was the leader. But do you know—and this is the odd thing—I still adored him."

"Good God, why?"

"Partly because I always had, and partly because," she frowned, "I wanted him to like me."

"Good God." He frowned, trying to puzzle that out. "So he'd stop teasing you," he said after a moment.

"Yes. I realized that later."

"What happened, Chloe?"

She took a deep breath. "My father held a house party the summer I was nine. My mother had died, so I'd lost the only person who ever truly cared for me. My father certainly didn't."

"Unfortunately, Chloe, children often don't matter to their parents in our set."

"I know. But, Michael, we won't be like that, will we?"

He leaned forward, suddenly alert, suddenly hopeful. "Chloe, are you—"

"No." She shook her head and then brushed back a strand of hair. "I so wish I were."

He reached out his hand, palm up, and after a moment she laid hers in it. "So do I," he said, though the idea filled him with sudden terror. Not for himself as a father, but for what she would have to go through.

"I know you need an heir—"

"Stubble it," he said roughly. "Is that all you think I care about?"

She smiled shyly. "I hope not."

"It isn't." He kissed her hand and then drew her back against him. "You'd be a good mother, Chloe."

"I hope so. I'd certainly protect my child," she said, so fiercely that he held up a hand in self-defense.

"Pax," he said, smiling. "I would, too."

"I know." She sighed, and he could sense the lightness ebbing out of her. "A child so needs two strong parents."

"And you had neither."

"I know."

"Tell me the rest of it, dear."

She sighed, and leaned against him. "Oh, very well. The house party was wonderful at first. Some of the people had children. Michael, I started to have friends for the first time in my life."

"Hempstead left you alone, then."

"Oh, no. The opposite."

"The opposite? Good God, how?"

"He was losing his control over me. He didn't like that." She paused. "He doesn't like it now."

He was suddenly alert. "Does he try to control you now?"

"Yes. He tries teasing me. Goading me."

Damn the man. "I won't let him," he said grimly.

"Shall I tell him that?"

"No. I'd like to have that pleasure."

"I'll give you it, gladly."

"Thank you." What did Hempstead do to tease her now? There'd been that incident when he'd somehow made her try to drive his phaeton, but what else wasn't she telling him? "What did he do, when you were young? During the house party."

"He really couldn't do anything, for a time. There was a boy there who was a bit younger, but already larger, and his sister was a particular friend of mine. He stood up for me if anyone started the teasing. Can you imagine that?"

"It must have felt good."

"It felt wonderful, until he and his sister—my best friend—went visiting with their parents."

They were getting to it, he sensed. "What happened?"

"We had an old oak tree that everyone climbed. Except me, of course. There were handholds all the way up the trunk, and some sturdy branches to sit on. It terrified me."

"Why did you climb it?"

She stared at him. "How do you know I did?"

"A guess. Hempstead was there, wasn't he?"

"Yes."

"Was it his idea?"

She frowned. "I don't precisely know. He's good at that, you know, thinking of something but letting someone else make the suggestion."

"Which was?"

"A dare of sorts. They called me a coward for not wanting to climb." She took a deep breath. "So I did."

"Even though you were scared?"

"Even then."

"True courage, Chloe."

"Do you think so?" She looked up at him. "If I'd had courage, I would have walked away and not cared what they thought, instead of going along with them."

"But you did something you feared, and you survived it."

She looked thoughtful. "Yes, I did, didn't I?" she said slowly. "I never thought of it that way."

"Did everyone climb?"

"Yes, they all went first. I suppose I thought I could get out of it if I held back. Of course, they wouldn't let me." She swallowed. "I don't know how I climbed, but I did. The trouble was, I couldn't get down. It was so high, and I was so scared. And I had no idea of how to climb trees."

"Damn him," he said quietly. "He knew that."

"It wasn't the worst part," she said, as if he hadn't spoken. "Even though I couldn't get down, even though I was crying and they were laughing at me, I begged them all please to be my friends. I wanted them to be my friends."

"Friends!"

"Yes. I know why, now. I thought friends wouldn't act as they did. It shames me so."

"It shouldn't." He stroked her hair. "What happened next?"

"They ran away."

"And left you there?" he asked incredulously.

"Yes." She looked away, biting her lips. "I was in the tree for three hours," she said, her voice unsteady. "It wasn't

until a footman saw me that someone got me down. My
father was furious when he heard about it."

"Good."

"No, you don't understand. He was furious at me."

"Good God, why?"

"That I didn't get down by myself. And he caned me."

Michael's hands tightened. If the man weren't dead, he'd
thrash him. "Were you caned often?"

"Of course. We all were." She looked up. "Weren't
you?"

"God, no. Not until I went to Eton." How the devil had
she survived her childhood? "Was Hempstead punished,
too?"

"All of them were. It only made them resent me. Do you
see?" She looked up at him. "Such a foolish thing. It happened so long ago, and yet—"

"It hurts."

She nodded, and then, without warning, broke down.
With a little exclamation he pulled her closer, and she burrowed against him, sobbing as he had never heard anyone
cry before. He wondered if this were the first time she'd
done so. She must have lost so much that day, her innocence, her confidence.

"This is so foolish," she said after a moment. "It was
such a little thing."

"Not so little." He rocked her in his arms. "Is this the
first time anyone's agreed with you about how much it
hurt?"

She looked up at him in surprise, her eyes and nose red,
her curls going straight. His Chloe. "How do you know?"

"Because after I saw James's lodgings, I told my friend
about it."

"And he didn't understand? Oh, Michael."

"As I said, the little things." He smiled wryly down at
her. "I am going to give you an order."

"Oh, are you going to be an overbearing husband, then?"

He smiled. "Overbearing and domineering. My dear, I'd
not see you hurt again."

"How would I be?" she said in surprise.

"I don't trust Hempstead, especially after what you just told me. I don't want you to see him again."

"I've already told him I won't, though he didn't like it."

"Power and control."

"Yes. So." She walked her fingers up his chest. "Pray do not be the domineering husband with me."

He bent to kiss her. "Only if I need to be."

"I never said I wouldn't obey you. Unless, of course, I don't think your orders make sense."

"Oh, of course. I don't know why I'd think otherwise." He bent his head and kissed her deeply. "You are an incredibly brave, strong woman, to have come through what you have."

"It doesn't seem so, most of the time. I feel like the most terrible coward."

"You face your fears, Chloe. Most people don't do that."

"I didn't, before. I hid away from them for three years."

"No wonder you did."

"Why?"

"The teasing, that awful name—it must have seemed like what happened in your childhood."

She went still. "How is it you know so much about me?"

He shook his head. "I don't know."

"You're right, of course," she said, looking up at him. Her eyes today were green-gold, reflecting the shade of her carriage dress. "You helped me face my fears again."

"Did I, dear?"

"Yes." She nestled her head against his shoulder. "You cannot know what it has meant to me, having you beside me."

Or what it meant to him, he thought in sudden surprise. "You cannot know how it has helped me to have someone to talk to about James," he said in a low voice.

Chloe looked up at him. "In what way?"

He was silent, struggling to find words to express the feelings that he hadn't known until this moment were there. "His death bothers me still. I suppose it always will."

"Michael, you weren't responsible for it—"

"I bear some of the blame," he interrupted her. "Had I not rocked the boat—"

"Who started it?"

Again he was quiet, concentrating hard to remember. "He did."

"There you are, then."

He shook his head. "I'll never be completely free of it, Chloe."

She laid her hand over his. "It was a terrible thing, Michael."

"Yes. You're the only one I've ever talked to about it."

"Mercy! Why?"

"There's no one else," he said simply.

"Not in your family?"

"My sisters never knew him, you see. As for my parents . . ." He took a deep breath. "I'm afraid to."

"Mercy, why?"

"I don't wish to upset them," he said, after a long silence.

"I don't think they blame you."

"Nor do I. My father can be abrupt, but 'tis just his way." He paused. "The most he does is to compare me to James, but he always did."

She looked up at him again. "They live with it as much as you do. It must be terrible, to lose a child."

He frowned. "What are you trying to say?"

"That mayhap talking will ease some of the pain, yours and theirs."

"Chloe, I'm not sure—"

She took his face between her hands. "Something needs to be settled between you, Michael. They need to know that you feel the pain as much as you do." She paused. "They need to know that you feel the blame."

" 'Twill bring it all back—"

"You're their son, and they love you. I've seen it." She peered closely at him. "I've seen it. Nothing can change that."

"I'm not so certain."

"I am. Trust me, Michael. Talking to you has helped me. Talking to them will help you all."

He gathered her close to him, doubtful still. Bringing up the past would only bring up the pain again. Yet, he thought, they lived with it, just as he did. How, he wondered, had he ever been so lucky as to have this girl in his life? And who would have guessed that he would come to need her as he did? "Perhaps I will," he said, and lowered his head. He nuzzled her forehead, kissed her eyes, her cheeks, her nose; traced the curve of her ear with his tongue, which he knew always made her moan, and then finally brought his mouth to hers, softly parted in anticipation. The kiss was long and sweet, reflecting relief that the past was past, that they had each found someone who understood, and yet the kiss was filled with growing anticipation.

"I've another idea," he said, when they parted for a moment.

"Mm?" She looked up at him, her eyes already heavy and soft. "What is that?"

"Shall we go upstairs, after all?

She pulled back abruptly. " 'Twill soon be time to dress for dinner!"

"Hang dinner. Well?" he said imperiously.

"Well, if you're going to be so domineering." She smiled slowly at him. "I suppose I must obey you."

"In this case I must insist." They rose. He put his arm around her waist and, knowing that for this moment there was only a total, all-encompassing closeness between them, led her upstairs.

Fifteen

"Too much traffic," Michael said some days later, as he and Chloe drove in his curricle in the park.

Chloe smiled up at him as he helped her alight from the carriage. "You would drive here at the fashionable hour."

"So I would," he said ruefully. "But I wished to display my fashionable wife to all the world."

Chloe laughed as she slipped her arm through his. "Oh, Michael, I'm hardly that."

"Of course you are." His voice was imperturbable. "You dress in the very best of styles, which suit you admirably—"

"You do not think this shade a trifle dark for me?" she asked in a stifled voice. She was wearing the carriage dress Edwin had so deplored—perhaps, she thought now in surprise, as a gesture of defiance to him.

"Too dark?" He gazed at her critically. "No, I believe it becomes you well. I like what it does to your eyes." His own eyes twinkled. "Cropped hair is fashionable as well."

"You are amazingly foolish," she said, but she smiled up at him, warmed by his compliments. In the past he had commented favorably upon her talent with numbers or with painting, but never her appearance. She wondered what he would say if she ever did learn to ride. She so wanted to share in his life. Maybe if she did, he would come to love her.

He gave the signal to his groom to attend to his team.

"We may as well walk, too. Lord knows we'd go faster than this crowd allows."

"Walking is more pleasant, I think."

"Lud, walking, Lyndon?" a voice came, and they turned, to see Lord Adam just behind them on the carriage path, astride a chestnut hack. "Where do you get the energy, dear boy?"

Michael grinned at him. "Come to that, how do you stay awake long enough to ride?"

"I am sitting, dear boy, don't you know?"

Michael laughed. "What do you here? I thought you despised the park at this time of day."

"Lud, but one must be fashionable. Actually," he said, abandoning his pose as he leaned forward in the saddle, "just trying to cut through to Mount Street." His eyes gleamed. "Been to Rundell and Bridges, you know."

"The wedding ring?" Chloe asked, interested now.

"Lud, no, she'd shoot me if I picked that out without her," he said, and then straightened. "Forget I said that, if you will."

"Of course," Michael said, after a moment.

"What did you buy?" Chloe asked, her own attempt at distraction, though her curiosity was piqued. "Or should I ask?"

"Something special. Green, to match her eyes."

"Emeralds. Oh, how lovely. A bracelet?"

"And earrings. Don't know how you women have the energy to wear those things."

Chloe burst out laughing. "Oh, give over! When I've seen you with any number of fobs and chains and quizzing glasses?"

Adam looked at Michael. "Teaching her cant, dear boy?"

"I didn't need to," Michael said wryly.

"Lud, married life. Don't know why I decided on a life sentence, myself."

"Oh, stubble it."

Adam grinned. "So I will, dear boy, so I will." He

glanced around. "I'm off. Chloe, lovely to see you, as always. Lyndon."

Michael and Chloe said their good-byes as he rode off. "I've never seen him like this over a woman," Michael said bemusedly.

"He loves her." She took his arm again as they began to stroll. "Michael, do you know if she does shoot? Something was said about it at Chimneys."

He was quiet a moment. "I gather there was something, but I don't know what. Whatever it was was kept dashed quiet."

"Did she shoot someone?" she asked in surprise.

"I don't know. One doesn't talk about something like that when it involves a lady. Adam certainly doesn't." He shook his head. "He's dashed protective of her."

"He loves her," Chloe said again, and turned to watch Lord Adam herself, pursing her lips as she did so. She wondered. Had she finally found a way to share Michael's life? The idea that had come to her just now, as she saw Lord Adam on horseback, wouldn't go away. He would be a good teacher, she thought, especially since he was so solicitous of his fiancée. Asking him would be an imposition on a friendship, and Elizabeth might mind. If, however, Lord Adam consented to teach her and she learned to ride, she could present her accomplishment to Michael, almost as a gift.

She turned to see Michael regarding her with a slight frown. "What is it?" she asked.

"Why do I have the strangest feeling I wouldn't like your thoughts just now?"

"Why, Michael. Such a thing to say."

"I mistrust that look in your eyes."

"Mercy, why?" she asked, this time in genuine surprise.

"Usually it means you are about to be outrageous."

"I'm sure I don't know what you mean."

"Don't you?" He looked at her suspiciously. "The first time I saw it was the day I proposed to you."

"Oh, well, I was outrageous that day."

"How many of those other incidents were due to that behavior?"

"What incidents?"

"The ones that made everyone think you clumsy."

Her amusement abruptly died. "I am clumsy, Michael."

He gave her a quick glance, and then laid his hand on hers. "I'm sorry, my dear. I didn't mean to hurt you."

"I know." She took a deep breath. "But how did you know about the other things?"

"Good God!" He stopped and stared down at her. "Then I was right?"

"Only about one," she confessed. "Well, perhaps two. I wouldn't show disrespect to the Queen in such a way, and I already had been feeling ill when I went to that ball."

"Ah. I'm sorry for that, my dear."

"Yes. That was when he—they began calling me Miss Bumblebroth."

"He?" Michael turned sharply toward her. "Who?"

"Oh, I don't know," she said vaguely. "I've always assumed it was a man who made up the name. I don't know why. Perhaps because men can be as spiteful as women at times."

"Certainly in our set," he agreed, to her relief. "Well? That leaves the incident of the lemonade."

She huffed with laughter. "Oh, I shouldn't laugh. Poor Lady Cowper. She's always been so nice to me. I certainly don't deserve it. Though when I explained to her, she did forgive me."

"Which means?" he asked, with forced patience.

"Oh. I forgot you don't know what really happened. I meant the lemonade for someone else, of course."

Michael blinked, and then let out a bark of laughter. "Chloe, only you would do something like that."

"I'm not sure if that's a compliment or not."

"Who did you intend the lemonade for?"

"Lady Anne Fairchild. That year's Incomparable."

He laughed again. "Did she deserve it?"

"More than you know," Chloe said wryly.

"Why? What did she do?"

"I heard her talking about me to another girl in the ladies' retiring room. I won't go into detail, but it wasn't very kind. I believe she meant for me to hear it."

He laid his hand on hers again. "You've had a lot of pain in your life, haven't you?"

"Don't pity me," she said sharply. "Everyone suffers."

"Not everyone gets revenge, though." A smile played around his mouth. "How did you set matters right with Emily Cowper?"

"Oh, I simply paid a call on her the next day, to apologize. Helena made me do so, but I would have in any event." She grinned up at him. "You see, she wasn't over fond of Lady Anne, either."

He shook his head. "As I said, outrageous. I'd best avoid angering you."

"Oh, yes, who knows what I might do?" she said lightly. "Perhaps I'll leave paint on your Belcher kerchief—not that anyone would notice—or decide to remodel the house."

"God knows it could use it." He shuddered. "Whoever decided to decorate the east room Nile green?"

"I know, 'tis hideous, is it not? But I have plans for it. I think we should do our own suite of rooms first, though."

"I'll give you free rein."

"Wonderful, but beside that and Chimneys, it will be expensive."

He shrugged. "Chimneys should start producing a good income for us within a year or two."

She let out her breath, relieved he hadn't taken the mention of money as an insult. Apparently he was used to the idea of it now. "I'm glad," she said simply. "You'll be able to plan your stud, then."

"Of course, you must spend your money as you see fit."

She sighed again. "I thought perhaps you'd reconciled yourself to it."

"Most of the time, I have. But sometimes it chafes me, Chloe," he said quietly.

"I'm sorry. Not that I have money, of course, but that it so hurts you."

"It shouldn't. Marriages more bloodless than ours are made every day."

"Is our marriage bloodless, Michael?" She spoke as quietly as he had a moment earlier.

He glanced at her. "No, my dear," he said, extending his hand. This time Chloe placed her hand in it, and his fingers closed about hers. If anyone remarked upon this very public display of affection from a couple who were already considered to be unfashionable for the way they were together so often, Chloe paid them little heed. For once, she liked being unfashionable.

Chloe stared stoically out the window of the town carriage as it brought her to pay a morning call on Elizabeth several days later, feeling rather like a martyr going to her doom. She finally had got up the courage to go to Lord Adam about riding lessons, but of course it wasn't done to go to his lodgings, wherever they were. Elizabeth, however, could tell him about Chloe's visit, assuming she didn't resent Chloe spending time with her fiancé. If she didn't, and if Lord Adam agreed, it meant Chloe would have to get on a horse again. It meant she would have to face her fears, as she had in the past. She wondered if this time she could.

Chloe was surprised when she was shown in to the drawing room at the Burnet town house to see Lord Adam. Apparently he ran tame here, as well he might, since it was his cousin's house. She suspected, though, looking at him and Elizabeth, who was of course no longer companion and governess to his cousin, Miss Kitty Burnet, that that wasn't why he was here.

"It's so very nice to see you again," Elizabeth said in her soft voice, handing Chloe a cup of tea, poured faultlessly.

"Thank you." Chloe smiled back. How much she had missed during those years of isolation. Lord Adam was very good *ton,* and so, by extension, was Elizabeth. She was lucky to have them as friends. Of course, she would never have met them had she not married Michael. "Have you decided on a wedding date yet?"

Lord Adam, slumped in his chair, raised his eyebrows. "She won't let us use our special license," he said plaintively.

"Families, Adam," Elizabeth chided with a smile.

He slouched even lower. "Families are the very deuce. What must her mother do but post up to London?"

"To help with the trousseau."

"M'mother wants to hold the wedding breakfast at Ware House, while m'aunt is arguing for here. All three of them are holding out for St. George's."

"Of course they are." Elizabeth sipped her tea. "They want only the best for us."

He looked at her. "All the world's marrying there just now, Beth."

"It won't take that long, Adam."

"Families," he said again.

Chloe smiled. "You're very lucky to have them," she said.

"Not always," Elizabeth murmured.

"Yes, that's true."

Adam looked quickly at Elizabeth and then back at Chloe. "Got some dashed smoky fellows in your family, Chloe. That Hempstead fellow. Loose screw if I ever saw one."

"Adam," Elizabeth reproved him.

"True."

Elizabeth shook her head. "Unregenerate."

"Do you see what she does to me?" he complained to Chloe. "Uses words that I never learned. Too lazy to study, you know."

"Nonsense, you took a first at Oxford. Now." She turned to Chloe. "Is something troubling you?"

Chloe frowned. "No. Well, not precisely." Chloe set down her cup. "Is my cousin a loose screw?"

Lord Adam abruptly straightened. "Has he been bothering you?"

"My knight-errant," Elizabeth murmured, smiling.

"Not precisely. If he does, Michael will take care of him." She sipped her tea again. "He did want to teach me to ride, and when I refused he was out of all reason cross."

He slouched in his chair, seeming less alert. "Ask Lyndon."

She smiled. "He tried to teach me to drive at Chimneys. I doubt he'd make the same mistake twice. I do wish we had the same interests in common."

"That's not necessarily important in a successful marriage," Elizabeth said.

"Ah. The practical Miss Hunter returns."

Elizabeth gave him the same level look he sometimes used. "Unkind, Adam. I was known as Miss Hunter when first I came to London," she explained to Chloe. "There were reasons."

"Oh, I'm persuaded there were," Chloe said, her curiosity piqued.

Adam was slumped down again. "Are you learning to ride?"

"No. Certainly not from Edwin." She paused. "Lyndon wishes me to have no further dealings with him."

"Good. Send him packing. As to that, Chloe, I might be able to teach you," he said, yawning.

Chloe and Elizabeth exchanged amused looks at this display of feigned ennui. "Oh, that would be beyond all things wonderful. 'Tis what I came here to ask."

"Lyndon's done me a favor or two in his time," he said. "Have you a mount?"

"Yes, Firefly," she said instantly, remembering a long-ago day spent in the Grantham stables. "A sweet goer, Lyndon said."

"Tut, sporting cant, Chloe," he chided, only the twinkle in his eyes giving him away. "I'll speak to Lyndon about having her sent round to my stables." He smiled at his fiancée. "To teach you to ride, of course."

"We must trust he doesn't know I already can," Elizabeth said serenely.

"Would you mind so very much?" Chloe asked her.

"Don't be silly. You and Lyndon have been good friends to me."

"Of course. Why wouldn't we be?"

"Others haven't been so kind, I fear. I am marrying above my station."

"Bosh," Chloe said bluntly. "The same people who mocked me, I imagine."

"Never mind, Beth," Adam said, his eyes serious. "They're no one we care to associate with."

She looked over at him. "They're friends of yours, Adam."

"Former friends."

"They're fools," Chloe said. "I was afraid you might be jealous if I asked Adam to teach me."

"Lud, not leg-shackled yet. Got some say in my life still."

Elizabeth handed her a freshly filled cup, her eyes twinkling. "Nonsense. Do just return him in one piece."

Chloe smiled at this bit of gentle teasing. "I'll try. You are sure you won't be jealous?"

Adam and Elizabeth exchanged one of those looks that filled Chloe with longing and envy. "I trust him."

"Lud, if I strayed, she'd have her pistols out."

"Adam," Elizabeth said, laughing. "As if I would."

"I know better than to argue with you." He laid his head back on his chair, and again Chloe and Elizabeth looked at each other in amusement.

"I do appreciate your doing this," Chloe said.

"Happy to. Early morning, I suppose?"

"Yes, that seems to be the best time. So few people are about."

"Lud, but I hate early mornings."

Elizabeth looked at him fondly. "My dear, you dislike morning altogether. At least," she added quickly, her cheeks pink, "so I've been told."

He grinned at her. "I do, at that. Very well, Chloe." He grimaced. "Expect to see you here tomorrow, early."

"Thank you." Chloe rose. "I do appreciate it."

"Oh, but please don't go," Elizabeth said.

"I fear I must. Lyndon will be missing me. Besides," she grinned, "if I stay any longer, I may ask for more favors."

"Fatiguing of you," Adam said with a feigned yawn, and Elizabeth looked up at him, her eyes dancing. Again Chloe envied them their relationship. "I'll see you out."

"Thank you."

Adam put a hand on her arm when they had reached the hall and she was tying her bonnet strings, causing her to look up in surprise. "Be careful of Hempstead," he said in a low voice.

"Why?"

"He's a rum one. Didn't want to say it in front of Elizabeth, but you're his family, worse luck."

"Unfortunately. What has he done?"

"Got blackballed at White's."

"Yes, something he said made me think that. Why?"

"Can't prove anything, but there's been talk he cheats at cards."

"He would."

"Another thing. There's more talk, no one knows how true, that he wanted to marry the Randall girl a year or so back."

"I didn't know that. Why didn't he?"

"Talk is her father gave him five thousand pounds not to."

She looked at him in shock. Even for Edwin, that was a bit much. "Not really!"

"Just talk, but sounds like the sort of thing he'd do." He helped with her shawl. "Watch out for him."

"I will." She smiled. "Thank you, Adam. You and Elizabeth are good friends."

* * *

Something was going on with Chloe. Michael was baffled as to what. Usually he spent his morning at White's, hearing the news of the day, making plans for a race or to go to see a mill. Sometimes he went to Gentleman Jackson's for a good round of sparring with the Gentleman himself. Sometimes he went to Manton's to practice shooting. However, for some reason, he would find himself restless and bored with his usual pursuits. He wanted Chloe, only to return home and find her gone. It was unusual, since they tended to be out late of an evening, meaning she usually slept in. Careful questioning of the servants availed him nothing. Their eyes slid away from his when he asked if they knew where she'd gone. They knew quite well but weren't telling him, and he had a good idea why. She was seeing someone. Devil take it, Chloe was his, he thought furiously. He would kill to keep her.

Sixteen

"You're quiet tonight," Michael said a few evenings later, as they drove to yet another of the Season's endless balls, given by—he had to think for a moment to remember the name. Ah, he had it. The Fullers, who prided themselves on their annual events. That they were usually undistinguished and boring mattered not. All the *ton* would be present, as usual.

"Hm?" Chloe turned from staring out the window, though in the darkness outside there was little to see.

"Is aught bothering you?"

"Of course not," she said, looking out the window again, and then sighed. "I do so wish we didn't have to go to this ball tonight."

In spite of her odd morning disappearances, Michael slipped his arm around her shoulders. "I'm rather tired of all the balls and routs and soirées, myself."

"We should have gone to a literary or political salon."

He made a face. "Not exactly my style, my dear."

"Well, a mill or a carriage race doesn't interest me very much, either," she said, but he could tell in the dimness that she was smiling.

"There's a way to do both."

"What is that?"

"Compromise."

"Do I need be in the carriage on a race to Brighton?"

He laughed. "No, not if you don't want to."

"Pity. I think I'd rather like to."

"You do?" he said in astonishment.

"I like driving with you."

"In the park, Chloe, not something like that."

"I've always been sorry, you know, that I took you away from your race that time, before we were married."

He shook his head. "You needed me."

"Yes, but—"

He reached out to lay a finger on her lips. "No buts."

"You weren't happy about it."

"I didn't know you then. And as you pointed out just the other day, I am rather too absorbed in sport."

"Michael, I didn't mean to hurt you."

"You didn't, dear. You simply pointed out something I should have seen long ago." He looked out the window. "I don't think I'll ever quite get over James's death, but I almost don't regret what my life's been like."

"Why is that?"

"It made me what I am today. I don't think I'd change anything."

"You've been doing some thinking," she said.

"Heavy work, for someone like me."

"Bosh. I saw what you were like at Chimneys."

"I'd like to go back there."

"I thought you preferred town."

"London's enjoyable," he agreed. "But Chimneys is home."

"It is, rather, isn't it?" she said softly.

"Yes. I'd like our babies to be born there." He glanced over to see that her head was bent. "Chloe, are you blushing?"

"No! Well . . . maybe a little."

Desire stirred within him. "I'd like to make those babies with you," he said huskily.

She rubbed her face against his shoulder. "I'd rather be home myself."

"Oh? Doing what?"

"I daresay we could think of something."

"I daresay we could. Damn." He looked out the window as the carriage came to an abrupt stop. "I think we're here."

"We could turn around."

He rolled up the window and looked out. Ahead he could see the lights of flambeaux and a long line of carriages. "No. Too many carriages."

"Damn," she said with feeling.

"Such language, Chloe," he teased.

"The situation seems to call for it."

"Hm. I wonder what we could manage in a carriage."

"Michael!" she exclaimed, staring at him.

He pulled her back against him. "It was just a thought."

She sighed. "We did accept the invitation."

"Yes." He was quiet for a time, remembering something that bothered him. "Dashed odd thing."

"What?"

"Burnet asked to borrow Firefly for Miss Collier."

"How very odd," she said, after a moment. "You'd think he'd have a mount for her."

"Or be able to afford one. He has money enough."

"Unless he doesn't think she will like riding."

"She grew up in the country. Does she not know how?"

"I don't know. Her father is a vicar."

"True." He pondered that. He knew Chloe and Elizabeth were close, but there had been an odd note in Chloe's voice. She was keeping something from him, he thought again. "Where do you go of a morning?"

She stiffened. "Have you been looking for me?"

"Occasionally, yes. 'Tis the best time for walking, or for driving out into the country."

"I am sorry," she said, with what sounded like genuine regret. "I sometimes go shopping with Elizabeth for her bride clothes, since her mother has no idea of what is fashionable, or with Lady Sherbourne. Do you know"—she looked up at him—"she knows of a shop which sells the most daring lingerie?"

"Really?" He brushed his fingers across the base of her neck and felt her shiver. "Such as?"

"The nightgown I wore the other night."

"Ah." Almost he was diverted by the memory of the gown of translucent silk. Almost. "By the by."

"Yes?"

"Someone mentioned to me he thought he saw you and Lord Adam the other day."

"Where had you that?" she said defensively.

"At White's."

"Oh, of course, where men gossip as much as women do. Excuse, 'tis conversation. Of course I go out on a morning to meet with Lord Adam. I can't think what Elizabeth must feel."

He grinned, though she was still tense. "My apologies, my dear." He glanced out the window again. "We're here."

"Oh, drat."

"I should have known better, of course," he went on, reverting to the former conversation. "I heard you were riding with him."

She was silent for a moment. "I wish I could," she said wistfully. "With you, I mean."

He tightened his hold on her. "I know," he said, and nearly sighed as their carriage at last stopped before the brightly lit mansion. It had seemed as if he might be near the truth of her odd disappearances. Likely she wasn't seeing another man. Still, he wanted to know. Still, he wanted to have his last doubts laid to rest.

The carriage door opened, and the footman put the step down. Michael sprang to the ground, and turned to help Chloe out. She held herself like a queen, he thought proudly, as someone in the watching crowd called out an undeniably suggestive compliment. "Courage, my dear," he said. "We don't have to stay very long."

She smiled up at him. "I'll plead a headache," she said, and let him escort her inside.

"Should I have the headache now?" Chloe murmured to Michael some time later. They were standing together, each rather warm after a particularly vigorous country dance. "These balls are all the same."

"Not quite. Some are duller," he said, and she laughed. Attending *ton* events was becoming tedious. It was rather like having a surfeit of sweets, he thought. One began to long for something more nourishing. Perhaps Chloe had a point about attending some intellectual salon, though he feared he would be as out of place there as she would be at Newmarket.

"Who is your next partner?" he asked.

She consulted her dance card and made a face. "Edwin." Michael's lips tightened. "Chloe—"

"I didn't realize he'd signed it," she protested, just as Edwin came up to them.

"Chloe." He bent over her hand, and then nodded to Michael. "Lyndon."

"Hempstead," he answered curtly. It was hard to be polite, after what Chloe had told him. If he bothered her now, he'd pay for it.

"I believe this is my dance, Chloe."

"Unfortunately," Chloe said, disgruntled.

Edwin let out a crack of laughter. "So, Chloe, as graceless as ever. No, no, Lyndon, don't start a dustup," he said, holding up his hands as Michael stepped forward. "Privilege of a cousin."

"No one has that privilege," Michael said through clenched teeth. "I believe you owe my wife an apology."

"Oh, Chloe doesn't mind. Do you?" He held his arm out without waiting for an answer.

Chloe stared at it with intense loathing. "I think I shall not dance this one."

"And not be able to dance anymore? Chloe, Chloe." He smiled. "Even you know better than that."

She threw Michael a look of such appeal that he moved closer to her. "Chloe was just saying she has the headache."

"Convenient."

Michael ignored him. "Shall I call for the carriage, dear?"

She turned to him in relief. "Yes, please."

"I shan't be long," he said, and made his way out along the edge of the crowded ballroom.

"Dear?" Edwin said, almost immediately. "My, my, Chloe, does he really call you that?"

She put up her chin. "Is that so hard to believe?"

"The Corinthian and Miss Bumblebroth. Who would believe it?"

"If you call me by that name one more time," she said through gritted teeth, *"I'll* call you out."

Again he laughed. "Brave words, from you. But have you not noticed, Chloe?" His grin was feral. "People are using the name again."

She stared at him, feeling her face go white, and then wheeled away, pushing her way blindly through the crowd. So that was what he had decided on as her punishment for not seeing him. Power and control. Because she had refused him both, she was going to pay.

At the doorway into the hall, though, she stopped. If Michael were to see her, he would know how upset she was. *Damn it,* she thought, relishing the rarely used swear. *I'm not Miss Bumblebroth anymore.*

She turned, making her way back to where Edwin stood. "Well, my dear?" he said, laying ironic emphasis on the endearment.

"This is the outside of enough," she said, so quietly that no one could hear.

"Why, Chloe," he said, in all innocence. "Whatever can you mean? I cannot help it if you deserve the name."

"It will fade again."

"Unless someone reminds people."

She smiled. "Do you know, Edwin, I really don't care?"

"Odd. I had the distinct impression you did."

"I have never understood," she said, her brow wrinkled, "why you have teased me so."

He gave her that same feral grin. "Because 'tis so easy."

"I shan't tell my husband," she went on, as if he hadn't spoken. "At least, not this time. Not that you deserve it, but I'd rather not create a scandal. But should you do aught else . . ."

"Chloe, Chloe. Do you think I fear you?"

"Mayhap you should." Her voice was quiet. "If not me, then definitely Lyndon."

"Really?"

"As you yourself said, he's a Corinthian."

For the first time, he seemed discomposed. His eyes grew hard, and his mouth was bracketed by tight lines. "Meaning, I suppose, that I am not? I may not be a member of the Four in Hand Club, or a crack shot—"

"Or skilled enough to spar with Gentleman Jackson, or to cross swords with Gianni."

"—but I do know how to ride."

She looked at him for a moment, then smiled. "What a paltry defense."

"Paltry? I don't know what you mean."

"For an empty life." She turned. "Good-bye, Edwin," she said, and walked away, feeling for the first time in her life triumphant over him; knowing that she wasn't Miss Bumblebroth.

Michael was just coming into the ballroom when she reached the door to the hall. "The carriage should be at the door soon," he said.

She smiled up at him. "Good."

For answer, he frowned. "You look rather odd, Chloe."

"I just had a confrontation with Edwin."

His fists tightened. "Damn him. Where is he?"

"No, you don't understand." She placed her hand on his arm. "I faced him down, Michael."

He searched her face. "Did you?"

"Yes." She smiled, feeling suddenly buoyant. "I don't know why I never did so before."

"What did he say to you?"

She shook her head. "Nothing of importance." She slipped her arm through his, still smiling. "Let's go home, Michael."

He gazed down at her for a little longer, and then hugged her arm to him. "Yes," he said. "Let's."

"Are you sure you want to do this?" Lord Adam asked Chloe as they rode from his stables toward Hyde Park.

"I'm sure," she said serenely, sitting Firefly with more confidence than she'd ever thought possible.

"Riding in the park during the fashionable hour for the first time can be unnerving for even an experienced rider."

"I am determined to do this, Adam."

"Lyndon will have my head," he muttered.

"Bosh. 'Twill make him so happy to see me ride that I doubt he'll even notice you."

"He'll notice."

"Don't be so downpin," she said as they entered the park. "All will be well. You'll see."

"I hope so," he said pessimistically. "Why did I agree to this?"

"Because you're Lyndon's friend."

"Not after this."

"I simply want to share in his interests."

"He seems to like you as you are, Chloe."

"But I'm clumsy and more interested in quiet activities. I think he'd like it if we could ride together."

"Doubtless. But he won't like it that I taught you."

She hesitated. Lord Adam was probably right. Still, for a reason she couldn't quite articulate, it was something she needed to learn without Michael. It had something to do with all that had happened to her in her childhood. It had everything to do with being Miss Bumblebroth.

They were nearing the other people now, enough so that Chloe could make out the individual faces of those who were walking or riding or being driven in carriages. "Well," she said. "Here we are."

"God help us."

"I'll do quite well, Adam. You'll see."

At first, she did seem to do well. Before her all she saw

were people sauntering or riding or driving in shiny phae-
tons and curricles and broughams, all stylishly and gaily
attired. Nothing there to panic her, she thought, except that
there were more people than she had expected. If she stayed
relaxed, though, and didn't lose her head, she should be all
right.

Coming toward her was a man riding a dappled stallion,
which tossed its head or sidled every few paces. The horse
was large; the man was large and plump, serenely unaware
of how unsuited he was to his mount. Chloe eyed him in
some amusement. So must she have looked when she was
learning to ride, clutching the reins for dear life and bounc-
ing up and down, except that this man beamed with obvious
pleasure and pride. It was a wonder Adam hadn't despaired
of her.

Chloe pulled farther to the side as the man—she recognized him now as Mr. Richfield, an innocuous, pleasant
person—neared her. She might be inexperienced, but she
was not stupid.

The stallion, however, put the seal on her fate. Though
Firefly wasn't in season, apparently she was of great interest
to the stallion. Again he tossed his head; again he sidled,
this time toward Chloe. Firefly, having a bit of spirit herself,
took instant exception and danced a bit.

"Are you all right, Chloe?" Lord Adam asked in obvious
concern.

"Oh, yes, I'm quite up to snuff," she said confidently.
"I can handle her. Easy, girl."

Firefly settled down. Mr. Richfield seemed also to have
regained control of his mount, though he now rode in the
very center of the path, nearly crowding Chloe and Lord
Adam onto the grass on either side as he passed. There,
that wasn't so hard, Chloe thought, and at that moment the
stallion lunged at Firefly. Mr. Richfield let out a startled
exclamation, Chloe loosened the reins for just a moment,
and Firefly reacted as she had been trained. She took off
at a gallop on the path.

"Firefly!" Chloe cried, all the training she had received

gone from her head. Instinctively she pulled the reins back, hard, to halt the horse, but to no avail. The quick, hard pull must have startled and hurt the horse, which only increased its pace, as if trying to outrun the pain.

As tightly as Chloe was holding the reins, one of them slipped from her left hand. *Oh, my dratted clumsiness,* she thought with an odd detachment, as she tried to grab it back. For a moment her seat became frighteningly precarious, and then she regained control. *All I need now is to fall and show the entire world my petticoats!*

The thought struck her as immensely funny, as Firefly veered to the left. Even Chloe knew that was due to her continuing inability to regain full control of the reins, if control it could be called. Ahead of her a man whom she had seen before strutting through the park with his three poodles, parading before him with equal hauteur, leaped to avoid her, while the poodles forgot their fine training. They reverted to the normal behavior of all dogs, struggling at their leashes and barking and baying at Chloe. She had an impression, as she streaked by and the dogs tried to give chase, that in the man's desperate efforts to hold on, somehow the leashes had become gloriously entangled and entwined around his legs, leaving him teetering and swaying. *He looks rather bound up for the moment,* she thought, and giggled.

People scattered before her as she continued her mad dash through the park; those on horseback had to fight to keep their mounts under control. Other horses, harnessed to carriages, plunged and reared as much as they could in their traces. One team bolted altogether, adding to the confusion. *Oh, a race!* she thought. *How terribly sporting of me.*

So caught up was she in her own struggles that Chloe didn't see a man on horseback suddenly pull his horse to a standstill, making his mount rear in surprise and apparent resentment. With superb horsemanship he fought for control, and won. "Chloe?" Michael stood in the stirrups and stared after her as she madly galloped through the throng.

"Good God!" he exclaimed, and, wheeling Thor about, set off after her.

And still Firefly ran, wreaking havoc in her wake. *Oops! Was that Lady Abernathy I just knocked down? Oh, no!* Her mind went blank for a moment while she tried, and failed, to remember why that was so bad. *Well, I never liked her anyway. But, oh no, Lady Jersey! Oh, I'll never be admitted to Almack's again. My children will never be admitted! Oh dear, and I do like her so. Oh, no, Firefly, what are you doing?*

For Firefly had, for some reason known only to herself, decided to leave the carriage path altogether for the freedom and relative peace of the lawn. *Thank heavens the Serpentine is on the other side,* she thought, but, oh, this was bad enough.

Ahead was a wall. Firefly had probably been trained to jump much higher obstacles, but Chloe had not. She did not know how to gather herself or how to give Firefly the proper signals, and she certainly didn't have control of the reins. It was too much for the horse, which had had a trying few minutes. With an inexperienced rider and faced with a wall, the horse simply balked. Abruptly she came to a complete halt, and Chloe was tossed free, to land with an *Oomph!* onto the ground.

"Oops," she said, quite distinctly, and succumbed to giddiness and nervous exhaustion and reaction.

Seventeen

"Chloe!" a voice called, and she opened her eyes the merest slit to see a horse draw up from a gallop. A man, silhouetted against the sun, threw himself off. *If I never see another horse again, I shall not repine,* she thought, closing her eyes.

"Chloe," that voice said again, urgent now. *Oh, dear Lord, Michael.* It needed only this. She didn't fight, though, as he grabbed her hand. "Darling, wake up. Please. Open your eyes. Talk to me."

Again she opened her eyes. "Am I your darling?" she asked with mild interest.

Michael abruptly dropped her hand. "Damn you, Chloe, what the hell did you think you were doing?"

"Tut, tut, Michael. Such language!" She raised her hand and then let it drop again, though she very much wished to investigate the whereabouts of various parts of her body. "Michael, where is my head?"

"On a platter, if I have my way."

She chuckled. "You have such a way with words."

"Chloe," someone else called out. *Oh, damn, another horse,* she thought, even as, more lucid now, she identified the rider. "Lud, Lyndon, is she—"

"What do you here?" Michael demanded.

"I was with Lady Lyndon," Adam said with great dignity, as he held Thor's head.

"So you're the one."

"The one?"

"The man she's been slipping out mornings to meet."

"Firefly," Chloe said.

"Firefly appears unhurt," Michael said after a brief silence. The horse was standing some distance away, contentedly munching grass. "Which is more than I can say—"

"I was meeting Firefly in the morning."

"Damn you," Michael said again. Chloe peeped up at him, but he was glaring at Adam. Better for her not to look. "Were you teaching her to ride?"

"Discretion is the better part of valor," Chloe said.

"Yes, Lyndon, I was," Adam said coolly. "Did you know Hempstead wanted to teach her?"

A thunderous silence fell. "Chloe, look at me," Michael said.

"Before you ring a peal over me," she said mildly, "you may wish to remember where we are."

Michael followed her gaze, and his lips tightened. In the few minutes since he had pulled up beside Chloe, a milling crowd had gathered about them, looking on with varying degrees of interest. This was indeed not the time to rip up at her, with all the *ton* waiting to see the Lyndons quarrel. What he would do when they reached home was a different matter. "Can you rise?"

"I don't know," she said in that same mild voice that was beginning to bother him.

"I'll be only too happy to help," Lord Adam began.

Michael threw him a murderous look. "I'll deal with you later."

"Er—yes." Lord Adam backed away. "I'll just go along home now."

"Come, madam." He grasped Chloe's hand, trying to pull her up. "You'll have to ride pillion on Thor."

"I am never getting on a horse again."

"I doubt anyone will give us the loan of a carriage after what you did today."

Someone cleared his throat, making Michael look up. "I say, Lyndon," Lord Farrow said. "I'd be happy to let you use my brougham. Lady Lyndon's been kind to me, you know."

Michael nodded. "That's decent of you."

"You're with Lady Sarah," Chloe said.

"Er, yes," Lord Farrow said after a moment.

"I'm so glad."

"Well, Chloe?" Michael said in exasperation.

"I don't think I can get up. No, Michael," she said, as he tugged at her hand again. "I mean it."

"Are you hurt?"

"I don't know."

"Had the air knocked out of her, eh?" someone said, and several people snickered.

Michael quelled them with the same look he'd turned on Adam, and then returned his attention to Chloe. "Where, Chloe? Can you move your arms and legs?"

With that same dispassionate look on her face, she tested her limbs. He was relieved to see them moving. "Yes, but I don't doubt I'll have a prodigious headache." She looked up at him. "I'll deserve it."

Michael's eyes were opaque, but he shook his head. "If I lift you by the shoulders, will you be able to get up?"

"I don't know," she said doubtfully.

"Let's try, shall we?" He slipped his arm under her. "There. Easy, now." He peered down at her. "All right?"

"Y-yes." She paused. "Just let me catch my breath."

"A moment only, Chloe." With his arm about her, and his free hand under her elbow, he pulled her to her feet.

She leaned against him for a moment, dizzy, shaken, but filled with a determination she'd never known she possessed. "Michael, please let's go home," she said, in a voice so weak and thready she barely recognized it.

"Yes, Chloe." His arms supporting her every step of the way, they made their slow progress toward the carriage, which seemed very far away to her.

"There goes Miss Bumblebroth," someone in the crowd said.

"Damn it, she's hurt," Michael snapped as he stopped abruptly, glaring at the crowd. Some people had the grace to look down, or away; too many others wore expressions of avid interest. "This will make the broadsides," he muttered.

"It won't be the first time." She looked up, relieved that they were finally near the carriage. "Do you mind?"

He was quiet for a long moment. "No."

That pause held a world of meaning to her. Oh, what had she done to this man? She had brought so much trouble into his life, and he didn't deserve it. "I'm sorry," she said in a small voice.

He looked down at her. "When we get home, you are going to explain to me how you got on Firefly in the first place."

"I can ride, Michael. Really."

"It didn't look like it to me. Here." He stopped. "We're at the carriage."

"I can't climb in," she said, eyeing the step, which appeared to be impossibly far from the ground.

"I'll help, my lord," the footman said, bowing.

Michael nodded. "I'll climb in first. You hand her to me."

"Michael," Chloe protested, but at that moment strong hands were at her waist, practically lifting her into the carriage. Another pair of hands reached for her, catching her about the waist and swinging her in. The unexpected movement brought the dizziness rushing back, making her stagger into Michael and forcing him to stumble backward.

"Hell, Chloe, don't push me out," he said, gaining control of himself enough to push her into the seat. She leaned her head back against the squabs, grateful not to have to walk anymore. "I expect an explanation from you, madam."

His voice was at its sternest, and yet his arm was around her, holding her against his shoulder and shielding her from the worst of the bumps. "Please, don't scold me. Not yet."

He was silent for a moment. "Very well then, madam. Tomorrow, when you are feeling more the thing."

"Thank you," she murmured, sagging against him. She thought she heard him speak again, as his other arm embraced her. She thought he said, "Ah, Chloe love," but she had to be mistaken.

She burrowed her head against his shoulder, giving in to the strength and security of his arms about her. "My love," he said, though it was surely a dream. "My love."

Chloe crept down the stairs the following morning, wary of what she might face. For one of the few times in their marriage, Michael had slept in his own room, coming into hers only as she was making an indifferent breakfast of tea and toast. "The bookroom, madam," he said crisply, in a tone of voice she'd never heard him use before, with an expression on his face she'd never seen. "At your earliest convenience."

"Yes, Lyndon," she said meekly, watching him despairingly as he stalked to the door. Oh, she'd truly done it this time. She'd created another major bumblebroth.

"I hope he doesn't mean to beat you," Patience said with familiarity of long service.

"I'll him hit right back," Chloe said swiftly, without thought as to the consequences.

"The staff will surely join you."

Startled, Chloe looked up. "But you'll likely lose your positions! Please don't. I'd feel so guilty."

"Very well," Patience said, her face set. "But I hope he doesn't expect good service should he hurt you, because he will not get it!"

Chloe ducked her head to hide her smile. She had strong allies, indeed. She wondered if Michael knew it.

Yesterday Michael had shown only concern for her, once they were in Farrow's brougham and he was holding her. Nervous reaction had set in as they left the park, making her shake and gasp and cling to him. "I shall never ride again," she repeated over and over. "Never. Never."

"Shh, Chloe." He held her so close she could hear the steady, if somewhat fast, beat of his heart. "Shh," he murmured, and whispered nonsense words into her hair, words of comfort that warmed her to her toes and eased the shaking. At home he helped her into the house, but once they were inside he caught her up, high in his arms, and carried her upstairs, to lay her carefully and tenderly on her bed. Once she was settled in bed in her nightgown, Michael sat beside her, gripping her hand, until the doctor arrived.

That had been yesterday. Today was likely to be far different, especially since her injuries had proven to be minor. All things considered, she'd brushed through the incident well enough. She had only aches and bruises to show for her experience, and a possible mild concussion, which left her with a headache that bedeviled her and attacks of dizziness should she turn too quickly. The shock was gone, however, and she felt steadier, stronger. Except for what Michael was about to say to her.

Taking a deep breath, she walked down the hall and rapped on the bookroom door. "Enter," Michael called from within. Caswell, his raised eyebrows the only indication of his lordship's mood, opened the door for her, and she walked in.

Michael didn't rise. Instead his head was bent over some papers upon which he was writing. The gesture was so breathtakingly insulting that a little spark of anger awoke within her. Dropping into a chair, she leaned forward and rapped on the desk. "Well? Do you plan to ring a peal over me, or don't you?"

He looked up, his eyes icy, his face set in harsh lines. For the first time since she'd known him he appeared very much an aristocrat, arrogant and aware of his consequence. "Can you give me one good reason why I should not?"

"I did it for you."

"For me!" He threw down the pen, and ink splattered across the papers. "Hell, Chloe, when I saw you on the ground, I thought you were dead."

"I wanted to impress you—"

"You didn't. Adam has much to answer for, and the head groom. I gave him his notice this morning."

"Oh, Michael, no," she said in dismay, leaning toward him. "He knew nothing of what I was doing."

"Someone drove you to meet with Adam each day. Were you in riding habit?"

"Not then, no."

"Then?"

She studied her fingernails. "Elizabeth called for me each day. I changed my clothes where she lives."

"Oh, Elizabeth. That makes matters ever so much better."

"I was never unchaperoned," she said, stung. "Michael, for heaven's sake!" She leaned forward. "All I wished to do was learn how to ride. I wished to share in something you enjoy."

"I never asked that of you."

"You asked it all the time!"

"I expected to be the one to teach you, though after I tried to teach you how to drive I decided against such a crack-brained notion."

In spite of herself, a little smile touched Chloe's lips. "That was truly dreadful, wasn't it?"

"It took about ten years off my life." His gaze had relaxed, too, though his eyes were still stern. "Well? Why did you do it?"

She looked down at her hands again. "I wished not to be Miss Bumblebroth anymore," she said in a low voice, and then put up her hands to ward him off as he rose from behind the desk. "No, Michael!"

"Hell, Chloe, I wasn't going to hit you."

Without raising her head, she could see he was perched on the edge of the desk before her. "I know that. But I don't deserve any sympathy from you."

"You'll not have it," he said, so calmly that she looked up at last. "It is time you forgot this Miss Bumblebroth nonsense."

"But 'tis not just I who uses the name."

"We all do foolish things."

"I am persuaded you never did."

He grinned briefly. "You never saw me at Oxford. What the *ton* says or thinks about you doesn't matter, Chloe," he said. "What you think of yourself does."

"You weren't happy to marry me. The Corinthian and Mi-me."

"Not in the very beginning, before I knew you, no. Chloe, you've much to give, if you would but let yourself."

"Such as?"

"Digging for compliments? Very well. You're smart. You're funny and honest. You paint well, and I cannot even begin to imagine what you do with numbers. You care about people. You work hard. There." He clasped his hands around his upraised knee. "Is that enough for you?"

"It will do, as a start."

" 'Tis all you'll get. There is one other thing."

"What?" she asked, wary of his serious look.

"You can be clumsy. No, I don't mean to insult you. 'Tis the truth, at least part of the time."

"I try so hard not to be—"

"Which is one reason you are. 'Tis not a matter of trying," he went on, more gently. "Think, Chloe. Remember our betrothal ball? You had trouble dancing until you had congenial partners."

"Well, yes."

"And in Dover you did well, once you forgot about yourself."

"True, but I'll never be good at it. Or at sports."

"No, likely not," he conceded. "But you do stammer when you're with people who make you uncomfortable, such as Hempstead."

"Not anymore."

He eyed her suspiciously. "Why not?"

She waved her hand in dismissal. "Oh, I seem to have lost my fear of him. But do go on. Pray tell me more of my defects. 'Tis quite fascinating."

"Very well. You befriend people others shun."

"But that's only kindness!" she protested.

"To an extent," he conceded. "But also easier."

"They become true friends."

"With one or two exceptions."

Now it was her turn to look suspicious. She'd distinctly noticed that several people who had been friendly before avoided her, once others accepted them. "Why?"

"They were taking advantage of your good nature."

"Hm." She wrinkled her brow, but decided not to explore that subject any further. "Do go on. I am all attention."

"You tend to hide away so people will not see you fail."

"I believe I failed rather spectacularly yesterday, don't you?" she said, smiling for the first time since this interview began.

"Quite." He smiled back at her. "Do please promise you'll not climb onto a saddle again."

"Actually I had been doing rather well. Lord Adam— well, never mind that," she said hastily, at the look on his face. "But this hardly seems fair, Michael. Are we not to hear of your defects?"

"Certainly. I can be arrogant—"

"True."

"And I am disgustingly self-assured."

"Oh, more than true."

"Chloe—"

"Not to mention overbearing, determined to have your own way, sometimes forgetting that not all people are like you—"

"For God's sake, Chloe!"

"And far too absorbed in sports."

"True," he said after a moment. "As we discussed, I don't feel quite that way anymore, though since talking to my parents."

"I know," she said.

"Are you quite through now, listing all that is wrong with me?"

"Yes."

"Good."

"I did forget to mention how kind you can be, and how caring."

"Ah, Chloe." He held his hand out to her, his gaze softening. "With you, 'tis easy."

She looked back at him, caught by his expression; drowning in the look in his eyes. She remembered all at once that yesterday he had called her "darling." He had called her his love. "I do not mean to worry you, Michael. Truly I don't. I simply wish to share in your world if I can."

"I know that." He covered her hand with his free one. "But it doesn't matter to me anymore, you know."

"I don't know why not."

"Believe me, it doesn't." He looked down at their linked hands. "Chloe, I don't care that you do something foolish or less than graceful at times. What does bother me is that you do things to prove something no one really cares about. Except, probably, you."

"Not even you?" she asked incredulously.

"Perhaps I once did, but believe me, my dear, I'd rather have you whole and well. I don't want you risking breaking your neck, as you did yesterday."

Her breath caught. "Really?"

"Really." He brought her hand to his lips and pressed a warm, open-mouthed kiss on her palm. The brief, very soft, touch of his tongue sent a stab of desire through her. "Pray do not, Chloe."

She leaned her cheek against his hand. "I won't," she promised. "I won't."

Chloe's riding lessons continued, once Michael found she could indeed manage a horse with some proficiency. Not that he let her ride alone, or with anyone else but him, for that matter. Someday, when he felt she had gained more skill and more confidence, the latter having suffered after her adventures in the park, he would allow it. Until then, however, he wished to be at her side, to grab the bridle should something go wrong, to laugh with her over her occasional minor mistakes, to be—oh, the devil, just to be with her, he admitted. Obviously she had worked hard to learn, he thought, touched and a little irritated, proud and yet empty inside. She should have come to him. Was he such a bear of a husband that she had been afraid to?

"Afraid?" Chloe asked one morning as they rode toward Hyde Park, and laughed. "Of you? Of course not, Michael. Whatever put that ridiculous notion into your head? Oops." This as Firefly, reacting to something neither of them could see, sidled unexpectedly.

Michael's hand shot out and caught the bridle. "Something did. Watch that, there." He tightened his hold on Firefly's bridle, as she shied again. "She's frisky today."

"She has spirit. Oh, Michael, she's a wonderful horse. I'm so glad you got her for me."

He smiled briefly at her. "Why did you not come to me?"

"For what?" She had Firefly well under control again. Likely she had all along, he thought, with that same curious mixture of pride and emptiness and loss. "Oh, to learn to ride? I told you, Michael. It was to be a surprise."

"It was that."

She threw him a quick smile, her hands on the reins steady, sure. "Rather one to me, too. But you must admit 'tis pleasant to be riding together like this."

"It is," he agreed, wondering why he wasn't more pleased with the idea. Devil take it, it should have been him.

"Do you mind so very much, then?"

"Mind? No, why should I?"

"You didn't sound particularly pleased just now."

"Of course I am," he said.

Chloe peered closely at him, a little line between her brows. "Michael, are you jealous?"

"Don't be more foolish than you can help."

"You are, aren't you? Because someone else taught me?"

"No, devil take it," he said, the words wrenched out of him. "This is *my* life."

"Michael!"

"I'm sorry, Chloe," he said, wishing he hadn't spoken,

though until he did he hadn't realized his feelings himself. "I can't help it."

"But I thought you wanted me to share it."

He stared ahead, jaw set. "So did I."

"I don't understand you," she said plaintively. "Why would this bother you?"

How could he explain, when he didn't fully understand himself? "You're so smart." Again the words felt as if they'd been pulled from him. "You can do things I can't imagine. This was my world, alone." He glanced over at her, to see that she had turned her head away. Though he couldn't see her, he suspected she had tears in her eyes. "I'm sorry, Chloe," he said helplessly. "I wish I didn't feel this way."

"So do I," she said, and set Firefly into a canter.

He caught up with her almost immediately. "Chloe—"

She pulled up. "Don't you know what it is? The way you live for sports."

"I do not—"

"You've admitted it yourself."

This time he cantered ahead, for the moment not wishing to be with her. He had little experience dealing with emotions, especially ones this tangled. Long ago he had learned to cope by running away, by pretending they weren't there. Long ago, when—God help him, but Chloe was right. When James died, he had become entirely absorbed with sport. He'd had to. It was the only way he could survive, until she had come into his life.

He reined Thor in and turned in the saddle. She held Firefly to a walk, as if reluctant to approach him. "Thank God for you, Chloe."

She stopped. "I beg your pardon?"

Controlling Thor with one hand, he held the other out to her. "You accept me," he said, trying to puzzle it out. "As I am."

Her face softened. "That's what marriage is about, Michael."

"I know. No, don't try to take my hand yet."

She returned his smile. Tentatively, true, but a smile, for all that. "I don't dare let Firefly go."

"I can't explain it, Chloe. I—"

"I can," she said softly, and sighed. " 'Tis unrealistic for us to live in each other's pockets all the time. We each had our own lives before. Marriage can't change us that much."

"Then what does it do?"

"I'll let you figure that one out on your own." She cantered ahead. "Are you coming?"

He set Thor into motion, frowning. What the devil did she mean? He let out his breath. Time enough to think about that later. For now, he wanted to be with his wife. "Hold up there, Chloe," he said, as he saw her setting Firefly to a faster pace.

She stopped for just a moment and turned to him. "Would you care to race?"

"Oh, the devil, Chloe, I don't think I could survive that."

Her laugh floated back to him as she cantered again. "Coward."

"You'll pay for that," he growled, digging in his heels. Because what else could he do but catch up with her, he thought, feeling suddenly lighthearted. He could never let her go.

Michael's good mood lasted through that day, and the next as well. At Gentleman Jackson's saloon, where he made so poor a show of sparring that the Gentleman himself reproved him, his friends hooted with laughter and teased him about being in love with his wife. Great wits, all, he thought as he pulled on his shirt and then tied his neckcloth in a simple knot. Could not a man have a good, strong friendship with his wife without this nonsense of love? He wasn't even sure he knew what the emotion was. He did know that he cared about Chloe, that he liked her and liked being with her. He would shelter and protect her for as long as he lived. But love? Nonsense.

He faced the same kind of raillery from his more political or pleasure-minded friends at White's the following day, when he went there to have luncheon. Only Lord Adam was silent, making Michael look at him quizzically as they sat down to eat. "Aren't you going to roast me, as well?" Michael asked.

"Lud, no." Adam waved his hand. "Too fatiguing by half."

Michael let out a crack of laughter. "Oh, cut line! You manage to express your opinions if you wish."

"Mm." Adam looked at him from under hooded eyes, twirling his wineglass by the stem, a gesture at odds with his languid, slouching posture. "You are in love with her, you know."

Michael's eyebrows rose. "You, too, Burnet?"

"Lud, yes. Have been anytime this age. What's more, so is she—I'd wager from the beginning."

"Imagine that," a voice said dryly from behind him. "Our Miss Bumblebroth in love with a noted Corinthian."

Michael slowly raised his head and turned. Behind him, Edwin Hempstead sat at a table with his cronies. "I beg your pardon? What did you call Lady Lyndon?"

"Miss Bumblebroth. Planning on calling me out?" He smirked as Michael loomed above him. "Or has being married to my clumsy cousin made you, ah, less of a man?"

The insult was so breathtaking that all in the room went still, awaiting Michael's response. "As a matter of fact, I am," Michael said pleasantly.

"He's pot-valiant, Lyndon," one of the men with Edwin put in as Michael returned to his table. "He doesn't know what he's doing."

Edwin waved the objection away. "Don't impugn me, Howard. Lyndon and I have a grudge to settle. I'm tired of skulking around him, the noted Corinthian," he sneered, rotating his glass on the edge of its base. "Might as well be hanged for a sheep as a lamb. Did you ever learn who hit on that pet name for her?"

Michael's jaw set. He had a vast suspicion he was about to learn. "Pet name? Is that what you consider it?"

"Oh, yes. Of course, I meant the name to be a joke from the very beginning." He looked falsely innocent. "How could I know everyone else would pick it up?"

Michael stared at him. Then he slowly rose, paced across the room, and very deliberately tossed his glass of burgundy into Edwin's face.

Eighteen

A gasp went up about the room at the traditional method of a challenge to duel, but the two participants didn't hear. Already mortal combat had been joined between them. "Have your seconds call on mine to settle the details," Michael said in a clipped voice.

"Lyndon," Mr. Howard called, "he's been drinking all morning. You can't call him out. He'll regret it later."

Michael ignored him. "Burnet, will you act as my second?"

"Of course. Lyndon, do you think this is wise?" he added quietly, all hints of laziness gone. "You could die."

"I doubt it," he said as they walked from the room. "I am a far better athlete than he."

"He's sly. I don't trust him."

Michael shrugged as he accepted his hat and walking stick from the porter. "I believe I can manage him."

Footsteps clattered on the stairs behind the two men as they reached the street. "Lyndon," Edwin said.

Michael turned, his attitude that of a man whose patience was much tried. "What now, Hempstead?"

"One thing more."

"You waste my time," Michael bit out. "What is it?"

He smiled, slowly, lethally. "Chloe, you must remember, has no sense of humor about some things."

"Meaning?"

"She's known about this all along. I wonder why she never told you."

"I give you precisely five minutes to be down the street and out of my sight," Michael said in that nearly pleasant tone again. "Or I'll have to cane you."

"What, and keep me from meeting you? I think not." He grinned. "You'll be hearing from me," he said, and, whistling, sauntered along St. James toward Piccadilly.

Michael's hands clenched into fists. "Why in *hell* didn't she tell me?"

"Protecting you, I think," Adam said quietly. "She loves you."

Michael swung on him. "How could you possibly know that?"

"Watch her. See for yourself." Languidly Adam pulled out his pocket watch. "Lud! I'm to take Elizabeth driving this afternoon. Must go, old boy, if I'm to make it in time, or she'll have my head."

Michael's smile was perfunctory. "I won't keep you, then," he said, as they reached the intersection with Piccadilly.

Adam sent him a curious glance. "You aren't going home, then?"

"I need to stretch my legs." He raised his hand in farewell and turned toward Park Lane. Mayhap a stroll through Hyde Park would help him think this through.

Half an hour later, no more enlightened than he had been earlier, Michael strode into the house. "Where is Lady Lyndon?" he demanded.

Caswell bowed. "In her studio, my lord. She did ask not to be disturbed, but—"

"She'll see me," he said, and took the stairs two at a time.

The door to Chloe's studio stood ajar. Quietly he pushed it open and stood in the doorway, watching her and feeling, in spite of himself, some of his confusion and anger drain away. She appeared to be absorbed in her painting, frowning at it as she often did, and she was, as usual, untidy, with streaks and daubs of paint everywhere, including on herself. A great uprush of emotion filled him. His Chloe. Had there ever been anyone else like her in the world? Had he ever once seriously not wished to marry her?

He must have made some noise, because she looked up, her eyes brightening. "Michael! I didn't hear you come in."

" 'Tis only been a moment." He crossed the room and, on an impulse he'd never expected, pulled her into his arms and kissed her soundly.

"Michael!" She stared up at him, her eyes round. "Whatever was that for?"

"Cannot a man kiss his wife?"

"Well, yes." Her eyes laughed at him. "Do it again?"

"Gladly." This time the kiss was longer, deeper, more thorough. Not surprised this time, Chloe returned it enthusiastically, and then let herself be held against him. "Ah, Chloe."

"I don't know why you did that," she said, sounding breathless, "but I'm glad."

"Mm." He kissed her once more for good measure, and then went to straddle a chair, folding his arms across its back. "Did I ever tell you how much I like it that you never care overmuch about your appearance?"

"What? Oh, no."

"What?"

"Oh, Michael, there's paint on your waistcoat."

He looked down, frowning. "So there is."

"Don't you care?"

"Not particularly."

"Well." Her brow was furrowed. "I don't know what maggot's got into your head—"

"A maggot? Because I wanted to kiss you?"

"—but I like it. Except for ruining your waistcoat, of course."

"Your bad influence, my dear."

For answer, she stuck her tongue out at him and picked up her palette. "I'm not sure I find that complimentary."

"It was, actually." He watched her for a moment, admiring the clean lines of her face—how was it he'd never before noticed what a nice profile she had—and the way she worried at her lower lip while she painted. His Chloe. "Seriously, Chloe. Why do you not care for fripperies, as you call them? You know you're beautiful."

She laughed. "I know no such thing!"

"Has it anything to do with Hempstead?"

"Edwin? Mercy, no," she said, but her gaze slid away from his.

"No?"

"No."

"Not Helena, or your brother?"

"Helena and I will never agree on any style. While you, sir." She glanced critically at him, her gaze traveling from the top of his head to his toes. "I do believe your valet could at least keep your waistcoats clean."

"Madam, you wound me."

"Silly. Perhaps you'll start a style. Spotted waistcoats to go with Belcher kerchiefs."

"I rather doubt that." He was not normally a perceptive man, yet he sensed he knew what, or who, had influenced her so. The others, as she called them. Edwin Hempstead, whose teasing had likely extended to her appearance.

"Chloe," he said, surprising even himself, "it was Hempstead who named you Miss Bumblebroth, wasn't it?"

Her paintbrush fell to the floor. "I beg your pardon?"

"Wasn't it?" he said again.

Her eyes slid away from his. "Yes," she admitted. "Though how you learned that—"

"Gossip. Did I not tell you that I would call out anyone who called you that?"

"You did."

"Did you fear I'd hurt him?"

She looked quickly at him. "Fear it? No! If anything . . ."

"What? Tell me, Chloe," he said, as she ducked her head.

She put her chin up at the command. "Very well, but you'll not like the answer. I fear he'll hurt you."

"Hurt me! Hurt me?" He took a brief turn about the

room, staring at her from several paces away, hands on his hips. "How the devil do you expect him to do that?"

"I don't trust him. If—"

"Yet you—"

"Yes, what?" she challenged him. "I went about with him once or twice? Are you implying something by that, Michael?"

"Mayhap I am."

Unexpectedly, that hurt. She turned her head quickly away. "Go away, Michael, before I—"

"Chloe." He raised her chin with his fingers. "Oh, the devil. I made you cry, didn't I?"

"It's just that I'm so angry."

"That's a corker, dear," he said, and pulled her into his arms. She tucked her head under his chin, wondering what had motivated his jealousy. "I am a fool."

"So you are," she said, and leaned back, wiping at her face with her fingers.

"Here." He handed her his handkerchief. "Of course I know he means nothing to you."

"He doesn't."

"Why did you not tell me he gave you that name?"

"I don't know," she said again, into his shoulder. *Fear,* she thought, and knew she could never explain. Michael, who seemed never to be afraid of anything, would never understand Edwin's particular form of terrorizing without experiencing it. Though just what she had been afraid of, now that she was grown, she didn't know.

"Chloe, he made your life hell with that name."

"I did do things to deserve it."

"Stop blaming yourself! He didn't need to be so cruel." She glanced away from his scrutiny, biting her lip. "You never once told me about it. Why not?"

Fear, she thought again, but not for herself this time. She well knew how underhanded Edwin could be. "Michael, he'd do you an injury if he could," she said, finally looking up at him.

He brushed that off. "He can't."

"You don't know him as I do."

"Which is the problem, is it not?"

"Oh, Michael—"

He kissed her briefly, but fully. "No, dear, I did not mean that as you think. I suspect you are living in the past."

She looked up at him warily. "What do you mean?"

"You hide away in here."

"Hide?" she said, genuinely surprised. "I'm not doing that."

"Oh, yes. You did so for three years, did you not?"

She fell silent. She hadn't expected such perception from a man known more for skill in outward things. "Yes, but not now, Michael. I do enjoy being here."

"I don't doubt it. But the past—"

"Is past! For heaven's sake, Michael, I am not some weak-willed ninny. Yes, of course growing up was hard. I did hide myself away for three years after my come-out. But do you know, I keep remembering something you said."

"What?"

"You once said that, except for James's death, you'd not change anything in your life. Well, nor would I. If I had taken during my Season, would you have married me?"

"Lord, I hope not."

She laughed. "You know what I mean. It was precisely because I wasn't successful that you married me."

"That and the fact that you bedeviled Helena so."

"Yes, a high recommendation for any wife."

"I believe so." His smile was soft. "We all need humor."

"And if I keep falling all over my feet, I'll provide it."

"But I'll be there to catch you."

"Why, thank you, Michael." Perhaps he didn't love her, she thought, but somehow they'd managed to make something of their marriage.

"Will you do something for me?"

Anything. "Yes, of course."

"Will you hire a competent dresser? Yes, I know Patience is a good enough maid, but I believe you require—deserve—something more."

She frowned. " 'Twill make little difference."

"On the contrary." He brushed her cheek with the backs of his fingers, his smile soft. " 'Twill make all the difference in the world. You have too much beauty to hide it any longer."

"I am not beautiful."

"And put yourself into my mother's hands completely as to clothes. No more shapeless or high-cut frocks, Chloe. You've too good a figure to disguise."

She opened her mouth and then closed it at that, but made herself hold his gaze. "Do you really think so?"

"Minx. Have I not told you enough times?"

She felt herself coloring at that. "Yes."

"I want the world to know how proud I am of you—"

"Oh, Michael."

"—and I want them finally to stop seeing you as that name."

"Do you really think that will change?" she asked skeptically. "People do tend to remember such things."

"Only if they're reminded. And, my dear, when you're at ease, you do little to remind anyone."

She gazed up at him. Another man would have demanded these things of her long ago and left her a stammering wreck, all to please his own vanity. Michael, however, understood. She still marveled at that. "And then I can really tell them to go to—"

"Chloe!"

"Well, I could." She grinned unrepentantly up at him. "Will you leave me in peace to paint, then?"

"Chloe—"

"What will I need to prove? Naught to you or to me. But as to them—why do I need them?"

"Because it will hurt you else," he said quietly.

She rested her head against his shoulder. "I don't need their good opinion anymore, Michael. Only yours."

He was quiet for a long moment. "I believe you may be wiser than I suspected."

She laughed into his face. "Oh, depend upon it," she said, and reached up her arms around his neck.

Pistols at dawn. The very words had an ominous sound, and yet Michael sat at ease the next morning in the carriage carrying him and Lord Adam toward Green Park. Already the days were growing shorter, he noted as he glanced out the window. Soon he and Chloe would repair to Chimneys for the remainder of the summer. He was looking forward to it.

He turned back inside to say something about where they would eat breakfast after the duel, to see Adam, a troubled expression on his face. "What is it?" he asked.

"Best be careful of Hempstead."

"That coxcomb? Bah."

Adam's eyes were guarded. "Has anyone else been talking with you about him?"

"Only Chloe." He sat forward, suddenly suspicious. "Why?"

"Elizabeth met some demmed odd sorts when she was learning how to shoot. She tells me Hempstead's been practicing."

"The devil, Adam! Did you tell her?"

"Do you think I did it deliberately? It—slipped out."

Michael knew well how bits of knowledge could be let slip between a man and the woman he loved. *Loved?* Good God. But he couldn't think about that just now, even were it true. "The devil, Adam. She'll go right to Chloe, and the last thing I want is to worry her."

" 'Pon rep, Elizabeth will stay mumchance."

" 'Pon rep?" Michael said, diverted in spite of himself. "And in what century did you learn that, dear boy?"

"Elizabeth won't say anything," he repeated, this time without use of thieves' cant.

I hope she can keep her mouth shut, Michael thought, his lips grim as he looked out the window, and nearly said so aloud. Adam was oddly protective of his fiancée, though, and to say anything against her would only damage their friendship. He would just have to trust him, as he did today.

The carriage drew to a stop. Looking out, Michael saw an expanse of green lawn. They were here. Carrying the box that contained his precious pair of dueling pistols, tooled especially for him by Manton, he descended from the carriage. Outside the sun, just rising, was burning off the early morning mist. A lovely day for a duel, he thought sourly, wishing instead that he'd stayed home with Chloe. True, he wanted to avenge the damage done her by her cousin; true, he wished to impress upon everyone that she was his, and that he'd protect her. Chloe herself wouldn't understand it, and yet he also knew that he would fight for her whenever necessary.

Hempstead was already there, standing some distance away, angled so that Michael could barely see his face, his hands thrust into the pockets of his coat. He was apparently lost in deep thought as he rocked up and down on his heels, and yet he seemed as relaxed as Michael had felt. He was tense now, as he usually was before any fight, the tension of coiling, repressed energy; the tension of unleashing that energy when the time came to battle. This time, though, the stakes were higher than they had ever been. He had never before fought a duel, but still he knew he could rely on his skill and prowess to see him through. This one he had to win.

Adam, along with Mr. Howard, Hempstead's second, was deep in conversation with the doctor who would tend to any wounds that might be inflicted during the duel. Michael gazed at them for a moment, then turned his look upon Hempstead. As if sensing it, Hempstead turned. They stood, each measuring the other across the wide expanse of lawn. Hempstead's face was calm, but his eyes burned with an emotion Michael had not thought to see, making him tense even further. Hempstead was looking at him with hatred. The stakes of this duel had suddenly risen.

Adam came up to him at that moment, and the spell was broken. "What is your plan?" he asked in a low voice.

"I thought to give him a flesh wound only," Michael said, still looking at Hempstead, still taking his measure.

Adam frowned. "You thought? Do you plan something different, then?"

Michael nodded. "Yes."

"Lud, Michael!" Adam stared at him. "If you kill him, you'll have to flee the country."

"I won't kill him." He was calm now. He knew what he had to do. "I'll injure him so that he'll not trouble Chloe anymore." *Or any other woman, for that matter.* Hempstead's confidence in himself as a man was about to be seriously threatened, if not damaged.

"Gentlemen." Mr. Howard walked toward them. "I believe we're ready to proceed."

"Good," Michael muttered, and strode toward him. Hempstead was doing the same, except that he sauntered, his hands still in his pockets. The posture set Michael's teeth on edge. He would not let this man bother Chloe again.

Adam looked gravely from him to Hempstead. "Gentlemen, as your seconds, Mr. Howard and I must ask you if there is any way this conflict may be resolved without fighting," he said.

"No." Michael and Hempstead spoke at the same time.

Adam looked at Mr. Howard. "Very well. You both, I believe, know the rules of an engagement such as this. However, it is as well to repeat them. You will stand with your backs together, there." He indicated a patch of lawn. "You will then take exactly ten paces away from each other." He looked from one to the other. "Agreed?"

The answer came in unison again. "Agreed."

"At Mr. Howard's signal, which will be when he drops his handkerchief, you may fire at will. You will each be allowed two shots. Mr. Howard and I have examined the guns and loaded them and find them to be satisfactory. Agreed?"

Again, together. "Agreed."

"The duel will be considered over when you have fired

your two shots, or when one of you is wounded enough not to be able to rise, or when Mr. Howard and I say it is. Agreed?"

"Agreed."

Adam nodded. "Mr. Howard? Have you anything to add?"

"Only that we expect a fair fight."

"Very well. Then, gentlemen, take your places."

Not looking at each other, the two men walked forward, Michael's heart filled with cold determination. He would fight fairly, but well. He had no intention of losing.

They both stopped, and for the first time looked at each other. Hempstead's eyes were narrowed; Michael looked back at him calmly, but with contempt. He felt transported out of time, felt the battle of wills between them stretch out endlessly. No matter what happened today, from this moment they were sworn, bitter enemies.

"Gentlemen, take your places," Mr. Howard called, and, pulled back to awareness of his surroundings, Michael turned, his back aligned with Hempstead's. Both men held their pistols high, facing upward. Again Michael felt that odd sensation of timelessness, until he felt Hempstead begin to pace off the distance. Deliberately he walked forward, ten paces precisely. Taking a deep breath, steeling himself, he turned to face Hempstead, and waited endlessly for Howard to drop his handkerchief.

False dawn was lighting the sky when Elizabeth, wearing one of her old dresses from her governessing days, tumbled down from the hackney. She bounded up the stairs of the Lyndon town house and pounded on the door with the knocker, shifting impatiently from foot to foot until she heard the snick of the lock. The door was at last opened, and a footman stood gaping at her. "Uh, the tradesman's entrance is around the back—"

Elizabeth thrust her foot against the doorjamb before the footman could shut her out. "Do I look like a tradesman?"

she snapped, slipping through the doorway and pushing past him. "I am Miss Collier. Pray tell Lady Lyndon I am here."

"Uh." The footman glanced around, as if searching for help, and then scratched his head. "I dunno as she's receiving."

"Of course she isn't at this time of day. Oh, Caswell." She relaxed as the butler, shrugging into his coat, came into the hall. "You can help me."

"Miss Collier." He stared at her. "I doubt Lady Lyndon is even awake yet."

"I know, but I need to see her anyway. Please." She thrust out her card. " 'Tis a matter of some urgency. Or," she said, struck by a sudden thought, "did Lord Lyndon not go out with Lord Adam Burnet early this morning?"

Caswell's eyes were shuttered. He knew what was about, then. "Yes, miss, he did."

"Then you know why I'm here." She stood firm. More people than this had quailed before the look she trained on him now, when she had been a governess.

"Very well, miss," he said, capitulating. "I'll speak with her maid. Do you care to step into this salon while you wait?"

Elizabeth did not care to at all, but she had little choice. Rousing a household at this time of day was bound to cause some consternation, but she would not be stayed from her mission.

Caswell returned within a few minutes. "If you will follow me, miss," he said. She walked behind him up two flights of stairs, until he showed her into a sitting room, far more intimate and untidy than the salon below. Chloe's room, she guessed, from the litter of books and papers spread across the cream and blue and peach furnishings of the room, and the painting of Chimneys on the wall. It was a comfortable sitting room, and yet she couldn't settle, moving from one chair to another. This was so urgent a matter. Why did not Chloe respond?

It seemed an age before the door to the bedchamber opened, though it was, Elizabeth realized later, only a few

moments. Chloe came in, her hair unbrushed, with a dressing gown thrown askew over her nightgown, and blinked
owlishly at her. "Elizabeth?" she said, and yawned. "Pardon
me, I'm not at my best in the morning. What do you here
so early?" She glanced out the window. "Why, it's barely
light out."

"Not quite dawn. Chloe, I had to see you. We may be
just in time."

Chloe sprawled into a chair across from her and yawned
again. "For what?"

"Do you know where Lyndon is?"

Instantly Chloe was wary. Michael had not been with her
when she woke a few moments ago. "I've no idea. Riding,
I presume. I sometimes go with him, but if I've had a late
night painting, he doesn't disturb me."

"He's fighting a duel."

"Bosh." She regarded Elizabeth for a moment, wondering why in the world Michael would do such a thing. Then
she remembered. He would challenge, he had said, anyone
who called her by that horrid name, which had made her
life so difficult during her come-out. "Did I just hear you
say something about a duel?"

"Yes. There's no time to waste. We must leave now."

Chloe continued to stare uncomprehendingly at her. "He
wouldn't do anything so foolish."

"Except for you."

"Then—" Chloe's eyes suddenly opened wide. "Good
God, Edwin?"

"Yes."

Almost involuntarily, Chloe shot to her feet. "Patience!"
she yelled. "I need you here."

"Yes, my lady, I'm coming." The maid appeared in the
doorway, looking much harassed. "May I do something for
you?"

"Where did Lord Lyndon go this morning?"

"I'm sure I don't know, my lady."

"Bosh. Servants always know everything." She raised her

chin. "Find my lord's valet, then, and ask him. And come back to me with the truth, if you please. Now, go."

"Yes, my lady," Patience said, and scuttled out of the room.

Elizabeth stared at her. "You do that well."

"What?" Chloe asked, whirling around.

"Behaving like a viscountess."

Chloe waved that off. "Where is this duel supposed to take place, and when?"

"At Green Park, at dawn."

"Then there's little time to waste. I do not understand, though. Edwin himself admitted he's not up to Michael's weight when it comes to athletics."

Elizabeth's face was troubled. "He's been practicing shooting."

"Hell! Excuse me," she added. "Michael's—Lyndon's influence. Then he might—"

"I've heard something. He doesn't intend to kill Lyndon."

Chloe went cold. Pistols at dawn. It had an ominous sound. "Will he delope?"

"No. He wants to wound Lyndon so he can never participate in sports again."

"Hell!" she said again, and sprinted to the door. "You wait here. I'll dress, and we can be off. Oh." She turned from the doorway. "How did you come here?"

"In a hackney. I told the driver to wait."

"Good," she said, and disappeared into her room.

Patience returned as Chloe was trying to fasten the buttons on the back of her dress, and, doing up the ones Chloe couldn't reach, reluctantly gave her the unwelcome news that yes, Lord Lyndon had gone to duel, taking his pistols with him. Chloe only nodded, dragged a brush through her hair, and took the shawl Patience handed her. There was so little time to prevent what could be a tragedy. She could not allow Michael to be hurt.

It was Chloe, once so uncertain of herself, who gave the orders to the hackney driver, telling him their direction and demanding him to spring his horse. She would have driven a carriage herself if she could have, had there been the time for one to be harnessed. This time she would not meet with disastrous results, of that she was certain.

It was frustrating, nerve-racking, to be only a passenger, aware of the consequences should she not arrive in time. From Elizabeth she learned the probable way Edwin intended to injure Michael, and the news chilled her. Though Elizabeth would not tell her how she had come by such information, Chloe trusted and believed her. If she could only get there in time . . .

The hackney finally drew to a jolting stop in Green Park. Chloe tumbled out, throwing far more coins at the driver than he had earned, and went running toward the small group of men clustered on the grass not so very far away. Three men stood together, alert, tense. She recognized only one, Lord Adam, and wondered with one part of her mind if Elizabeth had known of his participation in this nightmare. Then she saw the two duelists, facing each other across a wide divide, their pistols aimed toward the other. Oh, dear God, she had failed, she hadn't arrived in time to prevent the duel. If she were going to do something, she would have to act quickly.

"No!" she screamed, and, picking up her skirts, hurtled herself across the grass toward the two combatants. It was enough to distract them, though the pistols were still held at the ready, deadly, terrifying. "Stop!"

"Chloe, get out of here," Michael yelled, but she paid no heed. If she ran between them, neither could shoot. Michael would be furious, but that hardly mattered. What was important was saving him from the disaster that faced him.

She almost made it. Almost. But there was a slight rise in the grass that she didn't see, and she never had picked up her feet high enough, causing her to fall many a time. The toe of her boot caught in the grass, and she went sprawling against Edwin. The two of them fell in the grass, his pistol, held facing the sky, discharging harmlessly. From a distance she heard Michael yell something; she heard Edwin cursing fluently, repeatedly. Neither mattered. She had, after all, done it. She had prevented the duel.

Strong hands grabbed her arms and hauled her to her feet. "Hell, Chloe, what are you doing here?" Michael demanded.

She smiled up at him. "You're all right," she said.

"Of course I'm all right. This is no place for you." He looked past her, and she turned to see Edwin getting to his feet and dusting himself off. "This is between him and me."

"He was going to wound you."

"I expected that."

"In the knee, so you could never participate in athletics again."

He went still, and though he was already tense with anger, she felt him stiffen even more. "I planned on wounding him, too," he said, and bent to whisper into her ear just where.

Chloe jerked back. "Really?"

"Really."

"Good heavens!" she exclaimed. "How bloodthirsty men can be."

"We protect the people we love, Chloe."

"Michael." She stared at him, all other thoughts driven from her head. "Do you love me?"

He grinned. "Apparently, yes."

"But—"

"Well," Edwin drawled from behind them. "That was a remarkable thing to do, Chloe, even for you."

"Oh, do go away, Edwin," she said, burrowing her head into Michael's shoulder.

"Falling like that. It was quite amusing." He gave a dry, little laugh. "Miss Bumblebroth to the last."

Michael abruptly released her. "Excuse me," he said, and stalked across the grass. Putting his entire body into it, he lunged forward and planted a solid blow into Edwin's jaw. Edwin fell back in the grass again, and this time he didn't get up.

Chloe beamed at Michael as he walked back to her. "I think that's the nicest thing anyone ever did for me."

Michael gathered her close again. "He deserved it."

"Oh, yes, I quite agree."

"Are you all right? Did you hurt yourself when you fell?"

"No." If she had, she certainly didn't feel it. "Did I tell you I may be with child?"

Startled, he pulled back. "Chloe, only you would tell me that at a time like this."

"Are you happy about it?" she asked softly.

He stared down at her, his face going pale. "Lord, yes. Are you sure?"

"No, 'tis too early to tell. But it's possible."

"Oh, dear Lord." He held her so close that she nearly couldn't breathe. "You just fell. Are you all right?"

"Oh, Edwin took the worst of the fall," she said cheerfully. "All's well, Michael." She felt as if she were floating with joy. "Do you really love me?"

"Do you doubt it?"

"No one ever fought for me before." She drew back. "Let me see your hand."

"I've injured it worse than this before," he protested.

To Chloe, though, the sight of the reddened knuckles both thrilled her and hurt. She bent to kiss them, and then let herself be drawn close again. "I've always loved you, you know. From the day you proposed."

"It was a marriage of convenience, Chloe. A marriage for money," he said, and the words were dragged from him.

"Bosh. You treated me better than anyone ever had." She looked up him shyly. "And then there's what we share in . . ."

He grinned at her, her meaning obviously clear to him. "There is that, yes. Ah, Chloe." He tightened his hold on her. "I think I started loving you when you were so outrageous to poor Helena. I just didn't realize it until today."

"Well, if a duel can do that much good, perhaps I don't mind it so very much."

He pressed a kiss into her hair. "I needed you, Chloe," he whispered. "I didn't even know it. My life was empty, all I cared about was sports—"

"And you gained a remarkably clumsy wife."

"Who taught me that there were other things"—he paused—"that I could still love."

She laid her hand on his cheek. "I never doubted that, Michael. I simply never thought you'd love me."

"I'll have to love you all the more to prove it, won't I?"

"Yes, please." She looked up at him. "Would you please kiss me again?"

"If you insist." He lowered his head, and the kiss they shared was long and languorous. "Do you know something?"

"No. What?"

"Marrying Miss Bumblebroth was the best thing I ever did," he whispered, and kissed her again.

And, for once, Chloe didn't resent the nickname.

DO YOU HAVE THE
HOHL COLLECTION?